Cover by thecovercollection.com

CW01500682

About the author

Clive Edwards is an award-winning TV current affairs
filmmaker. He won a Royal Television Society Award for
Panorama: The Norway Channel which told the inside story
of the Israeli-Palestinian peace deal brokered by Norwegian
diplomats, and a BAFTA for the documentary series
Andrew Marr's History of Modern Britain. For six years he
was the Executive Editor of the BBC's TV Current Affairs
Department.

He lives in Lewes in East Sussex. *The Day You Die* is his
first novel.

For Elizabeth and Robbie

The Day You Die

Clive Edwards

Published by Barcombe Books 2025

ISBN: 9798284158944

Chapter One

He looked into her eyes and knew that she was going to die. In the next few minutes.

She was only five or six, a dark-haired, inquisitive little girl with a frank stare. Her bright blue dungarees had little pink badges all over, matching her coat and the backpack she carried on her shoulders. The picture of innocence.

She took in his stained clothes and his glassy eyes and no doubt some part of her young mind registered the alcohol fumes coming off him, even if she didn't know what they were.

'You smell,' she announced triumphantly.

Will Gray knew she was right. In fact, he stank. He had been on a prolonged drinking binge, and it had been a good while since he'd washed properly or changed his shirt, let alone his greasy cargo trousers.

It all helped to make sure that people kept their distance, but not this girl. She had not learned to stay away from human rubbish. He shifted on the street bench, pulling his grubby anorak around him, and made a shooing motion with his hands to get her to leave.

'Are you a tramp?' she asked with a little smile.

Will looked past her, searching for her parents. Where were they? Someone should be keeping an eye on her. He spotted two women talking twenty yards away. They looked like school-run mothers. Well, they were doing a very poor job if one of them was supposed to be keeping this little girl from harm.

'You look sad,' the girl said, waving to get his attention back. 'How can I make you happy?' she added, with childish optimism.

Will was surprised, for just a second, but a second was all it took. His gaze flickered past her fringe, and he found the palest cornflower blue eyes. Suddenly there it was, clear as crystal. The school bus approaching, her mother distracted again, a friend waving on the other side of the road. The young girl stepping towards her, a squeal of brakes, but too, too late. It was going to be that brutal, that unforgiving. A short, sharp blow and the end of this young life. In just four minutes' time.

Will shook his head, trying to clear away the vision, trying to pretend it hadn't happened.

'Your mother wants you,' he said to her, gesturing at the two women who remained engrossed in their pre-school chat. Didn't they realise the dangers they were supposed to be protecting their children from?

The girl was still there, staring curiously at him. And all he could see was her mangled body, legs twisted at unnatural angles, head bent back, eyes sightless, lying in the road.

'Piss off,' he said, the horror of it all ricocheting around his brain. The girl threw her hands to her face, uttered a little

2

squeal, a mix of horror and pleasure, and ran back to tug at her mother's arm.

'Mummy, that man said a naughty word,' she announced, loud enough for her mother and several other women passing with their children to hear. They turned to stare at him. The forgetful mother gave him a look of piercing distrust, grabbed her daughter's hand and set off up the road. He heard the words 'disgusting drunk' hang in the air and several of the other mothers shepherding their children to school flicked a dismissive glance at him.

Will slumped further onto the bench. In his mind's eye, he could still see the school bus ploughing into her. The wet thud of metal on flesh, the screams, the blood seeping over the road and into the gutter. His body felt taut, like an electric convulsion had seized him. He tried to steady his breathing. He tried to distance himself. There was nothing he could do. In four minutes, it would happen. Less now, in fact. At least a minute must have passed as he sat there trying to master his jagged breaths and the adrenaline that was coursing through him.

This was the worst one yet. The last few years since it started had been hell on earth, but this vision turned his heart and twisted his guts.

He reached for the whisky bottle in his pocket, but it was empty. Looking up, he saw the swiftly moving dark clouds and felt the first raindrops slanting across the face of the looming tower blocks. How had he ended up here drunk at nine in the morning in this gloomy council estate? He couldn't even remember where it was. The last recognisable place he'd passed was a Tube station – Ealing Broadway, maybe? And then he'd wandered south into unknown territory.

He cast around for a way out, and registered the street was nearly empty now, the last lone mother pushing her child ahead of her up the road. 'Hurry or you'll miss the bus,' he heard her say to her small son.

And then he realised what had been lurking in the back of his mind. There must be a school bus for this sprawling estate and the bus-stop must be just around the corner, out of sight. The parents and the children must be standing there, lined up, waiting for the bus and waiting for death. And though he couldn't see it, he would surely hear the squeal of the brakes applied hopelessly late and the piercing scream the mother would give, wrenched from her very soul, as she gazed at her crushed child.

For a second, he contemplated running in the opposite direction. Running far enough away not to hear the consequences, not to have them impinged on his consciousness forever. He usually made sure he was well away from the scene. It was bad enough knowing when someone was going to die, but he never wanted to witness it. He had seen enough sudden death in Iraq and Afghanistan to know exactly what it looked like. Whether it was friend or foe, long distance or close-up, a bomb or a bullet, there was an explosion of flesh and form and then the person had gone and that was that.

He had a hard and fast rule. Do. Not. Interfere. Whatever the circumstances. He had no idea what the consequences might be, and if he started saving people, where would he stop?

Yet this felt different, so much more urgent. His fellow soldiers might have signed up for their fate, but that dark-haired little girl with her mesmerising blue stare clearly hadn't, and if he could barely stomach their deaths, hers was insupportable.

He pushed himself quickly off the bench, stifling his misgivings, and started running up the road towards the distant corner even as the last mother dragged her reluctant child around it and disappeared.

How much time was left? It must be less than a minute now. He could feel the seconds speeding past, beckoning the girl's death closer. He could hear the ragged gasps of his breath, feel the tearing in his legs as he pushed them beyond their limits. God, he had let himself slip since his Army days. And the drink was still fuzzing his brain. Was he really doing the right thing? But then adrenaline and fear told him he must try.

He rounded the corner and there was the crowded bus stop fifty yards ahead, a dozen mothers with their children waiting in line. And there was the approaching bus, bearing down on them, just a few seconds away.

For a heart-stopping second, Will could not see the little dark-haired girl. Then he recognised her at the far end with her mother. They were almost the last in line, but the queue was stretching away from the bus stop and the bus would have to come past her and then all the other children before stopping. Except it wouldn't, of course. Will could see another mother and daughter on the far side of the road hurrying towards the stop. He could see the girl who would wave from the opposite side of the road. The still-forgetful mother didn't have hold of the blue-eyed girl's hand, and she would step out into the path of the bus, and that would be that if he didn't get there in time.

He ran past the beginning of the queue, sensing their anxious faces flicker at him. Who was this stranger approaching with such fury, at such a pace? Was he a threat? He felt their anxious, protective glances and saw mothers pull their children closer.

A little boy with bright ginger hair was staring at him with alarm. Without intending to he met the boy's eyes and felt immediately his future. A long life, a peaceful death in old age. Well, if he could have that why shouldn't the blue-eyed girl?

Then Will was just a few paces away and he could see his little girl had spotted her friend on the other side of the road. He could see as if in slow motion as she raised her hand and was about to step out. And he saw the bus just a few feet away with the driver not really paying attention.

Will grabbed her and lifted her off her feet. But then immediately he knew he had got it wrong. He had arrived at such a pace and his legs were weak and the weight of the girl was more than he expected. He discovered with a jolt of pure fear that he couldn't stop, and even as he sought to protect the girl with his body and arms, he took an involuntary step out into the road. He could see the startled face of the driver, registering the danger and stamping on the brakes. But the bus wouldn't stop in time, Will could tell. And so he stood there holding the little girl, waiting for the crunching impact, knowing that he had failed.

There was an unearthly silence, and then a squeal of brakes, just as he had foretold. But instead of oblivion, he felt the bus slide past his face, barely an inch away.

He thought he had got away with it. He opened his eyes and then he watched it all unfold as hope turned to ashes in a second.

The driver had locked the bus wheels and even as it moved past Will, missing him by a fraction, the back end was spinning round, wheels fighting for traction on the wet road and finding none. The back of the bus described a slow arc round into the middle of the road, completing a hideous one hundred and eighty degree turn until it was broadside on to the bus queue and sliding inexorably towards the shocked faces of the mothers and children. And before they could even shout out, it had ploughed into them with sickening force, sending bodies flying into the air. There was a moment's silence, and then time sped up and Will could hear the first screams, and he knew he had made the biggest miscalculation possible.

He could see children scattered and fallen like mis-shapen dolls across the pavement. The boy with ginger hair was lying in the gutter, a pool of blood forming round his head. One mother was caught under the back wheels of the bus, eyes cast to the sky, her face a rictus of pain.

This was hell on earth, and he had caused it. Then he realised he was still holding the child as her mother suddenly appeared in front of him. She snatched the girl out of his arms, her face contorted in panic and fury.

'What are you doing with my daughter?' she hissed.

'I was trying to save her,' Will said, but his words were lost in her rising hysteria.

'He did it!' she shouted. 'He caused the crash. It's his fault. He was trying to snatch my daughter.'

The sound of the impact had brought people out of the nearby flats and houses, some rushing to help, but others, attracted by the distraught mother, clustered around Will. She was gasping, fighting for breath, staring eyes fixed on him.

'He's a pervert. He was trying to take my Melanie.'

And then the crowd was advancing on him.

'I was just trying to stop her walking in front of the bus,' said Will desperately.

'He's lying. She hadn't moved,' said the mother, and Will registered with a shudder that she was right. He had grabbed the girl before she actually moved, and he had then endangered her by stepping onto the road, and he had caused the driver to swerve and the bus to skid. He was responsible for this carnage, and the fact that he had averted one girl's death was irrelevant when he had caused so many more to die. The knowledge settled on him like an overpowering weight. He could not move, he could not run, he could only watch as the angry crowd moved closer.

'Paedo,' said one. 'He's a filthy paedo.'

Will couldn't summon the strength to object. 'Lock him up,' said another. 'Throw away the key.'

And then Will's skull exploded into pain and the world went black.

Chapter Two

Light returned first, seeping past his closed eyelids, and with it a sharp, jagged pain in his skull. He felt sick to his stomach and there was something wrong with his left hand. He couldn't move it.

Carefully he turned his head towards where his hand appeared to be and opened his eyes a fraction. The room danced and shifted. White, very white, and then it came back into focus, and he realised his hand was fixed to the bed frame, and a second later that it was held there by handcuffs.

With a lurch he remembered the bus stop, the crash, the screams and the knowledge that it was his fault. His stomach convulsed and he vomited copiously over the bed, trying to be rid of the pain and the memory of it all.

'The nurses won't thank you for that,' said a rough voice behind him. Will slowly turned, little knives of pain making his vision shift and blur, and there was a stolid, bulky man in a battered suit surveying him with what Will could only think was contempt.

'You're not their favourite person anyway,' said the man. 'They've heard from their colleagues in A and E all the suffering you've caused, all the heartbreak. It wouldn't surprise me if they left you to rot.'

The man looked as if he thought this would be a just outcome. Will turned away. The stench of his vomit enveloped him. He could see no way out of this.

'You're lucky we came when we did,' said the voice. 'Someone hit you with a brick. It looked like they were about to hang you. Very angry they were. Beside themselves,' he finished with a humourless chuckle.

'Who are you?' Will finally managed to get out.

'Detective Inspector Tom Slater,' he said. 'I'm arresting you on suspicion of causing a fatal accident and anything you say could be taken down and used in evidence in court against you.'

Will's military training surfaced. Name, rank, serial number. No more. But this wasn't some mud hut in Afghanistan, and Slater wasn't the Taliban. At least there he had known who the enemy was. Here any danger Will was in he had brought on himself. Why had he given in to the urge to save the girl?

He had discovered too many times that death was impersonal, it happened when it happened and there was no changing that. Foolishly, he had tried to thwart it and instead only made it worse. Far, far worse.

'How many?' he said finally.

'How many what?' Slater said harshly. 'How many dead, how many injured? Well, at present it's three children dead and two of the mothers, but I'm informed that those figures could rise.'

There was a silence that stretched out as Will fought with the enormity of it all. He saw again the vision of the ginger-haired boy, due a long life that had been ripped away from him by Will's stupidity. How could he live with that?

'Perhaps you could start by telling me why you snatched the girl?' Slater consulted a notebook. 'Melanie Burton. Why you tried to abduct her there at a crowded bus stop?'

Will tried to focus. 'I wasn't trying to abduct her.'

'The mother is pretty convinced you were. She says you had noticed her daughter earlier and spoken to her. Then you followed them up the street. You ran up to the bus stop just as the bus was arriving and snatched her from her mother's side and then stepped in front of the bus.'

Will thought about how it looked from the mother's point of view, how it looked from the inspector's point of view. 'I wasn't snatching the girl. If I wanted to do that, why would I do it in front of so many witnesses?' he asked. He could hardly be bothered to defend himself. What was the point? There was no way out of this. And yet he couldn't bear to be labelled a paedophile child snatcher on top of all the other miseries he knew he had caused.

'I could have taken her earlier when she came up to me. If I'd wanted to. Her mother wasn't paying any attention.'

'You were thinking about it?' said Slater with a moue of distaste.

'No, no. I just meant a crowded bus stop was an unlikely place to choose. If I was a paedophile, which I'm not.'

'Maybe you wrestled with the impulse and only gave in after she'd moved off.' Slater contemplated this level of perversion and grimaced. 'Maybe you couldn't help yourself.'

'I am not a paedophile,' said Will as emphatically as he could muster.

'Why did you do it then?' said Slater flatly, staring at him. Will turned his head away. He did not want to look Slater in the eye. He did not want that knowledge on top of everything else.

What could he say? This solid lump of a police officer would never understand the curse that Will lived under. Slater wanted everything neat and manageable so he could jot it down in a notebook. He didn't want to know that death was there in his eyes, and Will could read when.

'I had a premonition,' said Will, knowing even as he said it how stupid it sounded. There was a strangled guffaw of laughter and when Will looked up he could see the contempt back on Slater's face.

'A premonition? Of what?'

'I thought the girl was going to step into the path of the bus.'

Slater was laughing properly this time, a hoarse, incredulous chuckle. 'Now I really have heard everything,' he said with a withering edge. 'You had a premonition that Melanie Burton was going to step in front of the bus, so you leapt in and instead caused the bus to crash and kill five other people.'

Will flinched.

'Not much of a fucking premonition, was it?' said Slater with a sneer. 'I think I prefer the paedophile explanation. More believable.'

He heaved himself to his feet. 'I guess you could try it on a judge and jury. You could say you knew she was going to die. But no one will believe you. You see, death isn't like

12

that. It isn't certain. I've seen enough, believe me, and mostly it catches people by surprise.'

He glared at Will, and Will didn't look away quickly enough. There it was, the kaleidoscope of images. Slater was at his desk in the police station. The tightening chest. The fleeting thought that he shouldn't have eaten that egg and bacon sandwich again, and then the sudden rising, escalating, monstrous pain, until he slumped over his desk and, within a few seconds, was gone.

Will blinked. Slater was still glowering at him, but Will could feel a touch of pity now. Just three days away. Slater would be dead, and there was nothing Will could do about it. He had more pressing problems of his own.

**

When Slater left he made a point of telling Will there was a police officer on guard in the corridor outside.

'In case someone tries to kill you,' he said with a careless laugh.

A little later the nurses came in to clean Will up. He could sense straightaway their distaste. A young Black woman with the name tag Joyce kept shooting him troubled glances. The other, an older white woman called Kerry, was much more direct.

'What a mess,' she said with disgust. 'You should've asked for a sick bowl.'

'I'm sorry,' said Will. 'If you leave one, I'll make sure it doesn't happen again.'

Will thought that they were being quite rough, and he could feel some sharp prods as they moved around on the mattress, hampered by his arm, which was still handcuffed to the bed rail.

'How are we supposed to do our job with this in the way?' Kerry said, rattling the handcuffs.

'You could get him to take them off,' said Will. 'There's a police officer outside.'

'Not being left in here with you free. Who knows what you might do?' Kerry announced acidly.

'I won't harm you,' said Will, but he heard her mutter under her breath, 'That's what they all say.'

Then she plumped up the pillows and her elbow caught on the side of his head. His vision flashed and for a second, he felt he was going to throw up again.

'Oh sorry, sorry,' said Kerry with a forced laugh, but he could see that she wasn't sorry in the least.

Finally, they finished. Joyce retreated with another troubled look in Will's direction, but Kerry made a point of turning on the television and changing the channel.

'I should think you'll want to catch up with the news,' she announced with a satisfied air and then bustled out.

Will sighed. This was what it was like to be hated. He had no doubt all the staff were talking about him. The pervert who had caused the bus tragedy. He cursed himself for ever having got involved. He had saved one girl and got three other children killed instead. Plus, two of their parents. A catastrophic bargain with fate, whichever way you looked at it.

The TV was droning on, but then he heard his name being read out. A big red caption 'breaking news' appeared, and the newsreader announced, 'They have named the man being questioned in connection with this morning's bus tragedy as Wilkinson Gray. We understand he is an ex-soldier who served in Afghanistan and was dishonourably discharged from the Army.'

Will winced. So, they'd got to that already. This was going to be a complete meltdown, he was sure.

The picture cut from the newsreader to a high shot of the bus stop, with the bus canted on its side and threatening white crime scene tents shielding the view of the pavement next to it. There were flashing blue lights from a dozen assorted police cars and ambulances and people milling around. Then the angle changed to a reporter on the pavement looking serious as he summed up the state of play. He heard again 'tragedy in West London, five dead, including three children. Three more seriously hurt.' Each polished phrase seemed like another blow to his heart. He was responsible for all that.

The reporter paused, then adopted his most serious face. 'I have here an eyewitness who is prepared to be interviewed.'

The camera shifted and there was a young blonde woman, face red, eyes darting around nervously. She was trembling, Will could see, still in shock. Not in the best state for national television.

'Thank you for agreeing to talk to us,' said the reporter unctuously. 'It must be very difficult for you. If you could just tell us what you saw.'

The woman swallowed, and with a visible effort concentrated on the camera. 'I was coming up to the bus stop, and the bus was arriving. Then this man ran up, very fast and seized the girl at the end, nearest to the bus.'

'Do you know which child that was?'

'Melanie. Melanie Burton, I think.'

'And then what happened?'

'The bus seemed to skid and the back end came round and smashed into the queue. And they all went flying, like ninepins. It was terrible.' She gulped and there was an audible sob. 'I've never seen anything so terrible.'

The reporter ploughed on regardless. 'That must have been awful, really awful. What do you think the man was doing? Was he saving.....Melanie?'

The woman glanced around distractedly. 'I don't know......er.... I don't know.'

Then suddenly a man's contorted face appeared over her shoulder. His eyes were red from rage or crying, his hoodie flapping around his face. 'He's a fucking pervert,' he screamed, his spit splashing the lens. 'He was trying to snatch her. String him up.'

The woman burst into tears, and even the reporter looked shaken. 'I'm very sorry about that. Back to the studio,' he gabbled.

The picture cut to a visibly shocked newsreader, trying to cover. 'Yes, I must apologise for that. And I should stress that no one knows the facts of what happened yet. We will, of course, let you know when we get any verifiable information. Moving on…'

Will collapsed back on the bed, his body taut. It could hardly be worse. Condemned like that for the world to see. He felt his vision shrinking and his limbs twitch, and then he knew he was going to be sick again. He grabbed for one of the cardboard bowls that the nurses had left and just got it to his mouth as he heaved up a string of bile. His chest tightened and his stomach spasmed and then, when finally it was over, he fell back on the sheets.

Was there any way out of this? He couldn't see it. He could hardly explain the real reason he had done it. 'Premonition' invited enough ridicule. The fact that he knew the precise moment and manner of everyone's death as soon as he looked into their eyes. Well, no-one would believe that. And anyway, now that he had seen the consequences of trying to alter things, he wasn't going to interfere again. He had tried to save one life and condemned five others instead.

He thought he knew the rules of this game. That what he saw was inviolable. It would happen. But clearly, the fate of those six changed in the blink of an eye. Changed when he interfered. He couldn't risk it again. He must never try to save anyone.

His gift, if that's what it was, was nothing but a curse. He was forced to know when death was coming but could only witness it as a mute and powerless spectator. It was too much.

He lay there, remembering how he first became aware of it as a child. How he thought it was just a nightmare. He knew his father was going to die, but he had pretended otherwise. He saw him rush out of the house, late, distracted, jump into his car, gun the engine and back out of the drive.

Watching from an upstairs bedroom, he told himself it was just a dream that wouldn't come true as his father sped down the road to the junction. He hardly dared to breathe as his father turned onto the main road without slowing down, and he flinched as the articulated lorry suddenly swept across, heard the distant thump as it obliterated his father's car and the long-drawn-out sound of the horn stuck on. The impact had mercifully swept the wreckage out of sight, so he didn't have that imprinted on his mind. But he knew with utter certainty his father was dead.

Finally, he went back to the floor of his bedroom and began mechanically playing with his toy soldiers. Tiny Airfix ones that he loved, ones where you could assemble platoons, whole regiments of little khaki figures on the bedroom floor and re-enact the battle of El Alamein.

He was still playing there when he heard the doorbell sound nearly an hour later, heard his mother go to answer it, and then heard her piercing scream.

He wondered then if maybe he could have altered it, stopped it, if he'd done something. But he ruthlessly suppressed those troubling thoughts. He was just a child. It was a nightmare. Something he had grown out of.

It hadn't troubled him for nearly twenty years, until the explosion in Afghanistan but then it all came screaming back, and he found that every eye he looked into showed their future death. And his world had become an endless nightmare.

Every time he considered intervening, he was afraid of what the consequences might be. Now he knew for sure. You couldn't change it, shouldn't change it, or it might be very

18

much worse. What will be, will be, in the worst possible way. Fate is fate.

Chapter Three

At 4pm, Slater returned with an anonymous middle-aged man in tow.

'Your lawyer,' he announced. 'God help him, having to defend you,' he added with a mordant chuckle.

The new arrival took in Will's handcuffs attached to the bed frame. 'Can you untie him please?' he asked.

'He's dangerous,' said Slater.

'You won't harm me, will you?' the man said to Will.

'Of course not.'

The man gestured to Slater and with a great show of reluctance Slater undid the cuffs. 'On your head be it,' Slater said. 'Call me when you're ready,' and then he left.

Will and the man exchanged wary glances. 'Robert Montgomery,' the man said, extending a hand. Will hesitated. Did he want to shake? It seemed a strange gesture in the circumstances. But then the lawyer had trusted him. Montgomery's handshake was as unforceful as his demeanour. There was, Will thought, a touch of Army bearing about him, but he seemed uncertain.

'Now, Mr Gray,' he said, setting out pen and paper. 'Perhaps we could start by you telling me exactly what happened.'

Will looked at him. Really? How on earth could he spell out the truth? And yet at that moment he felt too tired to care, to evade.

'I looked into her eyes and I just knew she was going to get run over by the school bus. I had to do something.'

'I'm sorry, which young girl? One of those who died?' said Montgomery, looking thoroughly startled.

'No, the one I picked up.'

Montgomery shuffled some papers. 'Ah yes, the one they accuse you of abducting. Er… Melanie Burton.'

Will bridled. 'I was not trying to abduct her. I was trying to save her. She was about to step into the road.'

Montgomery hesitated. 'And how did you know this? Had she moved towards the kerb?'

'She waved to a friend on the other side, and I just knew she was about to step out.'

'You just knew?' said Montgomery hesitantly. He shuffled the papers again and then pulled one clear. 'The police say you claimed it was a premonition.'

Will nodded. Montgomery looked at him and cleared his throat. He didn't look like he would be much good in court, Will thought. He looked nervous, as if he suspected Will really was a dangerous criminal who might round on him at any second.

'Yes, well, Mr Gray, it seems like it was a rather long-held premonition. You ran up the road to the bus stop, apparently intent on seizing this girl, whether to abduct her or save her, depending on your point of view. You say you knew she was in danger. From about fifty, one hundred yards away? How?'

Will had to accept his logic. It sounded absurd. Of course it did. But it was an absurd nightmare from beginning to end. He couldn't be bothered to lie.

21

'I looked into her eyes and knew she was about to die.'

The interview went downhill from there. He could see the disbelief in Montgomery's eyes, the shifting glances round the room. How do I defend a client like this, he must be asking himself?

Montgomery led Will painfully through all the facts as Will related them, and it only got worse. Finally, at the end, his note-taking slowed to a halt and Will could see him summoning up the courage to ask the big question. Will knew then that this would never work.

'Correct me if I got this wrong, Mr Gray, but you say that if you look into someone's eyes, you can tell when they're going to die?' Will nodded. 'But it doesn't seem to have worked here, does it? She didn't die.'

'Because I interfered. I wish I hadn't now.'

'You wish she had died?'

'I wish the others were still alive,' said Will wearily. 'There is no good outcome.'

There was a long silence. Montgomery finally raised his head and said, with a break in his voice, 'Well then, Mr Gray, when am I going to die?'

Will grimaced. This was why he should keep quiet. Either they wouldn't believe him, or he would become a fairground attraction. But then he really didn't have a choice, did he? He locked eyes with Montgomery, who was licking his lips as though he was afraid of the verdict.

White room, hospital bed, monitors around, a gaunt figure struggling for breath and failing. Motor neurone disease. Fourteen years away.

Will wondered if he knew. This was not the sort of diagnosis he should deliver right now. It could only go down badly.

'You may prefer not to know,' Will said.

Montgomery took a deep breath. 'No, I can handle it.'

'Very well. You die in fourteen years. Motor neurone disease.'

Montgomery went completely white. There was a tic lifting the corner of his eye. 'How can you know that? It's impossible,' he spluttered.

'I told you it may be better not to find out. I'm sorry,' said Will.

'No. I meant how could you know about the motor neurone disease?' Montgomery looked away, swallowed, and then added, 'I only got the diagnosis last week.'

There was a long, long silence as Montgomery struggled to regain his composure. Will couldn't think of anything to say. He had been proved right, but yet again, at what cost? Another life doomed to a miserable, painful end.

Finally, Montgomery stirred himself, made a few more notes and then closed the folder and looked at Will.

'Um, thank you, Mr Gray. I see you served in Afghanistan and Iraq as well. I think I should get you a psychological examination.'

'Do you believe me?' asked Will.

'We should cover every base,' said Montgomery, packing his papers away. 'I think we should consider all defences.' He looked at Will awkwardly, then added, 'maybe we should say you did it while the balance of your mind was disturbed. That would be the most believable.'

Will tried to stifle his anger.

'Maybe not,' Montgomery added quickly. 'Let's see what the psychiatrist says.'

And then he was hurrying to the door. 'In the meantime, it may be best if you say nothing more to the police. I will be there for interviews. Just let me do the talking.'

Montgomery tried to muster a reassuring smile. 'There's a guard outside. I'll ask them to leave the handcuffs off. We'll meet again soon,' he muttered, and then he was gone.

That went well, Will thought. Don't say anything ever again. Not unless you want to be locked up in a psychiatric prison like Broadmoor for the rest of your life.

Chapter Four

After hours of TV coverage going over the tragedy and speculating on the background of the ex-soldier who seemed to be responsible, the night nurse mercifully turned off the TV and gave him some pills she said would make him sleep.

Will eventually drifted off, his dreams punctuated by screaming children and hurtling buses, until it resolved into one of those nightmares where no matter how hard you struggle, you can't get to where you have to go. The bus was going to leave without him; then it was going to explode. The driver was screaming in anticipation, or was it agony? And without warning, it segued into an explosion straight from Afghanistan and there was more screaming, but this time it was a grown man.

Will woke suddenly, the screams still echoing in the room, to discover Kerry standing over him, shaking him.

'You're disturbing the other patients,' she snapped. Will struggled to sit up. He was in a room on his own. What other patients?

'We could hear screams down the corridor,' Kerry said, looking obscurely satisfied, as if the least he could do to atone was to scream in his sleep.

'What time is it?' Will asked groggily.

'It's quarter past six. Time to get up anyway,' she said, smoothing down the sheets. 'I brought you some papers in case you wanted to know what they are saying about you,' she added triumphantly, and dumped a sizeable pile of newsprint on the bed before marching out.

Christ, what a way to start the day, thought Will. Nurse Ratchet, followed by a visit from the lynch mob. He squinted at the top page. Even upside down, the headlines screamed at him. 'Child killer?' Good God, whatever happened to sub judice, he wondered, let alone being innocent until proved guilty.

He swung the papers round and saw they had tried to offset their headline with a further question. 'Did this disgraced soldier cause the bus tragedy?' It was pretty clear the conclusion they expected their readers to reach.

The rest of the papers were little better. They hadn't grasped the extent of his disgrace yet, only the dry words of his dishonourable discharge, and how his actions had put his fellow soldiers in danger. But no doubt that would come out soon.

The names of the dead had been released. Will forced himself to read the details one by one.

Top of the list was the ginger-haired boy. Jamie Cardale. Six years old. The accompanying picture showed him beaming impishly with slightly gapped front teeth. The tributes were conventional, 'our little angel', 'he lit up the room', but every one cut into Will like a knife. And the picture of his devastated, teary-eyed parents was even harder to look at.

He had taken seventy-five years of life from their son and blighted the rest of their lives too.

The stories of the other victims were just as bad. Ella Trent. Five years old. Lucy Maynard. Six. And then the parents. Sofija Huntsev, described as a chemist. And Margaret Maynard, a housewife.

It took Will a second to join the dots. Then he felt his stomach twist. Margaret was the mother of Lucy. They had both been killed, and when he saw the family photo it all fell into sickening place. Lucy, Margaret and a black-haired man that Will recognised. Colin Maynard. The same one who had screamed that Will should be strung up in the television interview. Lost his wife and daughter, no wonder he was demented with grief.

By the time Will had finished the reports, he felt sick to the depths of his being. He refused breakfast when Joyce brought it.

'You have to eat,' she said, but he ignored her.

Then the door opened, and Slater came in, wiping his mouth as if he had just finished another greasy breakfast. Too late to be worrying about that now, Will thought uncharitably.

Slater took one look at the papers on the bed and did a double take. 'Christ, who let you see those?' he said. He gathered them up quickly. 'Sorry about that,' he managed.

Will held his gaze, then pointed at the TV, which had been switched back on, albeit with the sound down. There was still an aerial shot of the crash scene on a split screen with a picture of Will and the caption, 'Did this man cause the bus crash?'

'Ah yes, you appear to be public enemy number one,' said Slater, with an attempt at joviality.

'What about sub judice?' said Will.

Slater looked momentarily shifty. 'We haven't officially charged you with anything yet,' he said.

'But you read me my rights yesterday. Isn't it from the moment of arrest?'

'You know the press now, completely out of control,' Slater said, avoiding Will's question. 'There's a lot of interest. They're all camped outside the hospital. And there are the relatives, some of them are pretty stoked. Just as well we've got you under guard. There's some would still like to lynch you.'

Will could see that Slater was enjoying his little speech. He turned his head away and stared out of the window at the scudding clouds. More rain, why not?

'Have you changed your mind about your ridiculous premonition story?'

Will didn't bother to look at him. 'My lawyer told me to say nothing,' he said.

Slater harrumphed. 'Well, I'll be back later, with your lawyer. You might usefully think about coming up with a more honest explanation.'

Will said nothing. He heard Slater mutter 'cunt' and then the door slammed behind him. It was going to be a long day, and it wasn't getting any better.

The doctor returned briefly, said his concussion was progressing satisfactorily and they could let him out the following day, as if he would be free to go home, rather than to a prison cell.

Will lay back and closed his eyes. Perhaps it would all disappear if he didn't see it, didn't think about it. No more news, no more pictures of the children who died with their parents. None of the hideous images that seemed imprinted on the back of his eyelids.

He must have dozed off because the door opening woke him. Slater was returning with his solicitor and another police officer. Montgomery looked little better this morning. Twitchy, downcast, his hand slicked with sweat when rather formally he shook Will's hand again.

'This is DI Meredith. Right, let's crack on, shall we?' said Slater with forced jollity, as if this was some awkward social event. He placed a tape recorder on Will's bedside table, switched it on, and launched into the official preamble.

Will let Slater drone on and wondered again about the detective's imminent death. You have no idea it's coming, do you? Of course, no-one had any idea about the date of their final reckoning, except Will, who tried to avoid the knowledge. No-one wants to know, he thought. It's an intolerable burden even if it's years away. At one stage, he'd imagined that knowing you were going to die of old age would free you from so many day-to-day worries about health and risk. But then he realised it was far too big to really comprehend, to definitely believe in. The only way to live was unknowing, treating each day as full of possibility and disaster. In fact, doing your best not to think about it at all.

The edge of Slater's voice changed, hardened, and Will zoned back in. 'Wilkinson Gray, you are charged with the attempted abduction of Melanie Burton and with carelessly and negligently causing a fatal traffic accident.'

Montgomery interjected with a little cough. 'Excuse me, officer, attempted abduction seems a bit rich. My client did

29

not flee, did not try to leave the scene. It's not much of an abduction.'

'He seized the girl,' said Slater impatiently.

'He was trying to save her life,' said Montgomery. Will was pleased to hear Montgomery's conviction. He could at least pretend, even if he didn't believe.

'You haven't fallen for that rubbish, have you?' said Slater with a sneer.

'That is what my client believes,' said Montgomery.

'And what do you say?' asked Slater, addressing Will.

Will looked him full in the eyes, seeing again Slater's approaching date with death. 'My solicitor has told me to say nothing,' he replied.

He watched the colour rise dangerously on Slater's mottled cheeks. This clearly wasn't helping. Will wondered if he was going to cause Slater's heart attack. That would certainly be ironic.

'You're not still sticking to that stupid premonition line, are you?' Slater spat.

'My client maintains the girl was going to endanger herself and he acted to intervene.'

'The jury will fall about laughing.'

'We'll see,' said Montgomery. 'I will, of course, want to arrange a psychiatric interview as well.'

'That's the first sensible thing you've said. He certainly needs one of those.'

'I imagine you will want to arrange one of your own,' said Montgomery. Will sighed. Two shrinks. That was going to be fun.

'You bet,' said Slater. 'Does your client have anything to say about causing a fatal traffic accident?'

'As you can see, Inspector, one flows from the other. He plainly didn't mean to cause the accident either way. If he was trying to save the girl, then the accident is simply a completely unforeseeable result.'

'You try telling that to the parents of those dead children.'

Montgomery ignored him. 'When will the court hearing be?'

'The doctor says he can leave here tomorrow. He will be taken straight from here to the court. We will ask for him to remain in custody while we continue our investigations.'

'In prison?'

'I imagine so,' said Slater. 'Probably best, given the number of people who seem to want to kill him.'

'I trust you will take every step necessary to ensure he isn't harmed,' Montgomery said.

Slater looked like he'd eaten something particularly unpleasant. 'Oh, you don't have to worry about that,' he said. 'We'll stop them stringing him up. All part of the service. Till tomorrow then.'

Slater gathered up his tape recorder and left with a still silent Meredith in tow.

'A real charmer, isn't he?' said Montgomery. A thought occurred to him, and he looked at Will. 'What about him?' he asked.

For a second, Will was lost, but then he registered what Montgomery was asking about. Good God, this was definitely a parlour trick now. But maybe it would convince Montgomery he wasn't crazy.

31

'This is confidential solicitor client information?' Will asked.

'Can't breathe a word,' said Montgomery, looking uncomfortably conspiratorial.

'Two days, heart attack,' Will said flatly.

'Dear Lord,' said Montgomery. 'Poor man. Makes mine seem a good innings.'

They looked at each other. Montgomery was shocked and embarrassed, as if he had been caught out. 'Right then, see you tomorrow,' he said hurriedly and left.

That was the trouble, thought Will. What he knew was knowledge that no-one wanted. Ever.

Chapter Five

Will slept badly, the bodies of the dead children chasing round his dreams again, interwoven with flashes from Afghanistan. Bombs, corpses, bullets flying past and then he was running, as he always did, running till he thought his heart would burst.

He woke bathed in sweat, disorientated, staring. For a second, he wasn't sure where he was. Was this an Army hospital? Was he still enlisted? And then the accident flooded back in, and he knew today things could only get worse. He was leaving the relative tranquillity of the hospital for court and prison. By tonight he would be lying on a hard cell bed facing God knew what threats from his fellow inmates. Accused of child abuse, responsible for three children dying, he would be a natural target.

I need a drink, he thought. But then he remembered how low he'd sunk and how much the drink had contributed, and he just felt sick. Never again.

Kerry bustled in, all efficiency and malice. She thumped the paper on the bed. The headline jumped out at him. 'From Afghan coward to child killer,' it proclaimed in screaming type.

'They seem to have found out your little secret,' she said. 'You get better every day, don't you? Ran away in Afghanistan, leaving your mates to die.'

Will wondered where she got such spectacular levels of self-righteousness from. 'It wasn't like that,' he said, but he knew she wouldn't listen. 'Whatever happened to the Hippocratic oath?' he wondered out loud.

'Oh, that's for doctors,' said Kerry blithely.

'Aren't you supposed to care for your patients?'

'I look after them. I don't have to like them,' Kerry snapped, and bustled out again, slamming the door.

Will picked up the paper with a sigh. Inevitably, they had found out. He could picture the snitch in the MoD or some obscure records branch who had dug out the details of his dishonourable discharge and sold it to the paper for money. And then they had picked out the juiciest parts and splashed them across the front page and an inside page spread. For thirty pieces of silver or the modern equivalent.

He read the bare details, a firefight near Sangin. He ran away. The rest of the patrol died. Shameful, shameful. And such a terrible way for a decorated soldier's career to end. He'd been a hero once, then he'd turned into a complete zero.

When he started, the Army had seemed like such a good fit. He liked the physical challenge; the camaraderie of facing danger together, and the adrenaline wiped out any chance of reflecting on the worries inside his head. He'd almost forgotten the nightmares of his childhood, thinking he knew his father was going to die. And in some funny way, surrounding himself with death seemed like an antidote.

He'd risen to corporal, got a couple of mentions for bravery and then a decoration. He felt like he'd carved a future for himself.

But then it all changed. The patrol through a village reduced to rubble, everywhere a loose stone that could hide a tripwire or a mine. The shout of terror from Hawkins up ahead as he saw the glint of a line moving followed by the punch of the explosion. It killed Hawkins instantly and lifted Will into the air, crashing him down on the hard stones with pain shooting through his skull, then darkness.

He'd woken up in a field hospital tent thinking he was lucky to be alive. Then a pretty nurse had leaned over him, concern softening her expression, and said, 'You're going to be alright.'

Will had looked into her amber eyes and unlocked his own personal hell. Suddenly, he could see her running desperately, whimpering in terror. Then there was a white flash and fire. When the smoke cleared, she was lying spread-eagled in the sand, those amber eyes gazing sightlessly, the life gone out of them. Somehow, Will knew it was a mortar round and, worse still, that it would happen later that day.

It was like his explosion over again, and he felt the blast and the pain rip through him and his body convulsed. Will screamed, and the nurse grabbed him, holding him down.

'Help, quickly, he's having a seizure,' she shouted, and other nurses came running.

Despite the pain and disorientation, Will tried to warn her, but all that came out was incoherent babbling. And then someone shoved a needle unceremoniously into his arm, and the darkness closed in again.

By the time he woke, it was evening. He lay there trying to sort it out and failing. It felt like the premonition with his father but a hundred times worse. It was as if he'd been there, lived the explosion again, died a little with her. And how could he possibly have known when it would be? When it had been, because if he was right, the mortar attack would have been while he was asleep, and the nurse would now be dead.

That was impossible, surely. Just another nightmare. He must be suffering from concussion, from shock. Perhaps the blast had caused damage to his brain. That would be better than the alternative.

He lay there wrestling with his tumbling thoughts until another nurse, not his nurse, came to check on him.

'Feeling any better,' she said as she took his pulse. But Will saw immediately that her hand was shaking and there were tears in the corner of her eyes.

'What's the matter?' he asked, dreading her answer, almost unable to breathe. 'Where's the nurse who was looking after me earlier?'

The new nurse had frozen, then uttered a little sob. 'While you were knocked out, there was a mortar attack on the camp,' she said, then she fell silent.

Will's mind was screaming. No, no, no. Finally, he managed. 'What happened?'

'She was killed. Direct hit. It was instantaneous.'

And that was it. Welcome to hell. Will soon discovered it wasn't a one-off. Everyone he locked eyes with gave up their ultimate secret. The cause and the time. And in an Army camp there were many people with not much time left.

Will felt like he was drowning in death. There was talk of shell shock and PTSD. His commanding officer tried to be sympathetic but failed miserably. There were sessions with psychologists, but Will couldn't tell them the truth. He

36

couldn't tell anyone. Who would believe him? He didn't want to believe it himself.

Instead, he quickly learnt not to look anyone in the eye. And when they finally sent him back on active service, he tried to make sure he was well away from any moment of death he knew about.

That was until he came up against Roger Alloway, a captain in the Black Watch. Not even a friend, thank God, not a friend. A rather loathsome officer with a Sandhurst swagger who had told him off for some minor insubordination. Will had become practised by then at letting his gaze slide over faces, without making eye contact, and never registering information he didn't want to see. But Alloway, the arrogant little creep, had barked out, 'Look at me when I'm telling you off,' and so he had, and seen clearly the sniper's bullet that would finish Alloway later that same day.

He had wrestled with his conscience and convinced himself that there was nothing he could do. But when the moment arrived Alloway jerked sideways, suspended for an instant on the force of the bullet ripping through his neck, and then collapsed to the ground and took an uncomfortably long time to die, gurgling as his blood flowed into the sand.

That was when Will discovered that knowing in theory when people would die was very different from seeing it played out right in front of him. And the long, slow burn of guilt had stayed with him ever since.

Shortly after, there was the final breaking point. It was the last days of the British involvement in Afghanistan before the humiliating pull-out. He was posted to a new unit;

he didn't know any of them. But he could see in their eyes that they were about to go out on a fateful and deadly patrol, go out and not come back. At the time he was trying to tell himself it wasn't his business when people died. He was pretending indifference.

So, he told himself he no longer cared. Except that when the moment came, and the bullets ripped into the platoon, he found he did care and he couldn't face seeing them all go down one by one. He ran blindly to get away from all the ineradicable horrors. One of the few who did survive saw him go and reported it. They arrested and court-martialled him, but it turned out the entire operation had been a gigantic cock-up. The Army didn't want to draw attention to this, so they threw him in a military prison back home for three months and then kicked him out with a dishonourable discharge.

Now it was all just another reason for people to hate him.

The door opened and Slater entered, looking marginally fresher in a clean if battered suit and with his hair slicked back behind his ears. His go-to-court outfit, Will assumed.

'Time to get ready,' he barked. Kelly followed him, gingerly holding Will's stained and smelly clothing.

'Sorry, they didn't get cleaned,' she said carelessly.

'Don't worry, lad. No one will look at your clothes. You don't have to dress up for court nowadays.'

Will hauled himself to his feet and dressed. His head was aching, and he was trying to block out the prospect of a humiliating ordeal in court. He couldn't care less about the clothes. Presumably they'd give him something clean in prison. But the journey from here to there was going to be deeply unpleasant.

He finished dressing, making sure he didn't look in the mirror. He'd seen his own death enough times, frozen and hunched under a makeshift cardboard bed in an alley somewhere. He didn't need to see it again. Slater gestured and followed him out into the corridor. There was a policeman on a chair outside the door who jumped up, took out another pair of handcuffs, and clamped them on Will's wrist and his own.

There were curious stares from nurses and patients. Slater led the way down a back stairwell. They reached an underground car park where a police van was waiting. Someone pushed Will into the back and made him sit in a window seat. Good for the photographs, he supposed. He got the feeling they wouldn't be protecting him much.

The van drove out of the underground car park and back past the front of the hospital, where a gaggle of photographers and TV crews were waiting. They ran up to the windows and fired off shot after shot, flash after flash. Will thought the van was going unnecessarily slowly. Helping them get their pictures, he guessed.

'That's just the appetiser,' Slater smiled wolfishly at him. 'You wait till the court.'

Will shrugged. As they wound their way through the suburban traffic, Will tried to prepare himself. His head started aching again where the brick had hit him. He wished he'd taken the painkillers Kerry had brusquely offered him earlier.

'Nearly there,' said Slater cheerfully, and then they rounded a corner into a road dominated by an imposing grey stone Gothic building with lofty towers. It looked like Gormenghast and Will had no doubt held similar horrors for him.

There was a large crowd waiting outside. As they drew nearer, Will could see people on the edges pointing towards the van, and then a mass of contorted faces swarmed across the road and surrounded it. They spotted him straightaway and thumped on the window. 'Bastard', 'Paedo', 'Child killer.'

After the shouted insults, there was more banging on the windows, and then gobs of spit landed on the glass. He could see a woman whose eyes were alight with a vivid rage and tears were running down her cheeks. She leaned close to the glass and despite the roaring of the crowd, he heard her clearly say, 'You killed my daughter. I'm going to make sure you die.'

Will pushed himself back in his seat, but he couldn't get any further away. The van slowed to a walk because of the crowd. The glass was covered in a haze of spit now, and the faces appeared contorted and blurred, but the noise pounded in his ears and the van rocked from the people pushing themselves against the sides.

Finally, Will could see the open gates of a courtyard and the van edged its way in. The shouting receded and Will opened his eyes and saw they were drawing up to a heavy door with a policeman waiting outside.

'Well, that was fun, wasn't it?' said Slater, but when Will glanced at the detective, he noticed a sheen of sweat on the man's forehead and a grey pallor on his skin. He saw Slater rub his left arm. Not long now, thought Will, and there's nothing I can do about it. Nothing you can do about it either.

They took him to an interview room and handcuffed him to the table. He could still hear the chants of the crowd in the distance. 'Hang him', 'Child killer' and 'Die, die'.

He shook his head. He just wanted this nightmare to be over. Prison would at least be quiet.

Montgomery shuffled in. The solicitor seemed smaller this morning and wouldn't meet Will's eye.

'This is just a formality. Say nothing except to confirm who you are. In the circumstances, there is no chance of bail, so I won't be going there. Understood.'

Will nodded. 'Is something troubling you?'

Montgomery physically flinched. He flicked his eyes towards the noise outside. 'Not very nice, is it? Try not to let it affect you.'

'What about the psychiatrist?' asked Will. 'When will I see someone?'

Montgomery blinked and swallowed. 'Soon. It's unnecessary for today.'

Will was certain there was something Montgomery wasn't telling him. 'But I will see a psychiatrist?'

Montgomery just nodded. 'See you upstairs,' he said and left quickly.

A few minutes later, they led Will up the stairs and into the courtroom. There was an angry murmur from his left. Will looked towards the sound and saw the public gallery packed with staring faces. He guessed most of them must be bereaved families. He distinctly heard 'Paedo' muttered

41

again and as he scanned the front row, he saw a familiar face, a dark, badly shaven man with glowing eyes. The same man who had interrupted the television report and denounced him, demanding revenge. Colin Maynard. Lucy's father, Margaret's husband. Maynard drew his fingers across his neck in the universal cut-throat gesture. Will knew Maynard would do it, given the chance.

'Quiet in court,' said an usher. 'Please rise.' A door opened at the back and the magistrate filed in.

The formalities got underway, but Will was hardly listening. He could only feel the hatred that radiated off Maynard in the gallery. It was like a wave of furious heat rolling across the courtroom towards him.

'Mr Gray, could you confirm your details to the court please?'

Montgomery was pleading with his eyes for Will to pay attention and get this over with. But even as Will turned back to the magistrate and confirmed his name and then listened to the charges, he could feel Maynard's venom beating down on the side of his head.

The magistrate pronounced Will would be held in custody on remand and there was a low growl from the gallery as if a predator was being denied its prey. But there was nothing they could do, and it faded away.

The proceedings had finished, and someone told Will to stand. He was ushered out of the box and was heading for the door when there was suddenly a piercing cry from the gallery. As Will turned, he saw Maynard launch himself over the railing and drop towards him. It was only a few feet and he landed on Will with an almighty thump, at the same time

42

delivering a solid punch to the side of Will's head. The room span and Will went down in a huddle on the floor, the man on his back. He tried to twist himself round and found the contorted features just inches away now, sour breath hot on Will's face.

'I should have killed you with that brick,' Maynard hissed.

Then hands gripped Maynard's arms and hauled him away. But not before Will had seen the consuming violence in his eyes and inevitably where it would all end. Five years, liver failure, an alcoholic who would drink himself to death. And all because of what Will had done. It was too much to bear.

Chapter Six

They hustled him out of the court down to the same interview room. Slater managed a muted apology. 'Sorry about that,' and left.

Will stared at the walls, wondering how long he would have to wait before they took him off to prison. His head ached, and he was trembling. The blow could not have done his concussion much good, but it was what he had seen in Maynard's eyes that had shaken him. Another one fingered for death, another shattered life, and this time there was no getting away from the fact that he, Will, was to blame. He couldn't wash his hands of this and just say it was merciless fate. He had caused this, no matter how good the reason. He felt sick to his soul.

He had never intervened before and clearly he never should again. It was just too much to bear.

Will sat sunk in misery for what seemed like an age, turning over his responsibility for everything that had happened.

Finally, the door opened and a man appeared. Will had never seen him before. He was tall, well-groomed, hair slicked back, an expensive suit, sharp blue eyes. He exuded a steely professionalism that looked completely out of place in this suburban courthouse.

He sat down opposite Will, smoothed back his hair with both hands, and opened the folder he was carrying. There was a long silence while he took in Will's hunched, defeated posture.

Finally he said, 'You were a soldier, weren't you? Sit up like one then, Corporal. Remember your training.'

What the fuck, thought Will. The last thing I need, some regimental type bossing me around. But an old dormant discipline triggered within him, and he sat up straighter in front of this aggressive stranger.

'Good,' the man said. 'I'm Dexter.'

'Are you the psychiatrist?'

'God, no. Although I will ask you to talk to one of those later. Just look on me as the one who controls your fate. I can decide what happens. You can go to prison, of course, or you can go somewhere… better.'

Will let slip a bitter laugh. 'Are you offering me a deal, Dexter? Dexter who?'

'Let's leave it at Dexter for now.'

Will watched Dexter warily. He seemed completely in control. Will had a powerful urge to puncture his cool demeanour.

'What's the deal, then? You'll set me free if I do what?'

'Well, soldier. You'll remember we don't do deals. You obey orders.'

'I'm sorry to disappoint you, but as I'm sure you know, I left the Army six years ago.'

Dexter picked up a piece of paper. 'You signed the Official Secrets Act. That never stops.'

'What's the official secret here?'

Dexter smiled. 'You are, Mr Gray. At least if you've been telling the truth at all. But why don't we start at the

45

beginning. You apparently claim that you can tell when people are going to die. Just by looking them in the eyes.'

Will bridled. 'That was supposed to be a confidential conversation with my solicitor.'

Dexter smiled again. 'Mr Montgomery is a former soldier too. Same regiment as me. He understands his duty. Do you?'

'Duty?'

'To the country.'

'Oh, come on. You're a spook, are you? What's that got to do with me?'

Dexter smoothed his hair back again. 'Let's come to that in a moment. I'm curious about this gift of yours. How does it work?'

Will stared at him, increasingly irritated. Was this urbane, civilised, controlled man ever likely to really believe him? Will allowed himself to look straight into Dexter's eyes. A looming truck, jagged metal, car crash, twelve years. Will flinched but also experienced something like satisfaction. That would puncture his unflappability.

But as if reading his mind, Dexter said, 'Go on, tell me then.'

'What?'

'I saw you look into my eyes. What did you see?'

Will met his eyes again. The squeal of brakes, a grinding thump. 'Twelve years,' he said flatly. 'Car crash.'

Dexter seemed completely unperturbed. 'I see,' he said with a small smile. Either he didn't believe Will at all, or he really had balls of steel.

'It doesn't bother you?' asked Will.

Dexter deployed the small smile again. 'In my line of business, Mr Gray, another twelve years is longer than I might normally expect. And anyway, you're assuming I believe you.'

This was beginning to feel like a dangerous game of chess. Will felt irritated again. He knew he was being played, but Dexter seemed to know how to press all Will's buttons.

'If you don't believe me, why are you here?'

'Montgomery told me you spotted his motor neurone disease. That seemed like more than luck. It was intriguing enough to check out.'

'You spend your time chasing fairytales?' asked Will bitterly.

'You don't seem to think it's a fairytale, do you?' said Dexter reasonably. 'In fact, if I'm a judge of anything, I'd say it causes you pain. Unbelievable pain.'

Will was wrong-footed again. The images of the scattered children, of the mother screaming under the wheels of the bus swamped him and he broke out into a cold sweat.

'It's hell, every day. But there's nothing I can do about it.'

'I believe you,' said Dexter. 'Most people don't want to know. It's too final. Knowing everyone's individual fate must be an impossible burden.'

Despite himself, Will felt tears spring to his eyes. The slightest hint of sympathy, and it all threatened to overwhelm him. He knew he was being manipulated, but he felt powerless.

'I'll ask you again, what's the deal?'

47

Dexter spread his arms on the table. 'Let's not rush this. I'm inclined to believe you, but I need to convince the people above me. Let's start with a little test, a demonstration, shall we say? Maybe we could organise an identity parade until we found someone who you saw was going to die shortly after, then wait and see if it happens.'

Will recoiled at the thought. More innocent souls, sifted just to find a victim. 'You don't need to do that,' he said flatly. 'I know someone. Tomorrow.'

Dexter's eyes gleamed. 'Excellent. Then I think we might avoid prison. We will take you to a rather more comfortable billet for tonight. And if it all turns out the way you say tomorrow, we can take it from there.'

Will nodded. Avoiding prison seemed like an attractive idea, and nothing would change what was going to happen to Slater. He certainly would not intervene after the dreadful consequences of his actions with the bus.

'Good. I think we have finished here then. Who is it?'

'That detective inspector, Slater. Heart attack. Four pm tomorrow.'

Dexter chuckled. 'Perfect. No doubt about that. We'll look after you and let's see if Mr Slater meets his maker at the appointed hour.'

Chapter Seven

Two hours later, they ushered Will back into the same police van and drove him out of the courtyard. There were fewer protesters, and they were kettled in behind barricades. But they hadn't lost their voices, and Will could clearly hear the screams of abuse. He stared fixedly ahead, trying to block the noise, trying to work out what Dexter was up to. Could he really be offering a way out? If he was MI5, then you could guarantee there would be a hefty price attached, no matter what.

Will's reverie was disturbed when the van turned down a deserted street and stopped behind a plain saloon car. Two men got out of the car and walked back to the van. The driver of the van wound down the window and the stranger flashed an ID card.

'We'll take him from here,' he said.

The driver seemed to expect it. He didn't object, simply got out and his colleague climbed out too.

'He'll give you a lift back,' the man said, gesturing at the saloon. Then the two new arrivals climbed into the van, and they drove on in silence.

'Where are we going?' asked Will finally.

'You'll see. It's about an hour from here. You need anything?'

Will shook his head. He may as well try to rest. They wouldn't tell him anything, and he would find out soon enough, anyway.

Will fell into an uneasy sleep and only woke when the van crunched over gravel and came to a juddering halt.

'Nice billet,' said the guard driving, with a hint of envy.

Will peered out. It was a classy Arts and Crafts Manor house, slates on the upper walls, a couple of faux turrets, some ivy and a few clipped yew bushes in front. It looked like a country house hotel.

Two men in suits came out of the lighted front door and over to the van. The guard unlocked the back door and Will jumped on to the drive. 'Come with us,' one of the suits said to Will.

It was a still evening. They must be deep in the country. There was no sound except the wind shifting in the trees, and the night sky was full of stars. To the right there was a glow over the hills, which must be the lights of London.

Surrey, guessed Will. A Home Counties safe house.

Will waved at the guards and followed one of them through the front door. He noted that the other man had fallen in behind, and that his hand was in the front of his jacket where no doubt he had a gun. This wasn't as relaxed and pleasant as it all looked.

The entrance foyer continued the country house feel with a marble table and an arrangement of flowers in a crystal vase. The muscle ahead and behind seemed even more incongruous.

They took Will up a grand wooden staircase and down a wood-panelled corridor into an enormous bedroom with a large double bed and thick carpeting.

'This is your room. There's a bathroom through there. Fresh clothes on the bed. Someone will bring you a meal shortly.'

The man nodded at Will and left. Will heard the key turn in the lock. Not really a hotel then. A quick check revealed heavy bars across all the windows. More like a luxury cell. Ah well, it was a lot better than prison. There was TV if you wanted it, and no fellow prisoners who fancied earning a bit of kudos beating up a man accused of child killing and paedophilia. It could be worse.

Will examined the clothes. Oxford shirt, cotton sweater, chinos, socks and trainers. All the right size. He stripped off, took a long hot shower and by the time he had dressed in the new outfit he felt almost human again.

Then he lay flat out on the bed and stared at the ornate ceiling as he considered the deal he had done. Had he just exchanged the frying pan for the fire? And what would they want in return?

***

A few hours later, as he was finishing the sausage and mash they had brought him, there was another knock on the door. Will wasn't sure why anyone would bother to knock. They had the key, after all.

Finally, the door opened, and a severe looking young woman came into the room, and then hesitated.

51

'You're still eating. I'll come back later,' she said.

'No worries,' said Will. 'I've finished,' he added, swallowing the last mouthful. He was keen to talk to anyone, find out more about this place, get the measure of the people who were holding him.

He gestured to the chair opposite him at the table, and she came and sat down. She was about his age, early thirties, he guessed, black hair, blue eyes, no make-up. Her hair was down her back in a ponytail and her clothes, black trousers and cardigan and a white blouse said professional, unapproachable, keep your distance. She looked like a hotel manager.

'Are you in charge here?' Will said, opting for flattery.

'No. Good God, no,' she said. 'I'm here to assess you.'

'Heart rate? Push-ups?' said Will. 'Or psychologically?'

'The latter,' she said, offering her hand to shake. 'I'm Alice.'

'All the nice girls love Alice,' said Will, smiling at her. 'It's a line from an Elton John song.'

'Never heard of it,' she said, with no hint of a smile in return. 'I'm a psychiatrist.'

There was a silence. Will decided he might as well co-operate. He would get what information he could, but he wouldn't look her in the eye, not yet. And he was pretty sure that she was avoiding looking directly at him, too.

'Fire away,' he said. 'Shall I face over here?' He shifted his position so that he faced away. 'More like the psychiatrist's couch.'

'There's no need,' Alice said, but when he flicked a glance at her, she was looking down, studying her notepad.

'Tell me, how long have you had this belief that you can see when people will die?'

Will let the question hang in the air. He remembered his army training and thought again about saying nothing. Name, rank, serial number. But he'd decided to co-operate, at least at first. He went on the offensive.

'That's a loaded question. It's my belief, is it? You're making clear you don't believe it.'

Alice made a note. 'You expect me to believe it too?'

'I expect you to give me a chance.'

'Are you always this aggressive?' she said coolly.

Will took a deep breath. So much for playing games. Two minutes and she had already forced him off balance. He made himself smile. 'Why don't we start again?'

'I agree,' she said. 'Let's start at the beginning. When did you first notice this, and how did it make you feel?'

'It was something I was aware of when I was a child, but for a long time I paid little attention to it. I thought they were just waking dreams or nightmares, and it seemed to go away as I grew up. But then it came back in a much more vivid way after an incident in Afghanistan, and now it's all the time. I just know when people will die.'

'And that's what you had with the little girl? A feeling that she would die.'

'It's very specific. I see the last few seconds. I know what happens and I know when as well.'

'A date, a calendar?'

'The date and time just flashes into my mind. It's always right, and that's when they die.'

'But the little girl didn't die,' said Alice quietly.

53

Will groaned. 'Yes, well, I made the mistake of intervening, and that just made it far worse.'

'You've never intervened before?'

Will looked at her, but her face was studiously down, writing notes, hiding her expression.

'I never wanted to admit that I could.' The images of so many deaths flooded through his mind, and suddenly Will was breathless and floored. It would be insupportable to imagine he could have intervened and saved all of them.

'Are you alright?' asked Alice. 'You're sweating.'

Will had a drink of water and tried to steady his breathing. 'Look what happened when I intervened. Carnage.'

'That would have happened anyway. Maybe that was what was supposed to happen.'

'No. It was my fault. It was me stepping out that made the bus swerve.'

There was a silence.

'How does that make you feel?'

'How does it make me feel? Appalled, guilty, responsible.' Will felt the words pour out in a rush. He felt the bile in his stomach rise. He thought he was going to be sick again.

'But you saved the girl.' Alice sounded reasonable, concerned.

'You believe me then?' asked Will. Alice didn't reply, then she seemed to change the subject.

'Let's go back to the beginning again. Tell me about the first time in your childhood you thought it might be true.'

Will knew immediately, and then he was back in the house, seven again, watching his father drive away.

'It was the day my father died,' said Will. He noticed straightaway that Alice had gone still.

'What happened then?'

'I'd seen it in his eyes that morning, but I convinced myself it was just a bad dream. How could it be so banal? A lorry hitting his car just as he turned out onto the main road.'

Alice's shoulders were rigid. Will sensed her tension.

'And?' she said finally.

'Somehow, as I watched his car drive away, I knew this wasn't just a dream. I ran upstairs to look out of a window and saw him reach the end of the road. Then he turned out without stopping and there was the flash of a lorry. I heard the bang clearly, but fortunately the lorry pushed his car out of sight. And that was that.'

Alice was immobile. Will was wrestling with his breathing, trying to still his racing heart, but he saw she was struggling with something, too.

'Did you just make that up?'

Will was surprised to see that she was furious. 'No, no. Of course not,' he said.

'You don't think you're just attention seeking. If you turn this round, isn't it just a desire to have the whole world revolve around you?'

'Good God, no.'

And now Alice was on her feet. 'You should think about that,' she said. 'Do you just want to be at the centre of everything?'

And then she stormed out, and Will remained staring at the door, blinking, as it slammed shut after her.

Chapter Eight

His night was full of restless dreams. He saw himself pinned under a bus, the wheel grinding through his stomach, shattering his pelvis. Then he was above the accident, watching it all unfold in slow motion. If only he had turned away, if only. He might have had a lingering regret about little Melanie, but he wouldn't have seen it all. Now instead he had indelible images of the broken children and misshapen limbs, the mother staring at the sky in agony. He woke, bathed in sweat, heart pounding as if he had run for miles.

He lay there, staring up at the plasterwork on the ceiling. Really, this was another prison. He couldn't get out. And anyway, the real prison was in his mind, and there was no escaping the images there.

He went into the bathroom and stood at the sink with his head bowed. It was time to find out whether his fate had changed. What would he see in his own eyes? If his intervention could change the death date of all the victims at the bus stop then surely it must have changed his too.

Slowly he raised his eyes to the mirror. Straightaway he could see it was different. Not a frozen night but bright blue sunshine. A country footpath, then the sharp and rising pain that he knew from the vision of Slater. Heart attack, but not for years. Seventy-two.

Will stared into the mirror transfixed. He had bought himself a full life, but at the expense of three dead children and two dead parents. How could he live with that? The guilt washed through him. He would be condemned to regret this Faustian pact every extra day of his life. He staggered to a chair and collapsed on it. Every time he thought he'd reached the bottom he discovered there was some lower state. Somewhere he could feel even worse.

Eventually he dragged himself off the chair. He had a long hot bath and changed into the new clothes that had been delivered to the room. They fitted well enough.

When a cooked breakfast arrived, he tried to eat, knowing that he needed to keep his strength up. He felt the need for a drink again, but ruthlessly suppressed it. They weren't likely to offer, and after what happened, he wasn't going to drink again for a long, long time.

There was a knock on the door mid-morning and Alice poked her head into the room. 'I'm going to start by apologising for my outburst yesterday,' she said, still not quite looking him in the eye. 'It was very unprofessional of me.'

She wore the same uniform of black and white, but this time she had on a black puffa jacket. 'I wondered if we could take a walk and talk,' she said.

'Will they let us?'

'There will be minders, but far enough away that they can't hear. I've borrowed this coat for you.'

Will took the coat and followed her out the door. She led the way down a series of carpeted corridors to a back kitchen and then through a back door into what turned out to be surprisingly formal gardens. This had clearly been a manor house of importance at some stage. They came past a series of box hedges into an expanse of lawn and flower beds. And there in the middle of the lawn was a peacock, putting on a display of its tail feathers.

'Very classy safe house,' said Will.

Alice ignored him. She set off at a pace on the flagstone walks that surrounded the large square walled garden. Will glanced back and saw the two shadows take a position on the corner of the square nearest the house, watching them.

'I'm sorry for making such accusations. It was wrong of me. I accept that you have these …er…visions of how people are going to die,' she said. 'But you surely must accept that they may be just that. Visions.'

She was staring fixedly ahead, talking with an urgent intensity. Will had to hurry to even keep sight of her profile, her eyes fixed on the stone path.

'They are not visions to me. They reveal the truth,' said Will.

'But how can you be sure?'

'I check in the newspapers. It's always true. And I have seen a few with my own eyes.' He described Alloway's death to her, but she only responded with a furious shake of the head.

'It could be a coincidence,' she said. 'There must have been plenty of sniper's deaths like that.'

Will shrugged. 'It's not just the same sort of death. It is very precise. I'm seeing the scene in detail.'

Alice lapsed into silence for a few minutes. Will studied the distant green hills as they walked. The countryside had a plush, well-tended air. Definitely Surrey.

'I don't understand why he believes you,' Alice muttered, almost to herself.

'Who's he?'

'My boss. Dexter.'

'I think he's just intrigued. He's asked for a demonstration.'

'What? What do you mean?'

'He wanted proof. So, I told him about someone who is going to die this afternoon at four.'

Alice stopped in her tracks. 'Who?'

'It's the police inspector on my case. A heart attack.'

Her face was aghast. 'But you've got to do something. Warn him.'

She whirled around, looking at him head-on. And there it was. An old people's home, a country house not unlike this one. The pervasive smell of urine and death. A younger man holding her hand. A relative, presumably, although he looked strangely familiar.

She was eighty-two. Not very dignified, but at least a long life. Will felt surprised at how relieved he was. He didn't want to have the dilemma of what to tell this intense young woman. He didn't want to have to lie to her.

Will looked her in the eye. 'I can't do anything. Look what happened with the bus crash when I intervened. There is no way of knowing the consequences it will have.' He felt the stab of guilt again when he remembered the extra years he'd been gifted. He wasn't mentioning that right now.

'But that was an act of violence, an accident. This is one man. You could save his life,' said Alice.

'And that could ripple outwards and kill someone else. It's impossible to know.'

Alice swallowed, clearly fighting for control. Then she stopped and looked at Will again. 'You saw, didn't you, when you looked into my eyes? You saw my death.'

Will nodded. Alice looked away. 'I don't want to know. I don't want to be manipulated by you.'

Will said nothing. He wondered why she was angry. She wasn't behaving like any psychiatrist he had ever met before. And there had been a few.

They walked on in silence for a while. Finally, Alice said, 'Do you believe in fate, in destiny? Because if you're right, it looks like we've all got a pre-determined fate we can't escape.'

'I don't know. That's not how I think of it. To me, it's just a map of what is going to happen. Everyone is free to make their own mistakes, and accidents intervene. I'm just able to see how it will end.'

'But where is the free will if you know the outcome, and there's no getting away from it?'

'Why are you so upset? You don't even believe it.'

Alice shot him a furious look. 'I'll see you later,' she said and stomped off.

The two minders shepherded Will back to his bedroom. They never came close enough to speak, but Will could see the direction they wanted him to go. He thought about running the opposite way just to see what would happen, but there seemed little point in antagonising them. Wait and see what happens at four o'clock, he thought.

The hours dragged past. They served him lunch on a tray. He avoided looking in the mirror. He watched television and felt relieved to discover that he was no longer leading the news. The hunt for a rogue terrorist cell was back in the headlines, and the country was on a red alert.

He thought about Slater and felt a moment of pity. But there was nothing he could do. There were people dying every second somewhere around the world. In terrorist attacks, in accidents, from illness. This was just the one he knew about.

He was relieved when four o'clock finally arrived. At least now things would move on. He didn't doubt for a second that Slater was dead. When Dexter finally walked back in at 4.20 p.m., he went on the offensive.

'I was right, wasn't I?' he said.

Dexter smiled, 'You were indeed,' although his face remained tight. He looked both angry and pleased at the same time.

'It was four o'clock?' asked Will.

'To the second,' said Dexter.

There was a silence. 'What's the problem?' Will finally said.

'Is there a problem?' Dexter shot back.

'I can see it in your face.'

Dexter stared at him, meeting Will's eye, not bothered. Broken windscreen, grinding metal, engine driven backwards into Dexter's lap. Will flinched and looked away.

'You see it every time, don't you?' said Dexter with satisfaction.

'I get used to individual ones, but it's always there, yes,' said Will, grimacing.

'Must get in the way of relationships. You look into someone's eyes, and you can always see their death.'

'I don't do relationships,' Will said shortly.

'Or sex?' Dexter added. 'Le petit mort and Le Grand Mort all in one. Maybe it adds some spice.'

'Hilarious.'

They were squared off across the room now.

'What's the problem?'

'Someone tried to warn Slater,' Dexter said curtly.

Will was shocked. 'Well, it wasn't me. It's the last thing I'd have wanted. You must know that by now. Anyway, how could I do it, locked in here?'

Dexter said nothing, but just watched Will keenly. Will scanned backwards, searching for the answer, until it came to him.

'It was Alice,' he said.

'You knew she was going to do it?'

'She wanted to, but I told her not to.'

'You didn't put her up to it?'

'I told you. I don't want to intervene ever again. There's no knowing what might happen.'

'Fortunately, we intercepted her phone call, so no harm done. Except to Slater, of course.' Dexter chuckled, pleased with his own joke.

Will grimaced. He was beginning to hate the man. 'She's not a very professional psychiatrist if she goes against the patient's wishes,' Will said.

Dexter looked away. Will got the powerful impression that this time he did not want to meet Will's eye.

'She's not a psychiatrist at all, is she?' said Will flatly.

Again, Dexter said nothing. Will shrugged. This wasn't getting him anywhere.

'Ok, you've got your proof. What happens now?'

'Patience, patience,' said Dexter smoothly. 'My bosses may require further evidence.'

'Bosses? I thought you were in charge here?'

'There is always someone higher,' said Dexter with a sly smile.

'And Alice? Will she be punished?'

'We'll see,' said Dexter.

'Will I see her again?' asked Will, and hoped the answer was yes.

'We'll see,' said Dexter. He moved to the door. 'Sit tight. I'll be back soon.' And with that, he was gone.

***

Will wondered what was getting to Alice? Why was she so furious? Why had she tried to intervene when Will had expressly asked her not to?

Still, at least she had engaged with him. Shown something, even if it was anger. Will was getting increasingly irked by Dexter's blandness. Nothing seemed to ruffle him at all.

63

There was a knock on the door, and Alice appeared again. 'Fancy another walk,' she said, as if nothing had happened.

Soon they were out in the manicured gardens again, the minders visible in the distance.

'I didn't think I would see you again,' said Will.

'Why ever not?'

'You seemed angry last time,' said Will.

'I'm sorry about that,' said Alice. 'There's something about your *gift*.' She said it with a heavily accented irony. 'There's something about it that freaks me out.'

Will decided to keep quiet about Dexter and see where this went. 'Go on,' he said.

Alice stopped walking and stared towards a distant copse of trees. Will noticed her long lashes and the electric blue of her eyes. He also noticed the sadness in them.

'I guess it brings back a lot of terrible memories,' she muttered. 'Things I'd rather forget.'

Will said nothing. Best often to let people fill their own silences. He had learnt that in interrogation classes.

Eventually Alice gave him a small smile. 'I lost someone who I think I could have saved. If I'd known what he was planning.'

'Planning?'

'He killed himself.' Will could see the tears forming in her eyes, threatening to spill over. She raised her hand and angrily wiped them away. 'If I'd had your gift, I would have stopped him.'

Will hesitated, then said softly, 'I'm sorry.'

Alice shrugged. 'Nothing to be sorry about. It was a long time ago. Ancient history.'

She started walking again with a determined stride. Will let her recover before he continued. 'It really doesn't work like that,' he said. 'If you'd have been able to intervene you would have, but really what is going to happen will happen.'

She stopped and glared at him. 'You intervened.'

'Yes and look at the result. Five people died who might not have otherwise. And that's just the beginning. What if one of those people was destined to come up with something world changing. A cure for cancer perhaps? Or the person I've saved turns out to be a monster, another Hitler maybe?'

'Like Melanie,' said Alice with a smile.

'Maybe not her,' Will conceded. 'But if it was someone important, a politician, a leader of some kind, it could have far-reaching consequences. The point is there's no way of knowing how damaging the knock-on will be. That's why I'm never going to do it again.'

'Dexter won't like that.'

'I've already told him.'

'He wants to use you,' she said. 'For the good of the country.' She pronounced the well-worn phrase with a heavy irony.

'I won't change my mind,' said Will.

'He'll find a way. He is very persuasive.'

Will decided on a change of tack. 'Dexter knows you tried to warn Slater.'

Alice shrugged. 'Of course. But I had to try.'

'Will they punish you?'

'I don't care.' She flashed him an angry smile. 'I'm already in trouble. Dexter's behaving like the shit he usually is. I think maybe I'm coming to the end of my time here.'

'You'd leave, just like that?'

'I guess I'd have to.'

'And go back to private practice?'

'What?'

'As a psychiatrist?' asked Will, keeping his voice deliberately even.

She looked at him for a second, then laughed. 'I'm not a psychiatrist. That was just to get your co-operation. Don't trust anything here. It's never what it seems.' She gave him a small wave. 'I'll see you later,' she said. 'Maybe.'

Will stopped her. 'Who was it? The person who killed himself?'

She looked at him steadily; the anger gone and only sadness left. 'My father,' she said, then she turned and walked away.

Chapter Nine

Will had barely returned to his room when there was a guard at his door beckoning him with a curt, 'Follow me.'

They went down to the main entrance hall and then walked off to the right along a plushly carpeted corridor to a pair of grand wooden doors. The guard pushed them open, revealing a large drawing room with heavy armchairs and a dark oak table in the bay window. Dexter was sitting behind the table, the middle of three. Will shifted his attention to the others and was shocked to discover his old army commanding officer, Colonel Grantley, sitting there on Dexter's right, staring at him. The Colonel nodded. Will knew he was gaping. The other man looked like an anonymous official, already writing on a pad, head down.

Dexter smiled that wolfish smile. 'This is where it gets serious. This is a colleague of mine, Thompson. He'll be keeping a record.' Thompson didn't even look up. 'And we thought you might appreciate the views of your old Colonel.'

Will doubted that. The last time he'd seen Colonel Grantley had been after his court martial. He was pretty sure the only words the Colonel had uttered to him then were that he had wasted his potential, and he was a disgrace to the regiment.

'Take a seat,' Dexter gestured unctuously. This beginning to resemble the worst-ever job interview.

Will nodded to the Colonel, who pursed his lips in distaste. Good to be back in your company, Will thought.

He couldn't help reflecting how it had once been very different. The Colonel had been his mentor, had promoted him and even given him a citation for bravery when Will had saved the Colonel's life. A rogue Afghani police officer had tried to kill Grantley at a passing-out parade. Will had spotted the policeman behaving oddly, and as soon as he pulled his gun out and took aim, Will had shot him dead.

But despite that history, when it all went wrong, Grantley had abandoned him. No soldier of mine ever runs away, he remembered Grantley saying, and even an initial diagnosis of PTSD hadn't changed Grantley's view.

'Let's get down to business,' said Dexter. 'We want you to use your particular talent in the service of your country, and we're here to discuss how best to do that.'

Will cleared his throat. 'I can see why you and your friend might be here to discuss that, but the Colonel?'

Dexter glanced at Colonel Grantley, who said curtly, 'I'm here to remind you of your duty.'

Will couldn't stop himself from laughing.

'You failed your country and your colleagues,' the Colonel said sharply. 'Perhaps you could make up for that now.'

'As I recall,' said Will, 'you didn't want to know why. You just kicked me out and covered up the fact that the operation had been a total shambles from the start.'

'You ran away.'

'I ran away, as you put it, because I knew all my comrades were going to die and there was nothing I could do about it.'

The Colonel was about to reply, but Dexter put a hand on his arm. 'Why don't we come back to that later and start at

68

the beginning? Perhaps you could explain, for the benefit of Thompson and the Colonel, exactly what you see when you look into someone's eyes.'

Will studied Thompson. He had his eyes fixed on his pad and would not look up. As for the Colonel, Will knew his fate from their earlier service together, but Will looked at him full on, just to confirm it. There he was sitting in a troop carrier, a blinding thump, and the vehicle disintegrating, shredding his body. Roadside IED. Clearly a terrorist bomb, somewhere hot and sandy. And now, Will was intrigued to discover, only eight days away.

Will felt the blast, but because he had seen it before, he was ready and controlled his instinctive flinch. He took a deep breath and looked back at the Colonel.

That would wipe the contempt off your face, Will thought. But he said nothing, just watched the man who had been his biggest supporter but then had drummed him out of the Army, become increasingly irritated.

'Answer the question, boy,' the Colonel finally erupted. Will held his gaze, seeing the flash, feeling the force of the explosion again.

'It's like a three-second movie,' he said. 'Just the moment of death and the sense of the surroundings. But I feel it too and that gives me a greater sense of where it is. As for when, somehow, the date and time flash into my mind.'

There was a moment's silence, then the Colonel muttered, 'What utter poppycock.'

Dexter put a restraining hand on the Colonel's arm again. 'Let's, for the sake of this discussion, assume he's telling the truth.'

'You must believe me,' Will said to Dexter. 'Otherwise, you wouldn't have organised this tea party so quickly. You didn't wait for Slater's death, did you?'

Dexter nodded. 'You're right. After what happened with Montgomery, I had a feeling, and I thought the information you might give us was too valuable to waste time.'

'Too valuable?'

Dexter hesitated for a second, clearly weighing his words, then pressed on. 'We have a problem, and by 'we' I mean not just MI5, but Britain. The terrorist forces ranged against us, Al Qaeda, the remnants of Isis, all those bent on our destruction, are becoming much harder to track. We are currently searching for a rogue cell. Traditional intelligence methods are falling short, and it's very dangerous to get people in undercover.'

Will noticed Thompson glance at Dexter, who registered the intervention but made a shushing motion with his hand. What was that about?

'We rely on turning people, persuading them to help us, but there is little in it for them, and they don't last long. In the last few years, the move towards isolated individuals, the so-called 'lone wolves', has made it even harder. They're not connected to any cell system, they come out of the blue. We can only try to spot them when they become radicalised, but there are thousands out there, and it may take months or years before they carry out an operation.

Dexter paused. 'Your gift could be very useful. You could help us cut to the end product, so to speak. You could look at all those radicalised, would-be terrorists and tell us

70

precisely which ones are going to go into action and die for their cause.'

Will thought for a second. 'What would you do then? Put them in prison for the rest of their lives? Or quietly dispose of them?'

Dexter looked at him, clearly weighing up the options. 'We could let them run. See who helps them.'

'But at some point you would have to intervene,' said Will. 'It stands to reason. You wouldn't be able to resist. It would seem like the best option, saving people's lives.'

'And what would be wrong with that?' asked Dexter mildly.

'I thought I was saving that girl's life,' said Will bitterly. 'But look how many more died instead. You can't know what the consequences would be.'

'You never can in a war,' said the Colonel. 'You just make the best choice you can.'

'But supposing hundreds of innocents die.'

The Colonel shrugged. 'You couldn't have known.'

'But that's the problem,' said Will. 'I could know. I do know. And I'm the one who will have to live with that.'

'Sounds like cowardice to me,' said the Colonel quietly, but Dexter raised an arm to silence him.

'Let's just pursue this a bit further,' he said smoothly. 'If we took no action, just viewed it as gathering intelligence, you might be prepared to co-operate. It could still be useful to us to build up a wider, more detailed picture.'

Will hesitated. 'I find it hard to believe that someone somewhere wouldn't act on it.'

'What about vetting our people? Senior people who are under threat?'

'Like who?' asked Will.

'The PM, the Cabinet, senior civil servants.'

'But if they were under threat, you would have to take action.'

'You wouldn't want us to let the Prime Minister get killed, would you?' said Dexter, as if it was the most unlikely suggestion in the world.

Will hesitated. 'Why is the Prime Minister any different from Melanie Burton?' he said. But even to him, it sounded lame.

'If you don't know the difference, there is no hope for you,' said the Colonel.

'I think what the Colonel means,' said Dexter with a smile, 'is that it might be worth some collateral damage to save the Prime Minister.'

'Yes, but that would be on my conscience.'

'You think a lot of your conscience, don't you?' said the Colonel.

Again, Dexter raised a hand. 'Have you considered the possibility that some intervention by you might be part of the plan?' he said. 'For all you know, it could be taking account of your intervention. You just haven't tried to do it much yet.'

'And the bus crash?'

'These things happen with the best of intentions. There's no way of knowing. What I do know is that you could save many people's lives. Do you really want to leave them to be blown up, shot, stabbed in the street when you could do something?'

Will felt trapped. Could he really ignore that plea, but what would happen if he helped?

'I'll have to think about it,' he said finally.

'That's a shame,' said Dexter softly. 'We would have preferred to persuade you, but we're running out of time.' Dexter looked past Will and nodded. Before Will could react, he felt a hand close over his mouth and a sharp pinprick in his neck. A needle.

A voice whispered in his ear. 'Sorry, mate.'

He had a second to register his surprise that they would drug him right here like this, and to take in Dexter and Grantley's cold, cold stares. Then the darkness enveloped him.

Chapter Ten

The first thing Will noticed as his senses returned was a familiar smell. Slightly antiseptic, slightly boiled cabbage. He knew straight away that he was back in a hospital. But then, behind and beyond it was a deeper, darker chemical tang that caught at his nostrils and made his throat constrict. The answer popped into his mind straight away. Formaldehyde.

He opened his eyes to find Dexter leaning over him with an apologetic smile. 'Sorry for the dramatics,' Dexter said breezily. 'Just a little sedation. We wanted you to see something, and we weren't sure you would agree.'

Will shook his head and focussed beyond Dexter. Institutional green walls, grey linoleum, steel doors. Two sharp suited heavies waiting in the background.

'You could at least have asked,' he said slowly, sitting up.

'Time was pressing,' said Dexter.

'Really. Why have you brought me to the morgue? I don't think any of these people are in a hurry.'

Dexter grimaced. 'The dead may not be, but those still living are. Follow me.'

Will stood up. He felt shaky, but the iron tang of formaldehyde mixed with blood was certainly clearing his head quickly.

He followed Dexter past the steel filing cabinets and their hidden bodies into a white-tiled room with several steel tables, which he knew must be the autopsy room. On one there was a body covered by a sheet. The stench of blood was suddenly much worse, like a physical blow to his throat and nostrils. He could see that some of the blood had soaked through the covering. This would not be pleasant.

Dexter gestured for him to stand on one side of the body and then went round the table and took up a position opposite.

Will swallowed. 'I can't see the point of this,' he said. 'The guy is dead. There's nothing I can do either way.'

Dexter said nothing, reached forward and folded back the sheet to reveal the man's head. He had short black hair cut close and dark olive skin. Immediately, Will could see cuts and abrasions across his forehead and bruising around his face. Someone had broken his nose, and there was a trail of blood down to his upper lip.

Unpleasant, thought Will, but not appalling. Then Dexter continued folding down the sheets, revealing the man's full Islamic beard and a jagged gaping cut on the side of his neck that went underneath the beard and emerged on the other side. His throat had been severed with significant force, and the wound was so deep that it seemed like they had been planning a decapitation. This had to be the work of fanatics, Will was sure.

Will looked up at Dexter. 'Isis?' he asked. 'A casualty of war?'

Dexter ignored him, continuing to turn down the sheets with a flourish like some bad conjurer. But he wasn't

75

revealing a dove, or a sawn-in-half lady miraculously rejoined.

Dark little circles of charred flesh covered the man's chest. Cigarette burns, hundreds of them, and then, as his stomach was revealed, Will saw there were deep cuts gouged into the flesh. This must be a revenge killing, a warning.

Finally, Dexter removed the sheet and exposed the area that had left so much blood on the cloth. The man's groin. Except there was nothing left. Just a sea of blood. They had cut off his penis and his testicles and left just the eviscerated flesh. Will shuddered. He hoped the man hadn't been alive when that was done, but he suspected the opposite.

Will looked up at Dexter, who was gazing at him keenly. He saw again like a shadow Dexter's own car crash death and understood why that must feel like a preferable option to this.

'He was one of your agents,' said Will.

Dexter nodded. 'He was undercover, infiltrating an Isis group.'

'And they found out,' said Will. 'A terrible way to die.' Will took a deep breath. 'But I still can't see what this has to do with me. I know how brutal they can be. I saw it in Afghanistan and Iraq. Taliban, Isis, they all have a hideous talent for torture. But it's too late for this guy. There's nothing I could tell you about his death that's not plain to see.'

'It's not about him,' Dexter said with a small smile, and then he looked behind Will and made a brief gesture of assent.

76

Will turned, and there was a newcomer. He was superficially similar to the dead man, same close black hair, same olive skin, same Islamic beard, if anything, a bit more abundant, a bit more faithful. But there was a tight energy in this man's movements as he strode across the room and a gleam in his eyes that said I'm very much alive.

Will knew instantly the game Dexter was playing, and that it was already too late to find a way out. The newcomer's eyes were fixed on Will's, and everything became clear. A wicked, serrated edge sawing into his throat, blood pouring out in a red viscous arc and his eyes rolling back into his head. And behind him a dirty brick wall with a tattered Isis flag hanging across it. A ritual execution, probably to the camera, and less than twenty-four hours away.

Will let out a little groan. He knew he was trapped. Dexter pretended he hadn't heard and carried on. 'This is Mo, though of course when he's undercover, his name is Mohammed. He is trying to inveigle himself into the same group as our friend here,' Dexter said, nodding towards the blood-spattered body on the table. 'We need to know if he's been compromised, too.'

There was a long silence. Will could feel Mo's anxious gaze and Dexter watching him carefully.

'I told you I wasn't prepared to do this,' said Will, feeling sick.

'You have to,' said Dexter flatly. 'What you know could save this man's life, and I'm guessing by your reaction that you do indeed know. Are you really going to let him go back and die?'

77

Will turned away, trying to think. Could he really say nothing, knowing that Mohammed would be dead within the day, knowing the terror and the pain that he would face? And if he did tell them would that set off another chain of unexpected deaths? Not to mention that he could kiss goodbye to his longer peaceful life.

Will could feel the bile rising. He hurried over to the sink and threw up, a cold sweat on his forehead. He fought the urge to throw up again and hurriedly turned on the tap, splashing water over his face and sluicing out his mouth.

'If you don't tell us, or you lie to us, he could end up on this morgue table. Your choice, your responsibility,' Dexter said remorselessly.

'You tricked me,' said Will. 'You've put me in an impossible position.'

'No, your gift has. But you can use it for good.'

Will looked at Mo again, at the man's vital, living face, at the death in his eyes.

'I'm imploring you, Mr Gray,' Mo said. 'Please tell me the truth.'

Will slumped back against the steel table, utterly defeated. 'It's a ritual beheading. Tomorrow, 8 pm.'

Mo blanched, the shock written large on his face.

'Do you know where?' asked Dexter.

'It looked like a warehouse wall behind. Bare brick, with an Isis flag draped over it. I got the feeling they were filming it.'

Dexter nodded at Mo, and he left the autopsy room.

'You saved his life,' Dexter said.

'Maybe, but who else will die as a result?' said Will.

Dexter looked at him. 'Just some terrorists,' he said, with the ghost of a smile.

Chapter Eleven

'Well, you got what you wanted,' said Will angrily. 'You all got what you wanted.'

Alice was silent. They were in Will's bedroom. He'd come back from the morgue in a fury. Dexter had tricked him blind. What chance had he really had?

'You saved that man's life,' said Alice quietly.

'But at what cost?'

'The trouble is you can't really know the cost,' said Alice. 'Why not do the deed and take the risk?'

Will could feel Alice studying him, but he didn't want to be talked round. The dead agent had been such a gruesome sight. How could he have left Mohammed to such a grisly fate? He was trapped whichever way he turned.

'I understand,' said Alice. 'You feel responsible. But believe me, it is much worse knowing that someone is going to die and then doing nothing.' She hesitated. 'We're the same, really. I never wanted the responsibility of my father's death. He put it on me. I would love to be rid of it too.'

She reached out a hand and touched his shoulder. Will was taken aback not only by the gesture but by the overwhelming reaction he felt. His chest heaved and tears sprang to his eyes. He couldn't bear this any longer and any sign of sympathy left him defenceless.

He had to stop her. Without really thinking, he seized her hand, but that only pulled her closer to him. And then suddenly he was conscious of her lips and her breath on his face, and without thinking he was leaning forward and trying to kiss her, desperate for human touch.

Alice brought up a hand to stop him, and her eyes flashed. 'What the hell do you think you're doing?'

Will felt like he'd been slapped. He turned away to cover his confusion.

'Let's just keep this professional, shall we?' Alice said. 'I don't get involved with the person I'm minding. I'm not a honey trap.'

Will stuttered. 'Sorry. Just a misunderstanding.'

'Not by me,' said Alice sharply.

'God, you're fierce,' said Will. 'I'm sorry, okay?'

Alice relented. 'Okay, forget it.'

An uneasy silence descended. Will looked at her. She was sitting rigidly on a chair as though she were ready to spring into action at any second, her face set, her mouth a thin line. She radiated a steely determination.

There was a knock on the door, and two of the minders came in with trays of food, put them down, and left.

'You're eating with me?' asked Will.

'We need to talk,' said Alice.

'You mean it's your job to persuade me. Maybe I don't want to be persuaded.'

Alice ignored him and gestured to the table. They sat and removed the covers from the food. It was a chicken breast with a nameless red sauce, Parmentier potatoes and French beans. More country house fare, but Will hadn't eaten for a long time. He suddenly felt hungry.

They said nothing and just ate until Will felt compelled to break the silence.

'If we're going to have this dinner date from hell, then maybe you could at least tell me a bit about yourself. Why are you so fierce?'

Alice looked as if she was about to bridle at that, but she swallowed the retort, and after a moment's consideration she said, 'I guess I've always been a bit like that. My father used to call me his little honey badger. Small and cuddly to look at, but quick to attack with very sharp teeth and claws. They're known for being ferocious and fearless, and they're immune to poison too.'

Will couldn't help but smile. 'That does suit you. Tell me more about your father. Why do you think you could have saved him?'

Alice tensed again, but then took a deep breath. Will hoped that she would open up.

'Looking back, I understand now that he was always prone to depression,' Alice said slowly. 'In my childhood, he was dark and moody and difficult, but then suddenly the sun would shine and I was his special daughter and it all seemed fine.'

She stopped, and Will watched the shadows flit across her face. 'But then my mother got cancer, breast cancer, and it was like the life leeched out of him too. The worse she got, the more he collapsed in on himself. I tried hard to lift him, but nothing could.'

Now he could see a tear in her eye. 'It was like I had mentally written my mother off. She was going to die. There was nothing I could do about it. But to lose my father at the same time was too much.'

'How old were you, then?'

'Eighteen,' she said bitterly. 'After her funeral, he just collapsed in on himself. He hardly went out of the house. He hardly got out of bed for months. I tried so hard.'

She was silent for a while, then she carried on. 'He appeared to get better. He encouraged me to take up my place at Cambridge. He made a big effort to tidy up and started talking about getting a job again. It was only afterwards I realised that he just wanted to create the space to kill himself. And to be fair, he wanted me out of the way so I wouldn't have to witness it. I went up to Cambridge and two weeks later he was dead.'

'And you think you could have stopped him? It sounds like he planned it carefully.'

'Yes, but maybe if I had said something. If I'd been there.' Alice shrugged despairingly.

'There was nothing you could have done,' he said. 'When someone's going to die, they are going to die.'

'But if I'd been like you and known, then I might have found a way. At least I'd have had that option.'

There was a long silence. Will could not think of anything comforting to say, and Alice was lost in her bitter memories. Then Alice's phone started ringing. She took a deep breath and answered. Will could see she had her armour back on again.

After a few seconds of listening, Alice simply said, 'Fine,' and ended the call. She went over to the television, turned it on, and flicked through till she found the BBC News channel. The tickertape proclaimed: 'Terror Cell Arrested. Four people have been taken to Paddington Green station and are being interviewed in connection with terrorist offences.'

The newsreader's voice had that urgent breathlessness that they saved for national emergencies. 'Police swooped on a house in Bethnal Green this afternoon and arrested four suspects. We understand they are part of the terror cell that the authorities have been concerned about and that led to the recent red alert. They have been taken to Paddington Green station for questioning.'

'That's your doing,' said Alice. 'That was the group that Mo had infiltrated. You saved his life, and we've picked them all up. Surely that was worthwhile.'

Will stared at the screen with a sinking feeling. What consequences would this have? And yet, how could he really regret preventing Mo's beheading? Maybe Dexter was right, maybe he was fated to save some people? There was no way of knowing. And as for the long life that had fleetingly been within his grasp? That had probably changed again after this intervention. It had been a mirage that was already gone.

Alice let the report finish and then turned off the TV.

'You really think I should do this?' asked Will.

'Of course,' she replied. 'I know it's my job to persuade you, but I'm sure. You have this power, use it. It's the right thing to do,' she added.

'Can I trust Dexter?'

'Definitely not. He's a complete shit. But sometimes you need shits on the side of the angels too.'

Will knew that he was being played, by Alice, by Dexter, by life, but he couldn't find it in himself to resist. He couldn't

84

face fighting against the flow any more. And there was no point worrying about his future. That would change and change again every time he intervened. He didn't think he would have a long life, and he didn't really care.

Maybe he would feel better about it all if he really was helping the angels. If it was for a good cause.

'If I do this, will you do something for me?' said Will. Alice nodded. 'I want to know everything about the people who died in the bus crash. I'm still worried that the victims who I accidentally got killed could have gone on to do something important for the world that won't happen now.'

'But you'll never know, particularly with the children.'

Will could see her point. 'Alright, but the adults at least. And I want to keep tabs on anyone who's an accidental victim of the knock-on consequences from now on.'

Alice looked troubled but eventually she agreed. 'I promise.'

Now was the moment. He couldn't shake a terrible foreboding, but there was no way of knowing whether it would turn out better or worse in the long run.

'Okay,' he said reluctantly. 'I'll try it.'

'Good,' said Alice. 'I'll tell Dexter. You try to get some sleep. I suspect it'll be a busy day tomorrow.'

Alice left and Will sat there, lost in thought. There was still a small voice at the back of his mind telling him he was making a terrible mistake.

Chapter Twelve

Dexter's face creased into its usual wolfish grin when he greeted Will the next morning. 'You've made the right decision. You won't regret it,' he said.

'I think I might,' said Will. 'But I'm going to try it. I have a couple of conditions, though.'

Dexter's smile returned to cold storage. 'Yes?'

'I will only tell you if it's something to do with national security, something terrorist related. And I want a time limit of five years in the future. I don't want it to become a blank cheque for future governments to interfere in these people's lives.'

Dexter's wary look was back. 'I'll agree to five years, but you'll have to tell me about the circumstances of every death. We will know if it affects national security, you may not.'

Eventually, Will conceded. 'One more thing, though,' he said. 'I don't want them to see me. I don't want them to know it's happening.'

'How's that going to work, then?'

'Easy. Get them to stare into the centre of a two-way mirror. I'm on the other side. Say it's part of a new vetting procedure.'

'And you'll still be able to tell?' Will nodded.

Dexter smiled. 'Okay. We'll try to get that set up where we can., But there may be one or two you will have to do on the hoof.'

'What does that mean?'

'It won't always be possible to persuade them to come to a pre-arranged session. Just wait and see. It suits me if we can use the two-way because then fewer people will know you exist. So yes, that will be the preferred option.'

And then it moved quickly. The next day Will was taken from the safe house to a flat in an anonymous modern block by the Thames, just a few hundred yards downriver from MI5. Near, but deniable, he supposed. He suddenly found he had new clothes, and some money, but since he was not allowed out unsupervised it was a limited freedom. They set up Alice in the second bedroom and had another minder on call. It was made clear that he wasn't to leave without either Alice or the minder's company.

Still, it was a measure of normality. Bedroom, bathroom, kitchen, sitting room and a view of the Thames with its dull grey expanse of water sliding powerfully and inexorably towards the sea. Will was surprised to find how pleased he felt when Alice moved in.

'Very stylish,' she said. 'They must want to keep you happy.'

'I think they just want to keep me. It's a high-class prison. Again.'

'With leather sofas, Egyptian cotton sheets and a view to die for,' said Alice, and they both laughed.

Later, when they were having supper, Alice asked him, 'Are you worried? First day tomorrow and all that.'

'How hard can it be?' Will said. 'I just look into their eyes and fess up about their futures, short or long.'

'Just be careful,' said Alice. 'They'll throw you in at the deep end.' And she looked away.

'Do you know what Dexter's planning?' asked Will.

'Not exactly, but it won't be easy.' And then she wouldn't say any more.

'Will you be there?'

'I'll be around,' she said vaguely. 'I'll be keeping an eye on you.'

'Is that your only job now?' he asked, and she shrugged. He was irritated at the lack of information. He would have to demand more from Dexter. But as he went to bed, he couldn't deny that knowing Alice was in the next room reassured him. His honey badger minder, ready to look after him at all costs.

Chapter Thirteen

The next morning he was up and ready by nine.

'Morning Mike,' Will said cheerily. He hadn't been offered a name of any kind, but he decided that the solid, suited minder with an expressionless face looked like a Mike, and that was what Will would call him.

Mike simply nodded and led the way down to the basement car park where a car and driver were waiting. Alice had gone in early so Will sat next to Mike in the back.

They drove out on to Nine Elms Lane and then east along the riverbank. It was a gusty day with the sun occasionally peeping through. Will was very conscious of the bulk of MI6's fake Art déco headquarters looming ahead, next to the river. Spies all around.

The car turned left on to Vauxhall Bridge and then right on to Millbank heading towards MI5's headquarters at Thames House. Will studied the drivers of the other cars, cocooned in their predictable, conventional worlds. For them it was just another day at the office where the most threatening problem was likely to be an overbearing boss and maybe worrying about how long they would keep their job.

For Will it would be death, death and more death. Every pair of eyes surrendering the most private of moments up to the spooks' gaze. Will felt slightly sick. And he knew he would have to watch Dexter every inch of the way, just as Alice had warned him. He was sure that Dexter had plans for Will that contravened every promise he'd been given.

They drove past the imposing neoclassical front of Thames House. The entrance had an enormous arch with a coffered ceiling that reminded Will of the inside of the Pantheon in Rome. Not exactly a low-key place to house half of Britain's spying community.

The car turned round the back of the building and down into an underground car park. Alice was there to meet him.

'This is your visitor's pass,' she said handing him a lanyard.

'Visitor?' asked Will.

'Just for the time being.' Alice seemed snappy, distracted. 'I'm going to take you up a back lift to meet Dexter and he'll explain what's going to happen next.'

Alice led the way to a back corner of the car park and used a key to open the lift there. Will saw there was only one floor button. Alice pressed it and they rose slowly up towards the top of the building. A private lift, then. But whose?

When they arrived Alice put her head out of the door and checked each way. She led him out into a wood-panelled and expensively carpeted corridor. This was clearly very senior level.

They entered a plain window-less room with just a table and chairs, a wastepaper basket and, by way of decoration, a large mirror along one wall. Alice gestured for Will to sit.

'No reception committee, then?' Will joked.

Alice smiled thinly. 'We don't want anyone to see you, certainly not yet. Everyone here keeps right on top of the news, so you're going to be recognised from the bus crash pretty quickly.'

The door opened and Dexter strode in. 'Good morning, Mr Gray. I'm going to be quite straight with you.' Will wondered if everyone who said that was always lying. It certainly seemed likely here.

'We have a bit of an emergency right now,' Dexter continued. 'I need to use you immediately.'

'What kind of emergency?' asked Will.

'It will become clear, but I don't want to forewarn you in case it affects your …er…vision.'

Dexter pressed a switch on the side of the table and the mirror suddenly changed to reveal the next-door room. It was much more expensively furnished with a large walnut table and a row of green leather chairs on either side. The opposite wall had two oil portraits of what looked like nineteenth century figures. Will was amused to see that one of the portraits depicted Admiral Nelson. The blind eye to the telescope opposite the all-seeing mirror. Someone had a sense of humour.

'I'm going to be bringing your target in there,' Dexter said, gesturing to the other room. 'We need you to look into their eyes and tell us the result.'

'They'll have to look straight at me,' said Will. 'It could be very hit and miss. Is it a man or a woman?'

'What's that got to do with it?' asked Dexter.

'Well, if it's a woman, you could say they have a smudge on their cheek and they'll come across to this mirror and check it, and then I'd definitely see into their eyes.'

'And if it's a man?'

'Just say it's dirt. They'll still want to check.'

Dexter looked put out but nodded his head. 'Ok.'

'This isn't a fair test,' said Alice.

Dexter fixed her with an icy stare. 'Stay out of it, Alice. It's not a test. It's the best we can do in the circumstances.' With that, Dexter left.

Will looked at Alice. 'He really doesn't like you, does he?'

'We don't get on,' said Alice. 'It's a mutual thing.'

After that, they waited in silence until the door in the other room opened and Dexter appeared in the corridor, indicating to someone that they should enter in front of him. A woman appeared and Will felt his chest tighten. It was the Home Secretary, Barbra Dent, her plain tight face set in its traditional disapproving glare, her mouth a thin, hard line.

Will was surprised to discover that a microphone was turned on.

'Why do I have to wait here?' Dent said irritably, looking round the room. 'Why can't Deborah see me now? I am supposed to be in charge here, you know.'

Deborah, Will thought, must be the head of MI5, Deborah Hillyer.

'She's very sorry to keep you waiting. She won't be long,' said Dexter, indicating a chair on the opposite side of the table facing the mirror that hid Will. As soon as she was seated, Dexter scurried round the other side so that when she looked at him, she would face the mirror.

But immediately Dent pulled out her phone and studied it, flicking systematically through messages. 'It's really very inconvenient,' she muttered to herself.

Dexter glanced towards the mirror, checking where he would have to get her to look. 'I'm sorry, but this really is a matter of some importance,' he said. 'We have credible evidence of a threat to your life.'

Will tensed, expecting the Home Secretary to look up and stare at Dexter, but she just flicked him a contemptuous glance.

'You spooks, you always like to wind us up, don't you? Keep us dancing to your tune. I've lost count of the supposedly credible threats to my life.' She went back to her phone.

'This isn't working. She's never going to look up for long enough,' Will said to Alice. 'Tell Dexter to do what I suggested.'

Alice tapped a message, pressed send, and there was a ping in the next room. Dexter glanced at his phone and seemed doubly irritated, but after a second he said, 'Home Secretary, that was Deborah's PA. She's ready now.'

'Thank God,' said Dent, rising quickly to her feet.

'I don't know how to put this,' said Dexter unctuously, 'but you have a smudge on your cheek. You might like to check it in the mirror.'

Barbra Dent gave him a look of pure malice, as if this was another cheap trick to keep women in their place, but she advanced quickly round the table towards the mirror.

Will readied himself. He wouldn't have long. She was too impatient. As soon as her cold blue eyes hit the mirror searching for the non-existent mark, he looked straight into them.

And there she was, standing in the open air at a podium, uncharacteristically smiling in a formal look-at-me-handling-government-business kind of way. It was an event of some kind. She looked as if she was about to start a speech. Then there was a blinding flash and an eruption of fire and pain. Will felt it like a physical shock coursing through him, firing up every nerve ending. It was a bomb, it must be a bomb. And the date was just fifteen days away.

Will felt the sweat start out on his forehead and his stomach heave. He looked wildly round, grabbed the wastepaper basket, and vomited into it.

'Christ,' said Alice. 'What was that about?'

Will couldn't find the words. His heart was racing, his chest was heaving, and his mouth was full of bile. He concentrated on trying to slow his breathing.

'What did you see?' asked Alice, but at that moment, the door opened and Dexter strode back in.

'Did it work?' Dexter asked urgently. Then the overpowering smell of vomit hit him. 'What's happened?'

Alice gestured at the wastepaper basket and Dexter glanced in with distaste. 'That was how you reacted? Well, it must be something big.'

Alice grimaced, and they both looked at Will.

He swallowed. 'It was a bomb. A terrorist bomb.'

'When?' demanded Dexter.

'Two weeks. May 10th,' said Will. He felt like he was going to vomit again. He doubled over.

'And where was it?' added Dexter.

'Couldn't really see, but it felt like a public event. She had a kind of professional smile the instant before, as if she was on show.'

'Anything else you can tell us?'

'Just a feeling that it was a suicide bomber, not a car bomb. Something about the blast.'

'You can tell them apart?' asked Alice with surprise.

'I've seen both. In Afghanistan. In a car bomb the air is full of metal. A suicide bomber feels more like a pure explosion. And more body parts.'

'Not much left of dear Barbra, then?' added Dexter with a slight smile.

'Not a lot.'

Alice looked disgusted. 'That was a rotten trick to play on Will,' she said.

'Sometimes needs must,' said Dexter. 'Don't create trouble, Alice, you don't want more.'

Alice looked as if she was about to spit out a retort, but instead she turned away. Will wondered why they were at such loggerheads. It wasn't very reassuring.

'Are you alright? I'd like to take you to see someone in a few minutes. We need to act on this.'

'I'd like a glass of water, and a chance to wash my face,' said Will.

'Of course. On the way. Alice, you can go back to the office,' he added.

Alice shot Dexter a look of pure hatred and left. Dexter led Will down several corridors and stopped at a single door with frosted glass.

'There's a toilet in there. Freshen yourself up,' he said with a smile, but Will could see that he was tightly wound underneath. 'Stay here till I return, please.'

Will went in and sluiced his face, and then took a long drink of water. What now? They would surely have to react to the Home Secretary's imminent death. If that is, they believed him. Will suspected he was about to get the ultimate going-over, and he wasn't looking forward to it much.

Dexter kept him waiting there for nearly twenty minutes, until, Will assumed, Barbra Dent had finished her meeting and left. Will knew he must be going to see the Head of MI5. Who else would have the final decision on this?

Finally Dexter re-appeared and led him round another corner, stopping at a big double door of polished wood. They went through and there was an anteroom with a woman guarding the entrance to another set of big double doors.

They went through into the room beyond, a long expanse of polished dark wood flooring and wood panelling leading to a wide window looking down on the river.

There was the Head of MI5, Deborah Hillyer, as Will expected. She was sitting behind a surprisingly modern desk reading a folder of documents, and there were others strewn around. She was a tall, angular woman, famous for her ferocious intensity and basilisk stare.

She gave Will a cursory glance and went back to her papers. Finally Dexter broke the silence. 'Mr Gray.'

'Good morning, Mr Gray,' said Hillyer, without looking up. She had a crisp, sharp tone. 'I've heard a lot about you. You have clearly made a big impression on Dexter. He's told me you're now predicting that our Home Secretary will be blown up in just a couple of weeks. Why should I believe you?'

She inclined her head and glanced at Will. Clearly she doesn't believe me at all, he thought.

'It's up to you,' said Will. 'Wait and see. You'll find out soon enough.'

Hillyer looked less than impressed. 'I say again, why should I believe you? It sounds like a fairground trick.'

Will started to get angry. He didn't need this. 'Look, I've told Dexter. I don't particularly want to help you. It costs me in pain and guilt. The one time I did intervene, it was disastrous. So I'm not forcing you to listen.'

Hillyer finally raised her head properly and looked squarely at Will. 'Dexter has told me about the police officer and the agent you may have saved and now the Home Secretary. I suppose the question is, can I afford to ignore you?'

Will stared into her steely grey eyes. He knew she was inviting him to read her. He was tempted to refuse, but what good would that do. He locked on.

There was a hospital bed, drips everywhere, nurses hovering, a doctor leaning forward to check her pulse, and then the final death rattle. Poison, of all things, and only twelve months away. Will couldn't help looking shocked.

'That good, eh?' she said with a hint of a smile. 'Well, I don't want to know right now, thank you, unless you're saying it's imminent.' Will shook his head. 'You're an uncomfortable person to be around, aren't you, Mr Gray?'

Will broke her gaze and concentrated on the view of the river out the window. He wasn't going to get into a staring match with her.

'Can we act on what Will has predicted?' asked Dexter.

'I suppose we must,' Hillyer said, 'but don't cancel the Home Secretary's event yet. See what you can reel in. Oh, and don't tell her either.'

'What about vetting the rest of the Cabinet?' asked Dexter.

Hillyer pondered for a second, then nodded. 'We may as well find out.' She looked at Will again as if he was some kind of insect under a microscope. 'You are going to be the keeper of a lot of secrets by the time this is over. Can I trust you?'

'You'll have to,' said Will flatly.

'I will indeed. Goodbye Mr Gray.' She turned back to her files again and Will was dismissed.

As he followed Dexter out he could only wonder just how complicated this was all going to get. The first few hours in his new job and he knew the Home Secretary was going to get blown up and the Head of MI5 poisoned. What on earth was going on?

***

They were having supper that evening when Alice asked: 'Does it always make you throw up like that?'

'You want to talk about this now?' said Will. Alice nodded. 'Okay. It's just the violent deaths. Usually bombs. The explosion seems to go right through me.'

'How can you bear it?'

'I've been through explosions before in Afghanistan. I'm used to it, in so far as that's possible. But the simple truth is, I don't have a choice.'

Alice gave him a sympathetic smile. 'I couldn't stand it. I'd go mad.'

'If I'd had it all my life, I'm sure I would have. But it's only been the last six years.' Will pushed away his plate. The food had lost its appeal. 'I don't know if I can take it forever. I'm just living day to day.'

Alice made to put her hand on his, then clearly remembered her last attempt to empathise.

'Don't worry, I won't misinterpret it,' said Will ruefully. 'It's just nice to have a little understanding.'

Alice carefully patted his hand, but then equally carefully took her hand away.

'You believe me then?' said Will with an attempt at a laugh.

'Let's just say I'm more inclined to, having seen how it affects you.'

'Well, that's something I suppose.'

They lapsed into silence, Will covertly sizing Alice up. She was a contradiction, so fierce most of the time, but there was a softer side somewhere. She was so small, but so strong. He felt drawn to her, but he knew already that was both unwise and unlikely. She'd bite his head off.

'What's Dexter doing about the bomb?' he asked.

'Running around. Checking this and that. Turns out the Home Secretary is due to attend a mosque opening that day, so it's a controversial target, killing Muslims too.'

'Far right then, or provocative jihadists?'

'Don't know. It's a bad time for a bomb attack. The G7's in town, so the PM is playing host to the world's leaders.'

'Why wouldn't any self-respecting terrorist go for that?'

'Security's too tight, but if they go for a soft target like a mosque and off the Home Secretary that's a pretty enormous coup.'

'When will they cancel the mosque visit? Hillyer said they might leave it late.'

Alice looked at him warily. 'It's complicated. If they cancel now, it will alert the terrorists and then they might turn their attention to the G7. There's maximum security in place but they've got all those world leaders coming into town for a big ceremony marking the State Re-Opening of Parliament after the reconstruction works. Everyone's nervous about that. If they stop the Home Secretary's event, it will be at the last minute to make sure the terrorists don't target Parliament Square.'

'If? What do you mean, if?'

'I meant when. I'm sure they will cancel it in the end. But this is a long game, Will. Sometimes you have to plan a long way ahead and consider all sorts of possibilities. Three-dimensional chess.'

'With people's lives?'

'It's always with people's lives.' Alice's face hardened. 'Someone dies, whatever happens. It's just a question of how many.'

Will changed the subject. 'What about you and Dexter? You really don't trust him, do you? And what did he mean by you getting into more trouble? Why are you still in trouble?' asked Will.

Alice's eyes shifted away, avoiding his gaze. 'You know, trying to warn Slater,' she said eventually.

'I thought that was history,' said Will.

'Dexter doesn't forget or forgive,' said Alice bitterly.

Will was certain she wasn't telling him the whole story. But then would she ever? She was a spy, a professional liar. That was her job, and he would have to become one too. He hadn't told them about Grantley's death, and now he had the bigger problem of what to do about Hillyer's poisoning. He had a feeling that tomorrow would only bring more unwanted secrets and impossible choices.

Chapter Fourteen

The next morning the same minder was there with a car.

'Hi Mike,' said Will.

'It's Patrick, actually,' said the man with a chilly smile.

'Okay, Patrick. Got it. Makes all the difference,' said Will.

Alice raised her eyebrows but said nothing. They drove into town towards Thames House, but instead of turning off Millbank towards the MI5 car park, they carried on to Parliament Square. They turned left onto Great George Street towards St James's Park and when Patrick turned right onto Horse Guards Road, Will had a sinking feeling.

'Are we going where I think we're going? he asked.

Alice nodded. 'If the mountain won't come to Muhammad, then Muhammad must go to the mountain.'

'Hilarious.'

The car turned into the far end of Downing Street and Will was guided through security at the back end of No.10 and then into a quiet side room where Dexter was waiting.

'Welcome,' he said. 'Ready for part two?'

'As I'll ever be,' said Will, suddenly nervous.

'Follow me,' Dexter said, and they went down a carpeted corridor to a room at the back of No.10. Will tried to remember the layout. He'd been in No.10 once before for an Army reception after he got his medal, but though he could recall the main staircase and the big reception room on the first floor, this was a different part of the building. Dexter opened a door and ushered Will and Alice through.

Again, it was a plain room without windows dominated by a large mirror. Another two-way? Waiting there was a short, dark-haired man, impressively dressed in what looked like an Italian wool suit with a crisp white shirt and no tie, his black hair swept back. He looked formidably self-assured; his smile even fiercer than Dexter's. Like a tiger welcoming its prey, Will thought.

'Good morning. I've been looking forward to meeting you, Mr Gray. I'm Zar Yelland.'

'Zar?' asked Will, for want of anything better to say.

'It's short for Zarathustra. My parents liked Nietzsche,' he said.

'Must have been tough in the playground,' said Will. Zar gave him only a sardonic grin. This was going to be fun, Will thought.

'Zar will look after you from now on,' said Dexter smoothly. 'He will report everything back to me. You can trust him absolutely.'

Will stifled a laugh. Sandwiched between a tall lion and a short tiger then. He would only trust them to stitch him up at the first opportunity.

Alice had taken up an unobtrusive position again on the back wall. She smiled reassuringly.

'Let's get down to it,' said Dexter. He gestured at the large gilt mirror dominating one wall. 'We arranged all this rather hurriedly. We've got some very senior people lined up next door. That's another two-way mirror. When Zar presses the button, you will see them, but they won't be able to see

103

you. They have been asked to look in the middle of the mirror and hold that gaze for twenty seconds. We're telling them it's a psychological test to see if they're comfortable looking into their own eyes for that long.'

Zar uttered a short, barking laugh. 'That should make them squirm,' he said with relish.

'The first one will be in two minutes, so I suggest you ready yourself,' said Dexter.

'Not much of a run-up,' said Will, feeling his heart contract and his breath shorten at the prospect.

'Best to get on with it,' said Dexter. 'If you stand here in front of the centre of the mirror, you should have a good eyeline.'

Will tried to steady himself. He remembered the Home Secretary yesterday and the physical blow of the bomb. Would there be more like that today? He took several deep breaths and tried to clear his mind.

'Twenty seconds,' said Dexter quietly, consulting his watch.

Will counted down in his head. It was like going into action. He sensed Zar behind him, leaning forward, keen to see how he reacted.

The mirror's reflection suddenly cleared, and he got two shocks in quick succession. First that he found himself looking at a large, classically proportioned room with a big mahogany table. The Cabinet room. He found it surprising that there was a two-way mirror looking into the room at the heart of the Government, although he was getting the feeling that everything was always being watched.

The identity of the man gazing at him through the mirror was less of a surprise given the location. It was the Prime Minister, Benedict Payton. They really were starting at the top.

His familiar features were set in an impatient scowl. Well-cut fair hair framing an open bluff face and intense brown eyes. Will noticed the lines creasing his cheeks and forehead. He had been a young, vigorous PM when he started, but now in his second term, the stress was ageing him.

Then Will heard his familiar, blokey voice. 'Bloody bollocks if you ask me. I could stare at myself in the mirror all day and neither you nor I would be any the wiser.'

There was a gasp behind Will. A voice said: 'A few more seconds please Prime….' Then the sound was cut.

Will focussed on the task in hand. He looked straight into the PM's eyes. A big solid wooden bed. Designer headboard. An emaciated figure propped up on pillows, wires trailing out to bleeping monitors. He could hardly recognise the handsome features. Cancer, and an aggressive one at that. And only sixteen years away. Will calculated that would make the PM only sixty-five when he died. A life maybe not cut short but trimmed of its retirement years. He felt a moment's compassion as the PM shrugged irritably and broke away from the mirror. He saw the PM's mouth move and was pretty sure he'd said, 'Fuck this.'

The screen shut down and became a mirror again. Will turned to find the expectant faces of Dexter and Zar.

'Well?' said Dexter impatiently. Zar simply raised an eyebrow. Both looked like they were hoping for drama.

Will took a deep breath. 'Nothing to report. Illness. Cancer. Beyond our time limit.'

'Oh, come on,' said Dexter, irritated. 'This is the PM. We need to know.'

Will wanted to stick to his five-year rule, but he could see straight away that would be difficult.

'What time limit?' said Zar.

'Will doesn't want us to intrude into private matters if it's years away. We agreed a five-year limit.'

'That's ridiculous,' said Zar. 'How can we plan ahead, then?'

'My terms,' said Will.

'Let's just say the PM should be an exception, shall we?' said Dexter, back to being smooth again. 'When is it?'

Will hesitated, then decided he could make use of the concession. 'Sixteen years.'

'Which would make him sixty-five,' said Zar. 'Poor bugger,' he added, although Will could hear no trace of genuine feeling in his voice.

'And you're sure there couldn't be any foul play?' asked Dexter.

'I didn't get that feeling. Just cancer.'

'Very well. Next one then.'

They waited in silence, Zar watching a screen that Will couldn't see, until he raised his hand and gestured to the mirror.

The mirror cleared and there were the rotund features of the Foreign Secretary. Should have seen that one coming, thought Will. They're going to make me work through the entire Cabinet. He couldn't hear this time, but he could see that Toby Benson was even more irritated than the Prime Minister had been. Benson had florid features, thinning hair and a Roman nose that had gone to fleshiness. He also had an air of cast-iron entitlement, a look of contemptuous disdain.

Will looked into his hard blue eyes. A bed, a hotel bed, judging by the bland beige décor. Benson's face creased in pain. A young woman, a very young woman, naked, leaning over him, looking concerned and irritated as if this wasn't the first client to peg out on her. A prostitute, a high-class call girl judging by the girl's immaculate grooming, and Benson was having a fatal heart attack. In four years, eleven months.

Will's chest felt tight and his breathing was short. This was going to be very difficult. How many more secrets might he discover? Where should he draw the line? He was glad this one was just under his five-year rule. It was easier to come clean.

The mirror was back in place. Will turned to find the same expectant expressions, desperate for his secrets.

'Heart attack. Four years, eleven months away,' he said in a bored tone.

Dexter was observing him. 'And?' he said finally.

'With a prostitute. A young prostitute.'

Zar whooped with glee. Dexter smiled. 'Our revered Foreign Secretary finally gets his come-uppance.'

'Revered?' said Zar savagely. 'Only by himself.'

'Any idea where?' asked Dexter.

'Looked like a hotel room. Could have been anywhere.' Then Will remembered a river picture on the wall. The Seine, surely. 'Maybe Paris', he added.

'And the girl?'

'Attractive. Maybe Slavic or Russian. Hard to tell.'

Dexter was digesting this. 'Well, that's a pretty scandal to come, isn't it? Thank you,' he said to Will with a nod.

'He'll have to be moved,' said Zar.

'That's not part of the deal,' said Dexter.

'The deal? With who?'

'With Will. We are merely observing. It keeps us ahead of the game. If it's terrorism or violence, that's another matter. But if it's day to day, then we simply have the advantage of knowing.'

'But that's ridiculous,' said Zar. 'This is gold.'

'He may be out of office by then anyway,' said Dexter. 'Let's just see what we get, shall we? This is already proving a rewarding day,' he added, giving Zar a stare. Zar seemed to take the hint and subsided into silence.

And there's the problem, Will thought. How will I ever know what they do with the long-term examples like this? They might wait and see with Benson, but if it got near the time surely there would be a quiet word in his ear. Best for the country if you spend more time with your family, old man.

They waited for the next one, then at an unseen signal the glass wavered and there was the Chancellor, Peter Denham, staring quizzically at the mirror, looking unsure. If it was a psychological test you'd bet he'd fail. An unwaveringly grey man, he only survived it was said because he had the PM's back.

Will looked into his watery blue eyes. A big bed, fine cotton sheets, plumped up pillows. A painting on the wall that Will thought looked like a Chagall. Wood-panelling. A grand setting for a final scene. Clearly dying of old age in 39 years, which would make him 95 if he remembered the Chancellor's age correctly.

Will faced Dexter and Zar again. 'Old age, peaceful, nothing to report.'

'Boring as the man,' said Zar witheringly. He looked disappointed, and he looked dangerous, Will thought. There was something restlessly febrile about the man.

'Never mind, can't all be interesting,' said Dexter.

'Are we doing the whole Cabinet?' asked Will. 'The process is quite tiring.'

'No, that's all for now,' said Dexter. Will looked at him inquiringly. 'We're going to find another location for the rest.'

Will breathed a sigh of relief.

'I'm going to carry on with the Home Secretary's case. Alice will take you back to the flat. Check the car is ready, will you Alice?' Alice gave him another withering look but followed him out.

When they had gone, Will felt Zar's eyes on him, but he said nothing. Finally, he glanced in Zar's direction. The man was staring at him, a small faint smile playing on his face. Will ducked his head. He didn't want to see Zar's death. Not now.

'Ok?' Zar said cheerfully.

'I'd like to go back to the flat, if that's alright,' Will said, anxious to be away.

'Alice will be back in a second.' Zar hesitated. 'I notice you haven't looked into my eyes. I don't mind, you know. Dexter's told me his prognosis.' Zar made a short, dry sound. 'It won't upset me.'

Will demurred. 'Maybe some other time.'

Suddenly, Zar was directly in front of him. 'I think not,' he said forcefully. 'Let's get it over with.'

Reluctantly, Will raised his eyes. He was conscious of Zar's falsely jolly smile. Then he saw the same face, tranquil, composed with just a faint downturn of the lips, a small grimace. A gun appeared at the side of Zar's head and Will realised it was Zar himself holding it. There was an explosion of sound and blood and brain matter, and Zar slid to the ground.

Will gasped. His mind was racing. Zar was going to kill himself. But it was the date that shocked him the most. May 11th. The day after the Home Secretary's death.

He came out of his reverie and found Zar watching him. 'That didn't look pleasant,' Zar said. 'Out with it.'

Will scrambled for a way out. 'I'm afraid it's violent. 'You're run over in a traffic accident.'

Zar emitted another short sharp laugh. 'Bugger me. We should be more careful with cars, don't you think? Dexter and I. Both dying in road accidents. Maybe it runs in the business.'

Will could see the disbelief in Zar's eyes. Why had he chosen something so similar?

'Does he run me over then?'

'No, no,' said Will. 'You're much later. Fifteen years.'

'Aren't I the lucky one?' said Zar sardonically.

Fortunately, Alice chose that moment to reappear. Will followed her quickly out.

That was a terrible mistake, he thought. He should have found a more convincing lie.

But bigger than that, much bigger, was the other question. Why did Zar kill himself the day after the Home Secretary was blown up, and what was the connection between the two?

Chapter Fifteen

When they arrived back at the flat, the first thing Alice said was, 'What did you make of Zar? Bit of a nutter, isn't he?'

Will looked at her. Was this an innocent inquiry, or was she fishing? He wanted to trust her, but in the end her job was to manage him and lie when necessary. He opted for a flippant reply: 'Bit like Dexter, but more teeth.'

Alice laughed. 'You're right, they are two of a kind. Fellow predators.'

'Tell me about them,' said Will.

Alice thought for a second. 'Well, in some ways they're very similar. Dexter McMichael, to give him his full name, went to Cambridge. Ferociously intelligent, straight into MI5, a classic middle-class career spy married to an academic, Amelia. He's incredibly ambitious and seen as a rising star on course for the top job.' Will noticed the contempt in her voice.

'And Zar?'

'He's a high-flyer too, and very much Dexter's protégé. Next in line. He went to the LSE. If anything, he's even brighter. But he has a very different backstory. He's of Persian origin, married to a Muslim woman, the very glamorous Rasha. '

'Is he Muslim?'

'No. Atheist.'

'And his wife?'

'She is Muslim, but not devout. They both drink alcohol, live a pretty cosmopolitan life. Oh, and Zar is even more ambitious than Dexter if that's possible.'

'They're similar, but different. Lion and tiger,' said Will.

'Exactly. You don't want to cross either of them, but Dexter will tell you exactly where you stand, and you'll never know with Zar.'

And yet in two weeks' time the high-flying Zar was going to shoot himself, thought Will. What would make him do that?

Will watched Alice, waiting for her next question, suddenly certain what it would be.

'How is he going to die, then? I would foresee a dramatic death for our Zar,' said Alice.

Will's heart sank. This was definitely fishing, and he had no choice but to lie. 'Just a traffic accident. Very boring,' he said.

'I bet he was disappointed with that,' said Alice. 'Too ordinary.'

She was right, thought Will. Much too ordinary for Zarathustra Yelland. But the truth was not ordinary at all, and he would have to figure out why on his own.

Time to change the subject. 'Have you found out any more about the adults who died in the bus crash?' Will asked.

'As a matter of a fact I have, but I'm not sure it's helpful,' said Alice.

Will shrugged 'Humour me.'

'Okay. Margaret was the wife of Colin Maynard.'

'And mother of Lucy,' said Will. 'I know.'

'She was a housewife. No career. No particular skills. I honestly don't think her death, sad as it is, is going to change the world,' said Alice.

'Still on my conscience though. And the other one?' asked Will.

'Well, she's more interesting. Sofija Huntsev, a recent arrival from Latvia. She was a single mother of one of the kids who survived. In the newspapers she was described wrongly as working in a chemist. In fact, she was a research chemist, working for a tech start-up. Apparently very promising. Could have gone on to greater things.'

'What was her field?'

'There's no point torturing yourself with it,' said Alice.

'Just tell me.'

'It was cancer. Something to do with the mechanics of cell reproduction.'

Will blanched. 'So she might have done a lot of good.'

'She might. But you'll never know.'

'And the child?'

'Alise. Went back to Latvia to live with her grandparents.'

Will sighed. The loss of a potentially brilliant scientist and the whole of a child's life blighted. Was he doing the right thing co-operating with MI5 and risking it happening again?

'You have to put it out of your mind,' said Alice. 'No-one is going to die from the knock-on effect of you just vetting people.'

'And the mosque bomb?'

'It won't be allowed to happen,' Alice said firmly. 'You just need to concentrate on the good you could achieve. The people you're going to save.'

Somehow Will didn't feel all that reassured.

***

The next morning Alice said, 'We've found a new location to do the vetting. It's a safe house in Pimlico. More discreet, and we'll get the targets to come to you. You'll be able to get through more in a session there. Patrick will take you there, and Zar will look after you. I'm going to catch up on some other business back in the office.'

Will felt curiously vulnerable at the thought of operating without Alice covering his back. He realised that he relied on her already.

Patrick drove over Vauxhall Bridge, but this time he turned left on the other side, away from Thames House. They were soon in the residential streets of Pimlico, full of stucco Georgian cottages, two stories, white fronts, potted bushes by the neat front entrances, the only distinction the different pastel colours of the doors. Finally, they stopped at a light blue door, and Patrick locked the car and led him inside. There was a small hallway with mirrors and a standard occasional table with a large vase of white lilies. Will wondered if he would find one at every MI5 safe house. Standard practice.

'Follow me,' Patrick said, and they went down a carpeted corridor to a room at the back of the house. Patrick opened the door and ushered Will through.

It was another plain room with a large mirror down one side. Will was surprised to see Zar and a new man standing next to a small battery of medical machines. One, he was sure, was an ECG heart monitor. He recognised it from the casualty stations in Afghanistan. There was also a brain monitor, a CGI.

'What's with the medical equipment?' Will asked.

'We'd like to hook you up and monitor your body's reactions when you do what you do,' said Zar with a smile. 'Help us understand it better.'

Will shrugged. He didn't much like the idea but decided to be compliant. 'Ok,' he said.

Zar gestured at the young Indian man, bending over the array of monitors. 'This is Bean. He's our techie genius. Understands all things computers, as well as these monitors. He'll wire you up. I won't be a second.' Zar left the room and Will let Bean attach the wires.

'Bean?' he asked. 'Is that your real name?'

Bean paused. 'Actually, it's Javanshir. But that's Zar's little joke. Javanshir becomes Java becomes Coffee Bean, becomes Bean.'

Will was shocked. Javanshir had his head down, studiously attaching the leads. 'But surely that kind of thing's not allowed any more,' Will said.

'It's pretty harmless. I've heard a lot worse,' said Javanshir, keeping his eyes averted. He had obviously been briefed and wasn't keen to look into Will's eyes.

And then Zar returned, and Will was back in front of the mirror, and he was soon working his way through the rest of the Cabinet. They were an unremarkable lot of placemen and women, mostly heading for as boring a death as their lives had been.

The one exception was the Business Secretary, Oliver Trotter, who was going to be shot dead by his male lover's wife.

'Now that'll cause a hiccough in the City,' said Zar with satisfaction.

Will could still feel the tremors rippling through his body from the impact of the bullet that he had seen.

'Look at this,' said Zar, peering at the monitors. 'Your heart rate spiked when you saw Trotter getting his just desserts, and it's still high. I suppose the brain can't figure out the difference. You see it happening, so the brain thinks it's happening to you. It triggers your fight-or-flight reaction.'

'Every day. All my life,' said Will bitterly.

'Can't be easy to live with,' said Zar sympathetically. Will was surprised. He wouldn't have thought Zar did empathy. So when Zar said he would give Will something to bring him down and relax him at the end of the session. Will agreed.

He woke a few minutes later, refreshed. 'What did you do?' he asked.

'Just a mild sedative. It will help you relax.'

Will noticed that Zar ducked his head and did not prolong the conversation. And Javanshir had his face hidden by the monitors. But Will felt so good he didn't care.

***

Over the next couple of sessions, Will settled into a routine, a succession of senior politicians, high-ranking civil servants and to his surprise, the occasional captain of industry.

When he was confronted with the first of those, a well-known buccaneering entrepreneur, Tom Roberts, Will challenged Zar.

'What's the point of doing him? He's not in the government.'

Zar smiled in his lightly threatening, tigerish way. 'You don't think he's important to the country?'

'Maybe to its wealth,' Will conceded.

'He makes a bigger contribution than most of the people you've done so far.'

'But national security?'

Zar smiled again. 'What if he died suddenly tomorrow? What would that do to the Stock Market? And when the economy stutters, that's an opportunity for the country's enemies.'

As it turned out, Mr Roberts was destined for a very long life, no doubt of great comfort and wealth. Will still wasn't convinced, but then a few candidates later there was another industrialist and this time a very different outcome.

Will looked into his eyes and suddenly he was in a helicopter plummeting towards the ground and the urbane, tightly controlled face of Jeremy Brenton was twisted into a rictus of terror. The picture disappeared in a flash of light and flame as the helicopter hit the ground. And it was only five days away, May 2nd.

Will was shaken again. No matter how many times he did it, the sudden, violent ones seemed to rip through his body. A helicopter, of all things. Will had always felt they were far too dangerous out in Afghanistan with the Taliban shooting at them and a ground to air missile round the next corner. Too prone to fall out of the sky or be blown out of it. Why rich people were so keen on them, just to save a few minutes, he couldn't fathom. Well, Brenton was going to pay a high price for his daily impatience.

Zar was staring at him with a voracious look. The monitors were pinging away, registering his racing heart and his short, panting breaths and Javanshir was scanning them with intense concentration.

'Well?' said Zar.

'Helicopter crash. Five days,' said Will, swallowing.

'That's a shame,' said Zar, although he looked as if it was the opposite. 'Doesn't he have a big launch around that time, Bean?' Javanshir nodded.

'Will you do anything?' asked Will.

'We're not supposed to interfere,' said Zar with a sly smile. 'Maybe we'll warn the Treasury. Poor Mr Brenton, all that time building up an empire worth £6.5 billion at the last count and it's going to be taken away in the blink of an eye.'

Will noticed that Javanshir had the grace to look embarrassed. He shrugged. He'd had enough of it for the day. It was like looking over the Grim Reaper's shoulder and he felt an intruder on grief again.

Zar stopped him as he was going. 'Change of plan tomorrow. You'll be going somewhere different. And Dexter will be there.'

'Nice to see him again,' said Will ironically. He had been pestering Zar for a meeting with Dexter and an update on the Home Secretary's bomb plot. 'Anything else you can tell me?'

'Need to know, old boy. Need to know.'

***

Alice wasn't any more helpful that evening.

'What's the big surprise?' asked Will.

'Just the next stage.'

'And you can't tell me what it is?'

Alice grinned. 'Need to know,' she said, and Will wondered if she'd been listening to his conversation with Zar.

This was getting irritating and worrying. He was being kept in the dark all the time. He had no idea what they were doing about the Home Secretary's bomb. Surely they were taking some action. He was also conscious that he had yet to tell Dexter about Hillyer and the Colonel. He had thought they were cards up his sleeve but the Colonel's date with death was getting perilously close, just three days away. Maybe he should tell Dexter tomorrow. And beyond that there was Zar's suicide.

'Have they done anything about the bomb? Have they cancelled the event?' he asked Alice.

'Like I told you, even if they were going to, they wouldn't do it yet. Ask Dexter. He might tell you more tomorrow.'

'But you must have some idea.' He knew he sounded petulant, but he couldn't help it. He saw a trace of irritation in her eyes. There was a flash of old people's home, the familiar scene, but it hardly registered now. He was so used to it. Instead, he just felt blocked out by her.

'What's the point of our relationship if you can't spill a few secrets?' he said, trying for lightheartedness and failing miserably.

'As I've made clear, we do not have a relationship. Just leave it. You'll find out more tomorrow,' Alice said, turning away from him to shut down the conversation.

Chapter Sixteen

The next morning Patrick took him down to the basement car park and he was put into a dark grey van with blacked-out windows.

'Just a short trip,' said Patrick, with a brief nod, 'but I'll need you to wear these.' He handed Will a blindfold and noise-cancelling headphones.

'You don't trust me?' he said, but Patrick just held them out. Will reluctantly put them on, and he was plunged into a world of blackness and silence.

Will felt the vibration as an unseen driver started the van, then they moved up the ramp and out onto the road. Will tried to keep track, left, right, left again, but when he worked out they'd gone round in a circle, he knew he was being deliberately confused.

He gave up and switched off. After about thirty minutes, the van drove off the smooth road onto a rough patch of ground and then stopped.

Will felt the headphones and blindfold being removed. The van door opened, and he could see they were in a large breeze block garage.

'You'll enjoy this,' said Patrick and led him through a back door into another spartan area with a concrete floor and steel rafters. It must be a small warehouse. At the far end was a table with a computer and a few monitors by the side, and behind it was an opaque glass wall. Dexter and Zar were talking quietly when Will entered.

'Will,' said Dexter. 'Welcome. This is where it gets interesting.'

'You've been very elusive,' said Will. 'I want to know what you're doing about the Home Secretary's bomb?'

'Well, this for one thing. Why don't you see how this goes, and we'll talk afterwards.'

Will was annoyed at being put off again, but Dexter was all business.

'Behind this screen you'll find some young men. They won't obey any instructions like looking at the mirror, so you'll just have to wait till it happens naturally.'

'Young men? Muslim young men, presumably?'

'Absolutely.'

'And have they done anything yet? Or are they long-term suspects?'

'A mixture. Let's just say they're helping us with our inquiries.'

'Then they might be entirely innocent?'

'No-one in life is entirely innocent,' said Dexter. The wolfish smile was back again, but Will would not be deterred.

'They might have only a glancing interest in Jihad. They might have been named by someone else just to take the pressure off,' said Will.

'I accept that some of them will be long shots, but look at Richard Reid, the shoe bomber. He wasn't on anyone's radar at all. Just see how it goes, eh? It might be boring, or we might strike lucky.'

'And some of them might be connected to the Home Secretary's bomb?'

'That's what we think.'

Will was suddenly conscious of Zar, keeping his head down, but listening to every word.

'No monitors this time?' said Will.

'Didn't think it was worth transporting them all the way out here,' said Zar.

'Or didn't want to leave too much evidence that you'd been here,' Will said, and he could see straightaway that this was the more likely. This was a below-the-radar operation that officially would never have happened.

Will shrugged. 'Let's get on with it then.'

'We'll just refer to them by number,' said Zar. 'No names, just the number.'

Will waited, then the mirror flickered and cleared to reveal another part of the breeze-block garage with a bare concrete floor and no visible windows. There were two simple metal chairs. In the nearest with his back to the wall was clearly the interrogator, just wearing a leather jacket and jeans, but with a short, tidy haircut and a sense of purpose in the heavily muscled shoulders that were leaning towards the suspect.

Will took in the man in the other chair. Dark hair, stubble, hooded eyelids. He was staring into the middle distance, not looking at the interrogator, and mostly in profile to Will. He was pretending indifference, but he radiated anger. Will saw that he was handcuffed to the chair, which was bolted to the floor. There was also a suspicious amount of water on the floor. Washing away bloodstains or worse?

'Number one,' said Zar unnecessarily.

'Can I hear them?' asked Will.

'I'm afraid that might give away their identity,' said Dexter.

'So we just watch and wait,' said Will.

As far as he could see, the interrogator wasn't getting far. Number one was resolutely ignoring him, pretending no doubt that he was somewhere else. And yet Will could see the fierce anger burning in him, in every twitch of his shoulders, every time he crossed his legs.

Finally, Will couldn't stand it any longer. 'You'll have to provoke him. Tell him his mother is a Cairo street whore and you look forward to fucking her. In fact, the whole service will take it in turns.'

Zar whistled appreciatively and looked at Dexter, who nodded. Zar whispered into a hidden microphone and the interrogator leaned forward and spoke.

It was like cracking a whip. The man reared up, his head shot round and he gave the interrogator a look of utter hatred. And Will looked straight into his eyes.

It wasn't what he was expecting. He had braced himself for a bullet, or a knife, or the flaming fiery end of a suicide bomber, but instead he found the shimmery blue of a swimming pool in the sun, Mediterranean judging by the light. The suspect, much older, was swimming when his face contorted with pain and surprise and then he quietly slipped beneath the water. Heart attack, forty-two years away, an ordinary death.

'Well,' said Dexter in his ear.

125

'A bit of a surprise,' said Will. 'Old age. Drowned. Heart attack whilst swimming in his pool. Over forty years away.'

Dexter, he noticed, looked particularly disappointed. Zar was impassive.

'I think you got this one wrong,' said Will.

'Maybe,' said Dexter. 'But look at the hatred and anger on his face. Where does that go?'

'In this case, nowhere. It seems he's innocent,' said Will. 'There's no way of telling, but his death doesn't seem suspicious.'

'Maybe he just gets away with it. Maybe he's so far up the chain he never has to do the dirty stuff,' said Dexter. 'Maybe he's really important.'

Will shrugged. 'All I can tell you is that he dies an ordinary death.'

'Quite a lot of terrible men manage that,' said Dexter. 'Look at Stalin.'

'And if I'd looked into Stalin's eyes, all I would have seen was him dying in bed, of a cerebral haemorrhage,' said Will. 'I wouldn't have seen any of his atrocities. Sometimes the death reveals the life. Mostly it doesn't. It's just the random end of one existence. All I can say is that this one wasn't violent.'

'Let's move on before we become too philosophical,' said Dexter.

They had to wait half-an-hour before the next one was ready. Then the mirror shimmered again and became a window and number two was sitting in the chair opposite the interrogator.

The first thing Will noticed was that number two was much younger. He had a paler skin and the beginnings of a moustache that young men grow to convince themselves they can. And he looked frightened. Very frightened. His eyes were darting around, not settling on anything. Where number one's shoulders had twitched with anger, with number two it was simply nervous movement. He couldn't sit still, and there was a sheen of panicky sweat on his forehead.

This shouldn't take long, Will thought, and within less than a minute, those restless, jumpy eyes had flicked up behind the interrogator and contacted Will's.

Another surprise. The man was running away and then suddenly his back arched. There was a bloom of red and he was thrown to the ground, shot. Will saw the fear and terror in his eyes as he lay there dying, and then as he let out his last breath a military-style black boot was by his face. Six days away.

Will doubled over. The shock of the violent death, but also the shock of the implication. Will heaved but stopped himself from vomiting.

'Well?' said Dexter impatiently.

'Must have been a cracker,' said Zar. 'He only reacts like that when it's bloody.'

'Thanks for that helpful analysis,' said Will, straightening up. He looked into Dexter's gleaming eyes, saw again the car crash and wondered for the first time if Dexter deserved such a straightforward death.

Dexter raised his eyebrows. 'Don't keep us waiting all day.'

'Shot in the back whilst running away. Looked like a military or police operation. I'd say judging by the boot I saw it was police. CO19.'

'Excellent,' said Dexter, and Will felt a tremor of revulsion.

'Not for him.'

'When is it?'

'Six days,' said Will flatly. 'May 4th.'

Zar whistled through his teeth. 'It must be connected to the bombing, surely?'

'Quiet, Zar,' said Dexter with asperity. 'Let's not jump to any conclusions.'

'But that's a crime,' said Will. 'Shooting someone in the back when they're not armed.'

'Was it? He might have just planted a bomb. He might have just shot a police officer. Let's wait and see. Do you need a break? Water, coffee?'

'Both would be nice,' said Will. 'And a five-minute breather.'

Dexter nodded. 'There's a loo behind that door. Take a moment.'

Will shut the door firmly behind him and sat on the loo seat. Dexter was right, of course. You couldn't tell guilt or innocence from the moment of death, but it was clear Dexter was going to convict them all, given half a chance. Will couldn't forget number two's fearful eyes. Well, he had plenty to be fearful about. In six days he would be dead, ruthlessly terminated, and Will had no idea whether he deserved it. Might never know.

Somehow these young men were more disturbing than the members of the Government. Politicians lived a public life that brought dangers, but these were unknowns who may or may not have harmful intent. Will felt anything he said was only going to be used to condemn them.

After ten minutes he emerged, still feeling shaky, but Dexter was all business again.

'Water and coffee there. Let's crack on, shall we?'

Fortunately, the next two were straightforward. They were both young men like number two, angry and fearful in turns. There was bravado and some resistance but they both turned out to have ordinary deaths, number three from cancer in middle age, number four from pneumonia in old age.

Both Dexter and Zar looked disappointed, but pragmatic.

'Just one more to come today,' said Dexter, but even as Will breathed a small sigh of relief, he saw a look pass between Dexter and Zar.

'Saved the best for last?' he asked.

Dexter gave him a blank smile. 'Let's see.'

Will's heart sank. They waited in silence, but he could feel Dexter and Zar on his shoulder, like predators waiting to pounce. Finally, the mirror shifted, and he was looking at number five.

Will noticed the difference immediately. This man was older, more contained, the same dark hair, a moustache, stubble, a similar sense of anger to number one. But there was no discernible fear, and the anger was well under control. He was looking at the interrogator with a hint of amused contempt, one corner of his mouth flicking up in a sardonic smile. He looked completely in control.

Will was totally unprepared for what came next. Number five's eyes shifted past the interrogator with a lazy insouciance. Will saw how intensely alive they were, then the picture changed and number five was hunched over a mass of circuit boards and wires, frowning in concentration. He moved a soldering iron into position, then there was a strange look of surprise on his face and the picture erupted. There was a blinding flash of white, then black, then fire and Will felt the blast rip through him. He doubled up again, but this time there was no stopping it and he threw up on the floor.

There was a long silence. His nose was full of liquid and the acrid smell of his own vomit. His head was ringing.

He felt a hand on his shoulder and Dexter passed him a towel and then a glass of water. Still, neither of them said anything.

Will wiped the bile from his face and sipped at the water. Finally, he raised himself to his feet and faced them. He thought both their expressions were rather smugly triumphant.

'Don't keep us in suspense, old boy,' said Zar.

'Bomb. He was, sorry is, a bomb maker, and it went off as he was working on it. Eleven days away, May 9th.'

Zar and Dexter exchanged glances. 'That is good news,' said Dexter. 'Any idea where?'

'No. I could only see him and the bomb in a pool of light from a desk lamp.' Will hesitated. 'There was one strange thing. He seemed to know just before the explosion.'

Dexter and Zar exchanged another glance, and this time they were openly triumphant.

'You're enjoying this,' said Will.

'Well, you have to admit,' said Dexter. 'It is satisfying to know that one of our mortal enemies is going to blow himself up with his own bomb. There's a sweet sense of justice in that.'

Will took another mouthful of water. He did not feel triumphant. He just felt drained.

'You've got what you wanted,' he said flatly. 'Now you promised me some answers. Were they all implicated in the plot to bomb the Home Secretary?'

Dexter looked as if he was mulling over his reply. 'They were all connected. Sorry, I should say they are all connected in some way, but what you've done today really helps us focus in on two of them, number two and number five.'

'And exonerates the others?' asked Will.

'Perhaps,' said Dexter. 'Perhaps not.'

'I'm sure three and four were innocent.' said Will.

'Maybe, but they're not keeping very good company.'

Will wondered if he would ever convince them of anyone's innocence. He had a sinking feeling again, that they were judge, jury and executioner and he was their useful idiot, providing them with just enough evidence to condemn.

'Are you going to cancel the Home Secretary's event now?'

Dexter's expression hardened. 'Not yet.'

'But you can't just let it happen.'

'You didn't want us to interfere,' he pointed out.

'You can't let her die like that.'

'Don't worry, it will be stopped in the end, but we are going to let it play out for a bit.'

131

'What and wait for number two to get shot and number five to blow himself up?'

'Not such a bad outcome,' said Zar.

'But you could save their lives,' said Will.

'Why on earth would we want to do that?' said Dexter. 'Anyway, we need to process all this, discuss it higher up, so let's not jump to conclusions. Thank you Will, a very useful day. Tomorrow will be back to bread-and-butter politicians and civil servants, I'm afraid,' he said with an insincere grimace.

'At least I'm less likely to throw up,' Will said, and Dexter and Zar both laughed.

They ushered him out rather quickly, Will thought. He had plenty of time on the drive back in the silent, dark van to consider the implications, and there was just one thought buzzing around in his brain. Why did the bomb maker look surprised in the instant before he died? Did he recognise his mistake, or was it something else?

And why had neither Zar nor Dexter mentioned the glaring implication? If the bomb maker was going to blow himself up, then who made the device that would blow up the Home Secretary?

Chapter Seventeen

When he returned to the flat, he wandered round aimlessly. He felt nervous and exhausted at the same time. He stared at the muddy Thames filling the view from the windows. It was high tide, and the river looked like it might burst its banks, a relentless, irresistible flow meeting the incoming tide from the sea.

Will threw himself on to the bed and fell into a fitful doze, the faces of the Muslim men sliding in and out of his dreams. They all looked angry, and then they looked guilty, or maybe he was the guilty one projecting his fears on them.

He woke with a headache and a sick feeling in his stomach. The morning's session had starkly illustrated his dilemma. Even if he felt they were innocent, the chances were that Dexter and Zar would ignore it. And if they were guilty, then apparently summary justice was OK. He was going to have a lot of dead young men on his conscience by the end of this.

He heard the front door open and felt a moment of panic. Should he tell Alice everything? How much would she know anyway? He was conscious he hadn't told her about Zar shooting himself. Was now the time, or should he keep that to himself? And above and beyond all that, could he trust her with his misgivings?

'Hi,' she said, smiling sympathetically. 'Difficult session?'

'Exhausting,' he said.

'Want to tell me about it?'

'Sure, but let's go for a walk. These walls are closing in on me.' He didn't say that the rooms were bugged. He was sure they were, but that was just another thing that he and Alice had never discussed.

Out on the river promenade he was conscious of minder Patrick trailing them fifty yards behind. He wondered if someone was using a long-range microphone to listen to them. There was no way of knowing. Alice might even be wearing a wire too, although he doubted that given how short a notice she'd had of their walk.

'Tell me about it then,' Alice said. 'It was rough?'

'It's always rough. Particularly when I see violence. Two out of five.' Will ran through everything he'd seen. 'The trouble is, I feel responsible. Dexter and Zar are certain they're all guilty, but I'm not. And beyond that, there's the inevitable question. Is my intervention making it more likely they will die?'

'Look,' said Alice. 'They're clearly all involved in the bomb plot. You've seen one of them get shot by the police and the bomb maker blow himself up. You're not responsible for that. That's something they chose to do.'

Will stopped to look out over the river. 'That's not good enough. The police could have set up the young man who was shot. Entrapment. I just couldn't see enough of the picture.' Will added, frustrated. 'And just by saying it out loud, I seem to confirm his guilt when he could be innocent.'

'And the bomb maker? Bang to rights, surely.' Alice gave an involuntary chuckle as she recognised the joke.

134

'I guess you'd think so. He's obviously jihadi. But there was something strange about it. Just before the bomb went off, he looked surprised.'

'He probably realised he'd done something wrong. Had a sense that it was about to blow,' said Alice.

Will shrugged. 'I'm not so sure. It was more like he'd found something he wasn't expecting.'

'You're overthinking. There's nothing to regret about him.'

'Except that he's out there now alive, and it doesn't have to end that way. If I'm doing this to avert death, shouldn't that apply all round?'

Will shivered. He suddenly had a sense that he was being watched. He spun round and scanned the fellow walkers on the riverbank. A mother with a child in a pushchair. A jogger, T-shirt stained with sweat. A man and a dog, an excitable, curious spaniel, sniffing at the traces of all the other dogs who'd been on this promenade. In the distance, a man in an overcoat was hurrying away. And of course, Patrick, keeping a wary eye. No jihadis, no suicide bombers, no-one of even Middle Eastern hue.

And yet. Will's eye was drawn again to the man in the overcoat. His shoulders were hunched, and he emanated a sense of furious purpose.

'What's the problem?' said Alice, interrupting his thoughts.

'I just felt someone was watching us.'

'Don't worry. Patrick is keeping an eye out.'

Will looked at their anonymous minder. Surely Alice must be right. Patrick stared stonily back, as if it was bad manners for the followed to eyeball the follower.

'What do you want to do?' asked Alice.

'I need more information. I need to know what's going on. Being shut out like this won't work.'

'Okay, I can tell Dexter that, but don't hold your breath.'

'Tell him I have some new information, something I've held back from him.'

Alice looked at him quizzically. 'Do you?'

'I held a few things back. For leverage.'

'What things?'

'So long as you don't tell Dexter?' Alice nodded. 'My old colonel, Col. Grantley, is going to die in two days. Roadside bomb. Middle East.'

'You're leaving it a bit late. Just that?'

'No, there's something much bigger, but I'm going to keep it to myself for the moment.'

'You don't trust me.'

'I would like to trust you,' said Will, 'but you're going to have to earn it. You've got to understand. They hold all the cards. I need some traction.'

It was Alice's turn to look out across the river. 'I can really help you, Will. Let me help you.'

Will imagined all the ways she could be betraying him, but the game had to go on.

'Okay, help me by putting pressure on Dexter. And there's another way. You could find out more about the Muslim men I saw today. Are they a known cell? How are they connected? Were they brought together for a reason, or are they just a collection of suspects? I got the feeling from the way Dexter and Zar reacted that they expected some of the outcomes.'

Will hesitated. Did he want Dexter and Zar to know his suspicions? Was he poking a stick into a hornet's nest?

'You know, the funny thing was, neither Dexter nor Zar asked the obvious question.'

'What's that?'

'If the bomb maker blows himself up, then who makes the bomb that kills the Home Secretary?'

Alice was silent for a moment. 'Okay, I'll ask around. Without telling them. I'm on your side, remember?'

'Then do this for me,' said Will. 'Please.'

***

Will had a troubled night. The faces of the Muslim men chased him through his dreams again. First, they looked like ogres, then they proclaimed their innocence and finally they cried out for justice.

Will woke with a start, sweating and panting. Immediately, he sensed there was someone else in the room.

'It's okay. It's me,' said Alice. 'You were shouting. Are you alright?'

'Just a nightmare,' Will said. 'Sorry I disturbed you.'

There was a faint glow of city light finding its way past the curtains at the window. Will could see Alice looming over him. She was wearing just a T-shirt and pants. Her legs were long and muscular. The nipples of her small breasts were pushing against the thin material of her top. He looked away quickly, but he knew he was aroused. Not very helpful.

'What was the nightmare?'

'The innocent, pleading for their lives,' said Will.

'The Muslim suspects?'

'Just because they're suspects doesn't make them all guilty. Some of the innocent will die and I will have helped kill them. That's the bottom line.'

Alice sat down on the bed and took his hand. Will groaned inside.

'You're far too sensitive. Think of the Taliban you were fighting in Afghanistan. They wouldn't lose a moment's sleep over killing you. And neither will jihadis here.'

'And the innocent ones?'

'Innocent people die every day. That's the fallout from war.'

'That's okay to say in abstract, but when you've seen their faces and a bit of their souls, it's harder to shrug it off.'

'Look, we take every precaution not to kill the innocent. It's not worth it. It always has repercussions.'

'You think Dexter and Zar are that fussy?' said Will. 'They seem to revel in the killing.'

Alice was silent. Will could feel her bare legs through the sheet. And then he noiticed he could smell her, too. There was a hint of lavender and something earthier underneath. Now he definitely had an erection. He twisted away to hide it.

'Look, I'll find out what I can on those Muslim men,' said Alice. 'How we got the names, and what else we have on them. OK? Now try to get some sleep.'

'Thanks,' said Will, but when she'd gone he lay awake for a long time thinking about her and the mess he'd got himself into.

Chapter Eighteen

The next day, at the stucco safe house, it was business as usual. Zar falsely jolly, Javanshir avoiding his eyes. When Will asked where Dexter was, all he got from Zar was a blithe, 'Busy, busy, busy….'

Will was conscious that time was running out, particularly for Colonel Grantley. He felt torn, given how close they had once been. But a roadside bomb was just a day-to-day risk in terrorist areas, and if he intervened with that, who knew where it would end? Still, it was one of his wild cards and he was in danger of leaving it too late to cash it in.

When the vetting got under way there was a familiar litany of civil servants with boring deaths, livened up only by a tired and distracted man from the Ministry of Agriculture who kept on running his hands through his thinning hair, his eyes flicking around like a guilty man who knows the game is up.

When he finally looked into the mirror, Will saw a deep despair, then the picture changed to his resigned face in a country field with the wind whipping the surrounding trees. He was wearing full shooting regalia, tweed jacket, deerstalker hat, knickerbocker trousers. He swung a shotgun round, placed the end in his mouth and without flinching pulled the trigger. Will felt the explosion and a flash of searing pain, then it was gone. Five months away.

Will staggered slightly. Zar put out a hand to steady him. Will doubled over so that he wouldn't have to look at Zar while he tried to work out what to do. He couldn't really withhold it. It looked like private despair, but it might not be. He had no way of knowing. The man might be involved in political corruption or worse. But Will would have to tell Zar without giving away any clue that this resembled Zar's actual death.

He straightened slowly, without looking at Zar. 'Shot himself. Five months.'

He heard Zar's breathing quicken. 'Where?'

'Looks like the middle of the countryside. He was in full hunting, shooting, and fishing gear. I'm guessing he has a country estate somewhere,' said Will as flatly and unemotionally as he could manage. He finally nerved himself to look up.

Zar was looking quizzical, amused. 'Poor man,' he said perfunctorily. 'Not a nice way to go.'

Did he know about his own fate? Was he laughing at it, and at Will?

Will shook his head. There was no way Zar could know. He must get his nerves under control.

'Where's the water?' he asked and Zar despatched Javanshir to get him a glass. Will staggered on for the rest of the morning. By lunchtime, he was tired of the litany of death, and very glad when Zar offered him a 'little something'. Again, he awoke refreshed and relaxed, but as soon as he looked at Zar he knew something had changed. Zar had gone from restrained to crackling with energy and barely suppressed excitement.

'Change of plan,' Zar said. 'You go home now and get some rest. You've got an early start tomorrow.'

'Am I going to see Dexter?'

'Need to know,' said Zar blithely. 'But you should pack a case. Pack for cold weather.'

'Where am I going?'

'Can't say, old boy. But don't worry. It will be fun.'

And with those words ringing in his ear, Will was ushered out the door.

***

Alice was no more communicative, and Will was driven through the early morning London streets with no idea of his destination.

When they turned left on to the Westway, he knew they were heading out of London and within a few miles he'd worked out the likely destination must be RAF Northolt.

'Do you know where I'm going?' Will asked the taciturn Patrick.

'No idea, mate. My instructions are to accompany you to the plane and then give you this.' He waved an envelope that was on the front seat.

'Can't you give it to me now?' asked Will.

'When you're on the plane, mate.'

Will spent the rest of the journey fuming at the unnecessary secrecy. By the time they turned through the gates of RAF Northolt he had prepared in his mind a suitably pompous speech telling Dexter where he could shove his job.

The car took them straight past the reception buildings and out on to the tarmac. A C-17 Globemaster was waiting at the end of the runway and Will's heart sank. This was not good news. A military transport like that could only mean a long flight somewhere operational.

There were half a dozen soldiers checking over cases near the open landing bay at the back. Will recognised the sharp efficiency and their determined manner. They all looked super-fit and hard as nails. They had SAS stamped all over them, and that made Will's heart sink further.

Patrick ushered him up the ramp and into the wide loading area. Will had seen it all before. The steel floor with pallets and provisions tied down in one corner. A jeep fixed in place in the middle. It looked like the SAS were bringing their own transport. And worse still, everyone was in desert colours. Chances are that meant Iraq or Syria. Will went cold at the thought. Could he face desert warfare again after everything that had happened when he was in the Army?

Suddenly, the full realisation hit him. The Colonel, his colonel, was due to die in a roadside bomb tomorrow. This had to be related, surely. The only person who knew about that was Alice, so who had she told?

Will rounded on Patrick. 'The letter?' he demanded.

Patrick raised an eyebrow but handed over the slim package. Will ripped it open and tipped the contents out. A passport fell into his hand. Will opened it and saw immediately his photo on the main page. But the details were different. He scanned the name Matthew Taylor. Well, that was anonymous and inoffensive enough, but why was it necessary?

He delved in to the envelope and there was a single sheet of paper.

'A favour for a friend. Be nice,' he read. 'Apologies for the subterfuge. I'll explain it all when you get back. Dexter.'

Will was still taking this in when Patrick waved at him. 'Have a pleasant flight, mate. See you when you get back.'

'Where am I going?' he asked, but Patrick just walked away. A member of the flight crew walked past, and Will tried asking the same question, but the man just looked at Will like he was mad and hurried on.

Will took a deep breath. He could cause a scene; he could run off the plane and get himself arrested. Or he could follow this through and find out what was really going on, and whether Alice had betrayed him. Though he hated the prospect, he might get some answers where he was going.

'Can you sit down please, sir,' said one of the aircrew, indicating hard seats along the edge of the fuselage. Will strapped himself in and was handed ear protectors. It was, he knew, going to be a long and noisy flight.

The SAS crew had taken seats as far from Will as possible, and they ignored him, never even glancing in his direction. Fair enough, thought Will. They're operational. I'm a stranger. Let's pretend we're on different planes.

The loading ramp ponderously lifted and slowly closed. Then the noise from the engines turned into a roar and soon they were accelerating down the runway into the air and turning east.

Will shut his eyes and went back to trying to work out whether he'd been betrayed and what was likely to happen in the next twenty-four hours.

***

Flying in the Globemaster was like being shut in a metal coffin. Will couldn't see out and it was only when the plane taxied to a halt and the rear loading door opened that he had his worst fears confirmed.

The first gust of hot and heavy air told him all he needed to know. Middle East. Desert. All the memories of Afghanistan flooded back: the endless patrols, the blood, the fear, the futility. He had never been so glad to leave anywhere, even in disgrace, as he had been when he had flown out of Kabul. Maybe this wasn't Afghanistan, but it was somewhere hot and very dangerous.

The SAS team continued to ignore him as they decanted all their equipment on to the tarmac by the plane and checked it again exhaustively. It was mid-afternoon and the heat bouncing back off the concrete was stifling. Will could feel the sweat running down his back. He cursed Zar and his little joke. Pack for cold weather. Will was going to be doing a lot of extra sweating thanks to him.

Finally, a soldier approached him. 'Mr Taylor?'

It took Will a moment to react when he belatedly recognised his false passport name.

'That's me.'

'Follow me, please. The Colonel is waiting.'

And there was Will's last fear confirmed. He did not need to ask which Colonel or why the Colonel wanted to see him. This looked like payback time from his old senior officer. The one big question that remained was, did Grantley know

145

he was due to die tomorrow, and if he did, then who had told him?

The soldier marched over to a Portakabin, opened the door and ushered Will inside. If anything, it was even hotter and more oppressive in there with only a small fan in a corner trying to move the heavy air around.

A sergeant sitting behind a desk looked up. 'Mr Taylor,' he said with a barely suppressed sneer. For a second, Will thought the man had recognised him from his Army past, but then he checked himself. Afghanistan was long ago. What were the chances that any of those men would be here, six years on. He was surely being paranoid. The disdain was probably the soldier's automatic reaction to civilians. And that's what Will was, he reminded himself.

'Col. Grantley will see you now,' he added and gestured at the door.

Will went in and there was his old nemesis, sitting at a makeshift desk surrounded by paper. Grantley looked up.

'Ah, Gray. Come in. Sit down.'

Will looked behind him. The door was still open. 'It's Matthew Taylor, sir,' he said, partly to remind Grantley of his alias and to reinforce it with the sergeant. He didn't want his real name getting out in case it reminded anyone of the bus crash.

Grantley looked taken aback at being contradicted. 'Of course, Mr Taylor,' he said crisply. 'My mistake.' He got up and closed the door.

'Alright Gray let's not muck each other around. I will call you Taylor in public, but you are always Corporal Gray to me.'

146

Will registered that Grantley was not his normal, overbearing self.

'What am I doing here, sir?'

Grantley looked away, as if faintly embarrassed. 'I have a situation here and some people thought you could be of use, so I asked as a favour if I could borrow you.'

Will noted the same use of 'favour' that was in the note.

'But you don't believe in what I can do,' said Will. 'You think it's...'

'Poppycock. Yes,' said the Colonel with a touch of his old asperity. But someone has prevailed upon me to take a different view. I'm told you are being quite useful back in London.'

'So what use can I be here?' asked Will.

'I have a group embarking on a very dangerous mission. Against an Isis cell here in the Iraqi desert. They are some of the best we have, but if this mission has been compromised, I need to know. I can't afford to lose them all.'

The pieces fell into place. 'The SAS Group on the plane I came out on. You want me to tell you if they're going to die?'

Grantley nodded. Will felt his anger grow. 'But I could have looked into their eyes back in London. I could have done it on the tarmac at Northolt, for Christ's sake. I didn't have to come all the way out here.'

Grantley had the grace to look faintly embarrassed. 'Operational security. I wanted it to happen here under my control, where I could assess the consequences.'

And then Grantley looked straight into Will's eyes, and Will saw again his face in the troop carrier and the explosion of dirt and metal and flame as the roadside bomb lifted the vehicle clear into the air and flipped what was left of it and Grantley upside down.

Will flinched and he saw the Colonel flinch too, and he knew then that the Colonel had been told and was only too aware that he was due to die tomorrow.

'Let's get on with it, shall we?' said the Colonel, taking a deep breath and straightening his shoulders. They clearly would not talk about the Colonel's fate yet.

Will suddenly felt sympathy for the old soldier. It must take some courage to do what Grantley was doing. Facing up to enemy fire depended on the belief that no matter what the odds, you had some chance of survival. Knowing that you were going to die required an altogether higher level of bravery.

'Very well. How do you want to do this?' asked Will.

'How do you normally do it?'

'Behind two-way glass so the subject doesn't know they are being studied and can't see my reaction.'

'You always have a reaction?' the Colonel asked flatly. Will knew he was thinking of the way Will had flinched moments before.

'It's hard not to,' said Will. 'Especially if it's a very violent death.'

Grantley smiled faintly. 'I see. Well, I'm afraid we don't have any two-way glass here, and it needs to happen right away, because they are due to set out at dusk.'

Will felt trapped, but now he was here, he guessed he had no choice. 'Alright, we'll do it head on. You'll have to introduce me. Say I'm a security consultant for the MoD monitoring the outcome of their mission.'

'They'll hate you,' said Grantley. 'A bean-counter who doesn't take the risks.'

'If it makes them angry, then they'll look me straight in the eye. Challenge, confrontation, those kinds of men thrive on that.'

'And you'll control your reaction?'

'As best I can,' said Will. 'I sometimes throw up if it's a nasty death, but I can always blame the Globemaster flight.'

Grantley laughed. 'They'll think you're a total wimp.'

'All the better.'

Chapter Nineteen

The SAS Patrol were relaxing under the shade of a canvas awning. They jumped to their feet when Grantley appeared but there were no salutes.

Grantley addressed one of the men. 'Randall. This is Matthew Taylor. He's a security guy from the MoD monitoring operations like yours and their outcomes.'

Randall, who was tall and sinewy and whippet-thin, looked surprised.

'He'd like to meet you all,' said Grantley. 'Introduce your men.'

Randall looked even more surprised but turned to a big, broad ginger-haired man with a craggy face who was already smiling threateningly. 'This is Tanner.'

Will shook Tanner's hand, ignoring the vice-like grip that was clearly supposed to intimidate him, and stared straight into a pair of intense brown eyes. Then he felt the impact of the bullet and he was staring at Tanner's face in the dirt, blood pooling around his head, those piercing eyes clouding over, going opaque. But it wasn't in the next few hours, it was seven months away.

Will tried to control a tremor, but Tanner had clearly felt something as their handshake ended.

'You all right, mate?' he said with a pretence of concern.

'Still a little unsteady after the flight,' Will said and heard a snort of derision behind him. 'Good to meet you. I like to know who I'm writing a report about.'

This time, Will heard a muttered 'desk-jockey'. He thought it came from the next in line who was introduced as Gregory. He was fair-haired, with a wide, amused face. Will shook his hand and stared into the man's clear blue eyes. Hospital bed, drips and the same face, but emaciated and shrunken. Cancer. Eighteen years on. Too young to die, but not a dusty, pointless desert death at least.

Will turned to the third soldier, a small ferret-like man who radiated toughness from his buzz cut tattooed head to the slab-like muscular hand that gripped his.

'Reynolds,' the man said for himself, and Will looked into dark eyes that were almost black.

Then it was a frosty night, cardboard boxes visible in the faint illumination of distant streetlights. The grey, raddled face of Reynolds expiring in an alcoholic haze on a freezing city street. And only ten years away. A cruel death for a fighting man.

Will shook himself and turned to Randall who was looking at him with complete contempt. It was hard to master his reactions when the visions came so quickly, one after the other.

'Thank you, Randall,' Will said, extending his hand. There was a moment's hesitation, then, as they shook, Randall pulled Will closer and said quietly, 'I don't believe you.'

Will looked into light grey eyes of surprising coldness. Then suddenly it was Randall's face screaming, 'Run, run' as he fired a burst from his machine gun and then incoming bullets were stitching a pattern of red across his chest, lifting him off his feet and depositing him in the dirt. 6.10 a.m., tomorrow morning.

Will heaved but swallowed his bile back down again. 'Sorry, something must have upset my stomach. Good luck with the mission.'

Randall stepped back and looked inquiringly at Grantley, who ignored the unsaid question. 'Thank you, gentlemen. Final briefing forty-five minutes.'

He led Will away. Will could hear them muttering as he left, 'What the fuck was that about?'

Will closed the door of Grantley's cabin office behind them and collapsed into a chair, feeling relieved.

'Well, that will have rattled them all,' said Grantley. 'I assume from your reaction it was not good news.'

'I told you it would be hard to conceal how it affects me. That's why I do it from behind a mirror.'

'What's the final score then?' asked Grantley.

'On the patrol. Just one fatality. Randall, I'm afraid,' said Will.

'Just Randall? You clearly found something with Tanner, too.'

'He gets killed. But in seven months. A different mission.'

'And the other two?'

'Cancer and alcoholism while living rough.'

Grantley looked sombre. 'And there you have the price of life in the modern Army.' He shook himself. 'What more can you tell me about Randall?'

'He was shouting what looked like 'Run, run' and loosing off a burst from his machine gun when he was cut down. It looked like they were ambushed.'

Grantley stared out of the window. 'He's a good man. I'm not sure the Army can afford to lose him.'

Will's heart sank. Here we go again, he thought. 'Are you thinking of taking him off the mission?' he asked. Grantley said nothing.

'Just remember what happened when I intervened in the bus crash. It all turned out far, far worse.'

Grantley looked at Will wearily. 'Thank you. I remember, but it's my job to make tough decisions. And to protect the lives of the men under my command. He took a deep breath and straightened his shoulders. 'Death comes for us all in the end. You should rest. We'll talk later.'

And then, Will knew, they would talk about Grantley's own date with death, which was now less than twenty-four hours away.

***

The memories were crowding in. Mostly terrible ones. Will lay in a cot in an airless tent and stared at the canvas, white from the sun beating down on it.

He remembered the adrenaline that flooded his body whenever they left the camp in Afghanistan. The step-by-step patrols where every movement could trigger a roadside IED or a mine. Where you didn't know whether to keep studying the road for tripwires or the ruined houses for the sniper who was already lining you up in his sights.

153

He felt his stomach clench at the thought. The endless unease created by a merciless enemy who you had no hope of understanding, who wanted to exterminate you in a religious crusade when you barely gave God a thought except to say what are you doing exposing me to this.

He could see the faces of so many dead comrades, some friends, some idiots, some hateful, but none who you could honestly say deserved to die at such a young age in such a god-forsaken place.

Why on earth had he allowed himself to be manipulated into this? He cursed Dexter. Sweat trickled down his back and he cursed Zar for his little joke about packing clothes for cold weather. He had nothing cooler to change into.

He was conscious of other pressing worries, too. He had noticed the odd quizzical glance from passing soldiers. Someone might soon remember him from the coverage of the bus crash. He needed to get out of here as quickly as possible.

Ahead was a tricky conversation with Grantley. Would the Colonel face up to it, or seek a way out? Will wasn't looking forward to that.

He drifted into a fitful doze, and then it was twilight, and a soldier was loudly clearing his throat outside. 'The Colonel asks if you would join him for a drink, sir.'

Will hauled himself off the cot and followed the man across the camp towards the Colonel's office. He saw another soldier pass them, glancing at Will as if trying to place him. He knew as soon as someone had a positive ID it would be round the camp like wildfire. Deserter, paedophile, child killer. And then who knows what would happen?

Grantley was sitting at his desk, staring into space. He roused himself when Will came in.

'Scotch?' he said, pointing at a full bottle sitting on his desk. It was an expensive bottle of Talisker. Will nodded.

Grantley poured them two generous slugs. 'You don't want water, do you?' the Colonel added, and smiled when Will declined. 'Never adulterate a good scotch.'

Will sipped the amber liquid and felt the warm bite at the back of his throat. It was good, but probably not the most ideal drink for a warm Iraqi evening. There was a silence, then finally Grantley looked at him.

'I owe you an apology, a big apology,' he said. 'I judged you too quickly.'

'And found me wanting,' said Will, deliberately locking on the Colonel's gaze, feeling again the explosion ripping through the armoured car. He shuddered and Grantley, noticing, smiled sadly.

'No reprieve then?'

'I'm afraid not,' said Will, swallowing another sip of whisky to wipe away the bile.

'What time?'

'Half past two tomorrow. Well, 2.28 p.m. to be precise.'

Grantley glanced at his watch. 'Nineteen hours away. Why didn't you tell me before?'

'You would never have believed me.'

'That's undoubtedly true. You had so much promise, and I was so disappointed when you ran away. I felt betrayed somehow. I didn't want to accept any explanation, even PTSD.'

'You made my life a misery.'

Grantley raised his palms in a gesture of surrender. 'I accept that. I'm sorry.'

'Why have you changed your mind now?'

Grantley smiled. 'Dexter seems to think highly of you.'

'You knew that before. Why now?'

'I suppose now I've seen how you react to it, I'm more inclined to believe. You look like you're taking a bullet, too.'

'That's what it feels like.'

'That must be difficult.'

Will let the statement hang in the air. 'It was Dexter who told you?'

Grantley nodded. But that didn't answer the bigger question. Who had told Dexter?

'And it's a roadside IED?' Grantley asked.

'As far as I can see.'

'Do I have any alternative?'

'What do you mean?' asked Will cautiously.

'Well, if I never left the camp tomorrow then presumably, I wouldn't get killed by that bomb.'

Will weighed up his response. 'Then someone else might die in the same explosion instead, or if it really is meant for you, the same people might regroup and get you on another day. There's no way of knowing.'

'I have an alternative.'

'You do, but as I said earlier, the knock-on consequences could be worse for others.'

Grantley sipped his whisky. 'Always been my favourite,' he said. 'Reminds me of home. The Isle of Skye. Which I guess I'll never see again.' He looked at Will. 'What about my men? The ones with me in the troop carrier?'

'I don't know. I'd have to look into their eyes. But that would only increase your dilemma,' said Will. He was becoming concerned about the direction of this conversation. There was a limit to what could be avoided.

'What did you do about the patrol?' he said, changing tack.

'I kept Randall back. I didn't want to lose him,' said Grantley.

'That may have been unwise.'

'My decision, my responsibility,' said Grantley, a hint of steel back in his voice.

'Did you tell him why?' asked Will, suddenly alarmed.

'I made up some cock-and-bull story. He was furious.'

'He mustn't be told the truth.'

'He won't be,' said Grantley. 'I know my duty. Corporal.'

And there was the old Grantley back again for a second. He passed his hand over his eyes. 'Thank you for your help, Mr Gray. I think I'd like to spend my last evening thinking back over my life. If you don't mind.'

Will took the hint and rose. 'I'm sorry,' he said. 'Truly, I am.'

Grantley gave him an absent-minded wave, whether of acknowledgment or dismissal Will wasn't sure, so he turned and left.

Chapter Twenty

Will woke the next morning to find himself staring down the barrel of a gun. Beyond the barrel were the cold, cold grey eyes of Sgt. Randall who was looking at him with absolute ferocity. Will could see that Randall's trigger finger was rigid, and he was clearly having difficulty stopping himself from firing.

'What did you say to the Colonel?' Randall demanded.

'I don't know what you mean.'

'What did you say to the Colonel?' Randall repeated. 'That made him take me off the mission.'

Will realised that something must have gone very wrong. Whatever had happened, this was not the moment to be honest. If word got out about his ability, the connection with the bus death soldier would be immediate.

'I'm just a security consultant,' said Will, struggling to sit up. Randall had his gun jammed against Will's chin.

'I don't believe you,' he said with frightening intensity. 'You don't smell right.'

'Ask the Colonel. He'll confirm it.'

Will noticed that Randall's eyes were fringed with moisture. He was close to crying. What on earth would reduce this hard-as-rock killing machine to tears? Will had a terrible feeling that he knew.

'What happened?' he asked.

Randall shuddered. 'They're dead. All of them. The whole patrol ambushed and wiped out. They were about to hook up with a guide and he saw the whole thing.' He swallowed, and the light shone again in his eyes. 'It's your fault.'

The look Randall gave him was of such frightening intensity that Will had no choice but to meet the man's eyes. Suddenly, surprisingly, it was an urban street in the half light of an early morning. Randall was in civvies, braced in the firing position, shooting his pistol at an unknown assailant and behind him there was someone running away. Then several bullets caught Randall in the chest, spinning him around and dumping him on the cobblestone street. The date hit Will like a blow, May 10th, the day of the bomb. What on earth could that mean?

'Answer me,' Randall growled, bringing Will back to his present predicament. 'How did you get me thrown off the mission?'

Will decided he must regain the initiative. 'It sounds like that saved your life.'

But that only made Randall angrier. 'I should have been with them.' He was shaking now, the gun scraping against Will's chin, tears leaking from his eyes. 'Don't you see? I might have saved them.'

Suddenly, a voice like ice cut through. 'Put down that gun, soldier. Now.' Randall hesitated, but there was a whip crack edge to the command that he clearly couldn't ignore. Slowly, he pulled the gun away from Will's chin. Over his shoulder, Will could see Grantley in the entrance to the tent.

Will was only momentarily relieved. He could see a glittering anger in Grantley's eyes that did not bode well.

'Stand back, Sgt. Randall.' Slowly Randall obeyed, every movement a battle between his desire to harm Will and a soldier's training to obey. 'The gun,' Grantley commanded, and Randall handed it over. Grantley weighed it in his hand for a second as if he would like to use it, then slid it into his pocket.

'Sgt. Randall. You will report to me later. In the meantime, you do not talk to anyone about this. Understood.'

Randall nodded, although the effort of restraining it all was clearly costing him.

'As for you, Gray, come with me,' the Colonel said and left the tent.

Will cursed. It was the worst moment for Grantley to forget and use Will's real name. Will saw Randall's head snap round and a dawning comprehension spread across his features.

Will left quickly, following the Colonel before Randall reached the inevitable conclusion about the identity of the so-called security consultant.

***

Grantley was almost as furious as Randall.

'Four men, Gray. I lost four good men. And you said at least three of them would survive.'

Will decided it was time to meet aggression with aggression. 'I told you the perils of changing your plans.

160

Maybe Randall was supposed to save the others, at the cost of his own life. He wasn't there, so they died.'

'Maybe,' thundered Grantley. 'Maybe, maybe. Those are people's lives you're playing with.'

'You think I don't know that?' said Will bitterly. 'You may recall I never wanted to be part of this. Once anyone changes the future, there's no telling where it will end.'

Grantley rounded on Will. 'How do I know you're right at all? You might be wrong about me dying today.'

Will stared straight into the Colonel's angry flashing eyes. 'There's only one way to be sure,' he said. He felt again the force of the blast. 'Same explosion, same roads, same time.'

Grantley sagged. 'Nothing's changed. I lose four men on the very day I'm going to die. That's a bitter pill. And if I try to change my fate, then even more could die too.'

Will said nothing. There was little he could say. The whole thing was a mess. He felt sorry for Grantley, but there was nothing he could do. Any further intervention could only make it far worse. And right now, he needed to avoid getting lynched by Sgt. Randall or some other vengeful squaddie.

'You know you used my real name back there in front of Randall. I could see he made the connection and I'm sure it will be round the camp soon. You have put me in real danger.'

'Why should that bother me?' said Grantley.

'Because as you know, I'm here on loan from MI5, who seem to rate me. I think they might be disappointed if I'm strung up.'

Grantley's eyes came back into focus. 'Alright, alright. I'll give you an armed guard to the landing strip.'

'And you need to make sure that Randall doesn't think of going to the papers. I have dropped off the radar since the bus crash, and it needs to stay like that.'

Grantley nodded. 'I'll talk to him.' He picked up the phone and gave his adjutant orders for the car and for Randall to come and see him.

There was an awkward pause. Will could see that Grantley looked a crushed man, defeated by the losses that were piling up and his imminent death.

'I'm sorry,' Will said. 'Really. I wish I could change it all, but every time that happens, it feels like the result is worse.'

Grantley said nothing, then he looked at Will. 'I wish it could be different too,' he said with a small smile. 'Goodbye, Mr Gray.'

Will left then, but found himself sitting outside Grantley's office, waiting for his armed guard and conscious that Randall was on the way over. He didn't think that Randall would try to kill him in the Colonel's waiting room, but he didn't relish another confrontation.

He was relieved when a private stuck his head round the door and said, 'Jeep for the plane', and the adjutant indicated Will.

He followed the private out, scanning the camp for Randall. 'Do you have an armed guard?' he asked.

'We pick them up at the gate. Don't need them inside the camp,' the private said with a laugh.

'I need to get my bag.'

'We'll stop on the way,' said the private, starting the engine and moving off. Will spotted Randall coming onto the open ground in front of the Colonel's office. He was fifty yards away, but Will could feel the hatred emanating from him. As they drove past, Will could see those cold eyes watching him and then Randall drew his hand across his neck in a cut-throat gesture.

'Dead man,' he mouthed, and Will could feel his eyes boring into Will's back as they drove away.

They picked up Will's bag and the guard and Will heaved a sigh of relief as they drove out of the camp. He would rather take his chances with the hostile Iraqi countryside than face Randall again.

He had a nervy wait when the plane was delayed, but no SAS squad burst onto the landing strip. Finally, they boarded. By the time they taxied down the runway, it was after two o'clock and the Colonel's bomb was due to go off in a few minutes.

As the plane left the runway and rose sharply into the bright blue sky, Will remembered the sharp flash of light as the roadside bomb exploded and the dirty black smoke rising into the air.

Will closed his eyes. Farewell, Colonel Grantley. He thought back to the years of camaraderie before it had all gone so wrong. The Colonel had gone to his death bravely enough, a true soldier.

Another fatality, and yet more questions. Had Alice leaked the details of the Colonel's death, or was it someone else? Since he hadn't told anyone except Alice, that didn't seem likely.

163

And now he faced an even more perplexing dilemma. How did Randall, who clearly wanted to kill him, come to be in London in nine days' time? And why, when he looked into Randall's eyes, had he seen someone running away that in the grey dawn light looked suspiciously like Will himself? Was Randall, in fact, trying to kill him or could he be saving Will's life?

Chapter Twenty-One

Will was close to shouting. 'I need an answer. Did you leak the details of how Colonel Grantley was going to die?'

Alice turned on him, her eyes flashing. 'I've told you once and I'll tell you again, I didn't leak it. I said you should tell Dexter, but I didn't leak it.'

'Why should I trust you? I could have been killed out there, and I now have another homicidal maniac who wants to kill me. The odds on one of them succeeding are shortening all the time.'

'Who's the other one?' said Alice with irritation.

'That bus crash father who tried to throttle me. He's out there somewhere.'

'He's gone. Forget him. He'll never find you. We'll take care of that.'

'And yet I get sent to Iraq and put at unnecessary risk there.'

'Trust me, Will. I'm on your side.' Alice put a hand on his arm, but Will was not in the mood to be mollified.

'Why should I? I know next to nothing about you. Is this just a job for you?' Will said, gesturing around the flat. 'Do you have another life? Do you have another home somewhere? You must do, but you've never told me anything about it?'

'Of course, I have my life away from this. I'd go crazy if I didn't.'

'Then show me. Take me into your confidence. Let's really work together.'

Alice looked at him for several seconds, weighing up the consequences.

'Ok,' she said finally. 'Let's go.'

***

They left the building and walked down the street towards the river, Patrick trailing a hundred yards behind. Will could see that Alice was scanning the sparse traffic. Then she said, 'There's one,' and flagged down a lone taxi.

'Inside, quick,' she said to Will, and 'Notting Hill, I'll give you the address in a second,' to the taxi driver.

Will twisted in his seat to see Patrick running up the road, but they were already moving off. Patrick was searching the traffic for another taxi, but Will realised Alice had picked her moment carefully. There wasn't another one in sight.

'He won't be very pleased,' said Will.

'He'll get over it,' said Alice, smiling. 'Digby Crescent,' she said to the taxi driver.

'Where are we going?' asked Will.

'My flat,' said Alice. 'My proper home.'

The journey passed in silence. Will decided he would just let it play out. Maybe he would get to know a bit more about the real Alice.

They drew up outside a big white stucco terrace in Notting Hill.

'This is your house?' said Will, surprised.

'A tiny part of it,' said Alice, leading him down the side of the wide stone staircase that led up to the grand front door. She stopped outside two identical front doors.

'The whole basement, then?' asked Will.

'Just half of it,' she said, leading him into a tiny, dark entrance hall. There was a strong smell of spices, a pot-pourri of some kind, he guessed, and when she turned on the light he was surprised to find a small hallway full of exotic patterns and hanging scarves. Then she led him into a small living room that was covered in floor to ceiling bookshelves crammed to the brim. There was a comfortable high-backed chair with a reading light and a soft collapsed sofa covered in a batik dyed cloth, and wherever there was space there were other exotically dyed scarves and throws and swathes of multi-coloured fabric.

Will stared at the books. Philosophy, psychology, a few Booker prize winners. Not much in the way of pulp fiction.

'What are you? Half academic, half hippie?' he said, gesturing at the books and the scarves.

'That pretty much sums me up,' said Alice.

Will turned his attention to the mantelpiece. There were just two pictures. One of a teenage Alice with a ruggedly handsome older man, both wearing walking gear, hair ruffled in the wind. The other of the same man with a smiling woman, cheeks flushed, laughing at something presumably that the man had said. Alice with her father. Her parents together. That was it.

There were no other photos. Will felt for her loss. 'Thank you for doing this,' he said. 'It's a lovely room. Very peaceful'.

'My little retreat,' said Alice. 'When my father died, I sold their house, and it was a choice between suburban splendour or a pretty but tiny place in central London. I chose this.'

'Good choice.'

'Do you want tea or coffee or a drink?'

'Coffee would be fine.'

Will followed her out to a tiny kitchen that was full of bright colours and had a small window looking out over a green courtyard garden.

'Lots of plants?'

'Another love of mine. I have a softer side.'

'You certainly do,' said Will appreciatively.

He watched how she brushed the hair back from her face and bit her lip in concentration as she poured boiling water into a cafetiere. He felt some of the tension slip away. This was almost normal. The flat where they were operating from was always on show, tidy and new and oppressive, with Patrick never far away and all the rooms undoubtedly bugged. Here they could behave like ordinary people, getting to know each other.

Alice handed him a coffee, and they went back to the book-lined sitting room.

'Will you get into trouble for this?'

'They won't like it, but if they want the best out of you, they'll have to lump it. Tell me about Iraq. Tell me everything.'

So, Will went through it all, blow by grisly blow. 'I felt sorry for Grantley at the end. So many bitter pills to swallow but he went to his death bravely.'

'What do you think went wrong with the SAS patrol?'

'It's simple. They were ambushed. Randall would have saved the other three at the cost of his own life. That's what he was doing when he shouted at them to run. It was only a couple of seconds' grace, but they would have got out. Now he blames me for the death of his comrades.'

'Not a good enemy to have,' said Alice. 'I'll have a track put on him, so we'll know if he comes back to the UK.'

'Thanks,' said Will. 'The big problem, though, is how did Grantley know? Who told him?' He saw her tense up. 'Look, I believe you. It wasn't you, but then who was it, and how on earth did they find out?'

'Dexter always has his ways.' Alice studied him for a moment, then took a deep breath. 'There's something you ought to know. About Dexter's agenda.'

Will leaned forward eagerly. 'Yes?'

'I did some digging into those Muslim men. As far as I can see, none of the younger ones had any track record or connection. Dexter thought they were just makeweights. He was as surprised as you when it was revealed that number two was going to be shot.

'I've delivered them into his hands,' Will groaned.

'It's worse than that,' said Alice. 'Dexter's pushing on them hard. He's already had number three back in for further interrogation.'

'But that could change everything. He said he'd wait and see. Instead, he's making it worse,' said Will.

'You can't trust Dexter at all. He says whatever suits him.'

169

Will took Alice's hand, and this time she didn't pull it away. 'Thank you for telling me. I really appreciate it,' he said.

She squeezed his fingers. 'You deserve it. I've seen what it costs you every time. I respect that and the least you can expect from us is that we're straight with you. Unfortunately, straight is not a word in Dexter's dictionary.'

'Why do you hate him so much?' asked Will.

Alice sighed and pulled back her hand. Her voice got harder.

'I shouldn't tell you this, but the last assignment I had went badly wrong,' she said, staring into the middle distance. 'I was minding a defector at a safe house in the East End. He was a Russian, Pavel. He'd fled one of the oligarchs, but he had information on Putin.'

'What kind of information?'

'Bribes paid to Putin, corrupt trading deals, that kind of thing. Anyway, he was terrified. He was certain that the FSB would come and get him. He was weeping with fear. I couldn't talk him down.'

'What happened?'

'I was there with Patrick, but he was called away in the middle of the night. He woke me and told me to look after Pavel. But I fell asleep and when Patrick came back Pavel had hung himself.' Alice's voice cracked. 'All I had to do was stay awake and I failed.'

Will was immediately suspicious. 'Do you think someone might have drugged you?''

Alice gave him a shrewd glance. 'I did wonder, but they tested me and said there was nothing. It would have been extraordinary timing for the FSB to have broken in just then when I was asleep, so I was suspicious. But then they confirmed Pavel hadn't been killed; he had committed suicide. Forensics were sure.'

'How did he kill himself?'

'Tied his belt round a beam.' Alice stared unseeing across the room. 'Dexter was furious. Said I should have taken his belt away.'

Will took Alice's hand again. 'It's tough, but surely those kinds of things happen.'

'Dexter can't let go of it. There's a disciplinary inquiry. I'll have to be grilled, and I could be reprimanded, maybe even kicked out.'

Will whistled. 'He's a vengeful bastard, isn't he?' Alice looked away. 'You don't suppose it was a set-up?' he asked.

'Of course I've wondered that, but it would have to be a pretty big conspiracy, and I've got no way of proving anything. On the face of it, I fucked it up, and that's that.'

Will had an idea. Alice seemed to be opening up, trusting in him. He should trust her, too.

'You need to fight back, and I'd like to help,' said Will.

'How? Kill the bastard?' said Alice with a wry smile.

'Not quite. We could investigate it together. I wonder how Patrick dies. I've never looked into his eyes. And I wonder if there is footage anywhere of Pavel being interrogated shortly before he died?'

Alice raised an eyebrow. 'There must be. Why?'

Will smiled. 'I'm just curious. What he looked like. What he said. Maybe I'll pick up clues that you might have missed. It's worth trying, if you can get the footage.'

Alice looked energised. 'I'll get it. It would be so good to get one back on Dexter.'

She looked him straight in the eye and he saw again the old people's home and the tableau round the bed. And that strangely familiar figure holding Alice's hand.

'I owe you,' she said, and went to kiss his cheek. But somehow when their faces touched, she didn't move away. Will could smell her lavender scent again and feel the soft touch of her breath on his face.

Without thinking, he twisted his head so that their lips met. He felt her freeze for a second and was expecting another eruption of anger, but instead she seemed to relax. She kissed him back and, amazingly, he felt the tip of her tongue trace the inside of his lips. And then they were kissing properly for a moment until she gently broke them apart.

'Ho hum. So much for all my principles,' said Alice with a smile. 'I think we should take a moment while I check I'm not being a complete moron.'

'Thanks very much,' said Will. 'Great compliment.'

'When I said I don't sleep with an assignment, I meant it,' she said. 'But, but, but. I admire your courage, and if you help me get one back on Dexter, I'll be forever in your debt. And besides, you're quite hot.' She laughed. 'Let's have a drink. A proper one this time.'

She fetched a bottle of white wine from the fridge, opened it and poured two glasses.

'Sorry. I'm not drinking. Since the bus crash,' said Will.

'Fair enough. But I'm afraid I need one. To doing down Dexter,' she said, raising her glass in a mock toast.

'The defeat of all shits,' said Will.

'Ok, I've decided,' said Alice, taking him by the hand. She led him through into the bedroom, which turned out to be another riot of coloured fabrics with a deep, luxuriant maroon throw on the bed and big cushions in complementary colours.

'My boudoir,' said Alice with a small laugh, and then she turned and kissed him gently but deliberately. Will was amazed at the transformation. She was soft and yet insistent. When he pushed himself against her, she said, 'Slow down, soldier boy,' and returned to her kiss, easing her tongue into his mouth again, probing softly then firmly for his response.

He knew this wasn't wise, but he didn't care. He was pretty sure she felt the same. They fell back on to the bed. She was sinuous and urgent now. There was a cascade of discarded clothing and then they were naked, hands feeling, touching, caressing, urging on.

Will felt himself melting at her passion and by the time she allowed him to slip inside her, he was shaking with desire. He came almost straightaway, so great was his need. 'Sorry,' he whispered.

Alice smiled. 'No problem. You were obviously worked up and we have plenty of time.' She snuggled herself into the crook of his shoulder and they dozed off.

When they woke, Alice went to get her wine. Will watched her nakedness with a kind of amazement. She was compact and lithe, and her body radiated strength.

She returned with the glass and sat up in bed sipping the wine. She had only pulled the sheet up to her waist and Will was conscious of her small, neat breasts and the hard nipples.

He let his gaze slip further down to her muscled stomach. He put out a tentative hand and touched her there. It was firm and unyielding.

'You've got better abs than I had when I was in the Army,' he said, smiling.

'It's my little obsession,' said Alice. 'I exercise all the time. This honey badger hasn't just got sharp claws, there's plenty to back it up. I will never be weak again.'

Will could see a shadow pass over her face, but she let it pass. She reached out and ran a hand over his chest. 'You look in pretty good shape to me.' She let her hand slip under the sheets. 'Hard where it counts,' she added with a little smile.

Will couldn't disagree and soon they were moving together again but this time easily, fluently, her legs wrapped around him. For Will it felt like a re-birth, a coming alive again, and when she cried out, he let himself join her and felt for a precious moment almost healed.

***

In the morning, she brought him coffee and toast in bed and they lay there talking quietly.

'What happened after your father died?' asked Alice. 'Did you tell your mother?'

Will felt his stomach churn as he remembered. His mother, sitting hunched in the living room, staring vacantly out of the window, the tear tracks visible on her face.

'I didn't know what to do. I had this enormous secret that was just eating me up. It felt like my skull was going to

174

explode with the awfulness of it all. I'd known my father was going to die, and I had done nothing about it.'

Alice watched him with a sympathetic expression. She looks as if she really does care, thought Will.

'Finally, I got up the courage to tell her. At first, she was sweet and said it was just a nightmare, and when something terrible happens to people we love, we all feel it must have been our fault somehow. But then when I persisted, she got colder and colder until she said I was just trying to make her feel guilty.'

Will swallowed. He remembered the distance that had grown between them. 'When I said I was joining the Army she didn't want to know. We haven't spoken since,' he said.

'You should get in touch with her again,' said Alice. 'You've still got one parent. It's worth hanging on to.'

Will said nothing. Maybe she was right, but there were so many years of distrust to get round now.

'What did you do after you were forced out of the Army?' Alice asked.

'I couldn't face anything much. After months in a cell awaiting my discharge, I couldn't see any way forward. I certainly wasn't going to look anyone in the eye. Couldn't face that responsibility.

'I got a place in a charity home. It was full of ex-Army types who couldn't cope with life outside, either. I had a few odd jobs, making sandwiches for a fast-food chain, night security, that kind of thing. And I started drinking on an industrial scale. The only thing I could think of was to blot it all out. Never face it again.'

Will tasted bile at the back of his throat. 'Of course, I lost all the jobs one by one, and I was running out of money. I was on my last legs and then the bus crash happened.'

Alice prodded him in the chest. 'And then you met me, and you were saved,' she said, smiling.

'And then I met Dexter,' said Will. 'From the frying pan to the fire. You were a surprise.'

'Now there's a compliment. An unexpected surprise.'

'A very welcome surprise,' said Will, kissing her. 'Possibly the one saving grace.'

And then they were making love again, and this time with even greater tenderness. They fell asleep in each other's arms.

Chapter Twenty-Two

Will was woken by the doorbell being rung repeatedly. Alice got out of bed and pulled a bathrobe off the back of the door.

'Guess the cavalry are here,' she said with a groan. She looked at her watch. 'Christ, it's lunchtime.'

He heard her answer the door, a muted whispering, then she was back, striding into the room. The old Alice returned.

'You'd better get dressed. There's been an incident. Several incidents, in fact. Dexter wants you in the office.' Will pulled on his clothes and followed Alice into the living room, where she had turned on the TV news. The strapline grabbed his attention straightaway.

'Second woman stabbed in attack on a London street.'

'There was an aerial shot of what looked like Oxford Street and a presenter's voice saying. 'There's not much information, but we understand the attack near Tottenham Court Road Tube station has been followed by another attack in Leicester Square. The first at noon, the second at half past twelve.'

Will's eyes flicked to the time on the screen. 12.57 p.m.? 'And the next one will be in three minutes,' he said.

'Are you predicting this?' Alice asked.

'No, it just makes sense, every half hour till who knows what, till their demands are met.'

'We'd better get into the office then,' said Alice.

There was a car waiting outside, and they were soon racing through the traffic towards the Embankment. Sure enough, a voice on the car radio said, 'We're getting reports of a third attack in Westminster.'

A terrible thought occurred to Will. Oxford Street, Leicester Square, Westminster.

'The attacks are heading south,' he said to Alice. 'Where would the next one be?'

'It's probably just a coincidence,' she said. 'Anyway, there's not much south of Westminster of strategic importance. Waterloo Station maybe.'

Will watched the traffic, which was virtually at a standstill as they neared the river. It must be backing up because of the Westminster incident, but then they were turning away along the Embankment towards Thames House. The pieces clicked into place.

'What if the next target is MI5?' said Will.

'Bit far-fetched,' said Alice. 'The street isn't crowded like the shopping and tourist areas so far. You'd be pushed to create as much panic.'

'But maybe that's not the point,' said Will. 'Maybe it's a message.'

He watched impatiently as the car approached the Thames House entrance. He scanned the pedestrians. Alice was right, not that many around. No gawking tourists, just a handful of people, mostly walking purposefully towards their destination.

The car screeched to a halt, and they jumped out. Will hesitated. Was he being crazy, paranoid?

'Come on, we haven't got time for this,' said Alice. Dexter wants to see us straightaway.'

Will glanced at his watch. 1.27 p.m.. Then suddenly, a movement caught his eye. An old lady with a wheeled shopping trolley appeared from behind a parked van. She was plodding down the pavement. An ideal target. Too old to fight back. Easy to get close without her noticing.

She turned and moved away from Will. Then a young man in a bomber jacket and jeans poked his head round the corner of the van. He had dark glasses on, but Will suddenly knew with a tremor of certainty that he had seen him before. It was number two, the boy who had looked so fearful and innocent and was going to get shot in the back. Now he looked very different. There was a cold, hard set to his face. He was muttering to himself, and Will realised he must be praying. He followed the old woman, who was barely ten yards ahead.

Will burst into a run. He had over fifty yards to make up. He would never get there in time. Number two pulled a large, serrated knife from his pocket. Will was still ten yards away. He wouldn't make it. Number two raised the knife, but then the noise of Will's pounding feet clearly punctured the man's concentration, and he whirled round.

Will launched himself into the air. He clattered into the man and they both lost balance. The serrated edge of the knife bit into Will's arm. A few more of those, and he would be the victim here. As they fell to the pavement Will used the momentum to drive his head into number two's nose. There was an audible crack, and the man cried out in pain, dropping the knife.

179

Will grabbed it and number two scrambled away, suddenly looking young and fearful again. He jumped to his feet and was running. Will made to follow, but he was breathless from the earlier sprint and the slice in his arm was suddenly hurting a good deal. He dropped the knife and sat back on his haunches, panting.

Then Alice was at his side with two minders. 'He went that way. Dark glasses, black bomber jacket,' she said, pointing in the direction number two had gone. The minders gave chase.

Alice put her arms round Will's shoulders and helped him to his feet.

'You were right,' she said, taking in the bloodstained knife. 'Are you wounded?'

'He's taken a slice out of my arm. He was going to stab that old lady.' Will looked round. The old woman with the shopping basket was a hundred yards down the road now, clearly oblivious to her lucky escape. She must be deaf, Will thought.

'How did you know for certain?' asked Alice. 'You were already running when he took out his knife.'

'I knew him. I'd seen him before. From the vetting.'

Alice gave him a warning look, and he turned to find a security guard and several more MI5 officers approaching. 'Let's get him inside before we cause even more of a stir,' said Alice. 'You'd better bring that knife. It's evidence.'

By now there was a small crowd of onlookers and Will could see a few people filming the scene. 'Stop them and get their phones,' he said to one officer.

Alice led him inside Thames House to a seat in the foyer. 'Wait here,' she said. Will could feel blood trickling down his arm, but he could still move his fingers, so he didn't think it was that deep a cut.

Then Dexter came striding across the foyer with Alice in tow. 'Fetch a nurse,' he said to Alice. 'We'll be in the Ops room.'

Dexter led Will to the lift. 'Quite the hero, aren't you?' he said sardonically. 'How did you know what was going to happen?'

'I had an idea just from the sequence of the killings. Going south, heading in this direction, but then I recognised the knife man.'

'Who?' said Dexter.

'Number two,' said Will.

Dexter paused and then roared with laughter. 'The one you thought was innocent. The one we're going to shoot in the back in a few days' time.'

Good God, thought Will, he's a cold-blooded bastard.

'I bet you wish we hadn't let him go now,' said Dexter.

'Why did you?'

'So he could get shot, just as you prophesied.'

Will felt sick. Number two being ushered to his death and if Alice was right, Dexter was playing cat and mouse with number three as well.

The lift stopped and Dexter led Will through into the operations room, dominated by its large screens and rows of people hunched over monitors.

'Have you let all the suspects go?' Will asked.

Dexter paused. 'We'll come to that later.' Alice appeared with a nurse in tow. 'Get that wound seen to and then we'll talk.'

Will followed the nurse to a side room and sat patiently while she cleaned the wound and bound it. It was a clean cut, not that deep.

'It should close, but if not, you'll need stitches,' she said.

Will nodded absentmindedly. His mind was still in turmoil. So, Dexter had released some, but maybe not all of them. It seemed likely he'd let two and five go because they were going to die, anyway. Was he admitting to re-arresting number three, and what about number four? What kind of game was he playing?

And beyond all that, he had occasional flashes of Alice's naked body, and a shiver when he remembered their lovemaking. This was all getting positively surreal. And now they were getting closer should he tell her about Zar's suicide? Did he trust her enough yet?

Back in the incident room, aerial pictures of police cars and ambulances at the murder scenes filled the screens. There was a newsfeed from BBC News on in the corner. Three fatal stabbings across London read the tickertape across the bottom. Dexter and Alice were waiting in a corner.

'Alice says you think these incidents were aimed at us? Why?' asked Dexter.

'The locations. Oxford St, Leicester Square, Westminster, all heading south. Thames House was a likely possibility,' said Will.

'Good luck you spotted our friend outside.'

'Like I said, I was expecting the possibility,' said Will. 'I think it was a message for you.'

'Why?'

'The last one was on your doorstep. If I was you, I'd be guessing it was the people you interrogated and released.'

'And what do they gain by killing three innocent women?'

'They get your attention. Maybe they're angry at the way they were treated.'

Dexter looked by turns taken aback, irritated and guilty, then his normal bullish demeanour returned. 'Well, two can play at that game,' he said.

'What does that mean?' asked Will, but Dexter ignored him.

'I'm going to make you a more integral part of the team here,' said Dexter. 'You've shown you're quick off the mark and maybe you'll see insights we're missing. In terms of the general office, we'll keep your real identity under the radar, and obviously don't tell anyone else about your er…gift.'

Will was getting angry now. 'They won't be very good analysts if they can't make the connection with the bus crash.'

'I'm sure they will,' Dexter conceded, 'But they'll know not to pry further.'

Will changed tack. 'What on earth was the point of the Iraqi trip? I could have vetted those soldiers back here.'

'It was all put together quickly. They didn't want to compromise security this end, so as I said, I agreed as a favour to Colonel Grantley.' Dexter looked straight at Will, and Will was reminded again of the car crash.

'The late Col. Grantley.'

'Perhaps that was something you should have told me,' said Dexter icily.

'How did you find out?' asked Will, but again Dexter avoided answering.

'Come with me.' He led Will down corridors and up several flights of stairs. Will thought they were heading towards the river side of the building, and he could guess where they were going. Hillyer's office.

'Is Deborah free?' Dexter said to the PA, and she waved them through. Dexter pushed open the double mahogany doors, and they entered the familiar expanse of polished dark wood with the river view.

This time there was no prevarication, and Deborah Hillyer looked up straightaway.

'Dexter. Mr Gray. Do sit down.' She gestured to the two chairs opposite. 'Thank you for what you did outside the building, Mr Gray. It would have been rather embarrassing to have an old lady stabbed to death on MI5's doorstep.'

She smiled, but Will could see the smile still didn't reach her eyes. He looked again into their icy depths and there she was in a hospital bed dying from poison in twelve months' time. He flinched and saw that she had noticed it.

'Let me make this easy for you, Mr Gray. The last time we met, I made it clear that I didn't want to know what fate had in store for me. You obviously knew. Given what happened with Col. Grantley, I have accepted that I was being foolish, and I should face up to it. So, I would appreciate it if you would tell me the truth now, please.'

Will hesitated. As usual, they were playing their cards very close, and Will still didn't know how they had found out about Grantley. But trying to be coy now would not help.

'You are going to be poisoned,' Will said. 'In twelve months' time.'

There was a long silence while Hillyer stared out of the window at the river. Finally, she said, 'Who by?'

'I'm afraid I've no idea. It looks to me like some kind of nerve poisoning, which I guess would reduce the number of likely culprits.'

'Russia?' she asked.

'You could make an educated guess,' said Will.

'They've got form,' said Dexter.

Hillyer shook herself. 'Well, I guess at least I have twelve months. Thank you, Mr Gray. Now why didn't you tell us about Grantley?'

'Look,' said Will. 'He thought it was all, what was his word, poppycock. And it was an ordinary death, at least for a soldier.'

'Plus, you didn't like him.'

'He used to be my mentor. I saved his life once. But when it all went wrong, he didn't want to know, so I guess he wasn't my favourite person any longer. But that wasn't why. I didn't want to interfere. There's a lot of death in the Army. Where would I stop?' There was a silence as they faced each other down. 'The bigger question is, who told you about his death date?'

Hillyer glanced at Dexter, and Will was almost sure he saw a slight shake of the head. Hillyer changed the subject.

'We've decided you've been too much at arm's length, Mr Gray, so we're bringing you inside.'

'What about my security?' asked Will. 'There were several members of the public filming on the pavement downstairs.'

'We'll round up the footage and make sure the newspapers don't publish anything.'

'And the team itself? They're bound to work it out.'

'You're on the same side. They know the national interest outweighs everything.'

Will decided to forge ahead. 'What about the Home Secretary's bomb attack? Dexter won't tell me when the event is going to be cancelled.'

Hillyer looked at Dexter with a questioning eyebrow raised. Dexter said nothing.

'We will not endanger the Home Secretary's life,' said Hillyer. 'But we have several tricky operational demands to balance. As I'm sure you know, we have the world's leaders at the G7 summit in Kent. On the day of the mosque bombing, they are due to be coming into London for the ceremony re-opening Parliament after its reconstruction works. That's a big event with vast levels of security. We currently have a rogue Isis cell killing women on the streets. I'm sure you can see there's an operational advantage in leaving a cancellation till the last minute. More time to round them up, less time for them to decide to transfer their efforts to Parliament Square.'

'But by letting it drift, you may have cost those three women their lives today.'

'That is possible, but it may have been they were going to do it anyway. It may have been a separate attack that was already in the works,' said Hillyer.

'Except for number two,' said Will. 'He connects both.'

'Then it's your team's job to find out everything about him, and most importantly, to find him.'

'So that the police can shoot him in a few days' time instead,' said Will. 'Whether innocent or guilty.'

'He's hardly innocent now, is he?' said Dexter. 'If you hadn't stopped him, he'd have knifed an old lady to death.'

'Just find him, Mr Gray,' said Hillyer sharply. 'Good day to you both.'

Dexter took him back down two floors to the main operational office. In a corner of the open plan he saw Zar and Javanshir in what looked like a heated conversation. Zar put an appeasing arm on Javanshir's shoulder, but the young man brushed him off. Will could see Zar raise his eyes at Javanshir in what was clearly a signal of Will's approach. Javanshir looked hurriedly in Will's direction, and keeping his head down, rushed back to his desk and hid behind a computer.

'Welcome,' said Zar to Will. 'Welcome to the madhouse. This is our little corner here where we plot and probe. We can call on all the resources out there,' he said, gesturing to the scattered figures intent on their computers round the rest of the room. 'Analysts, language specialists, techies, James Bond, that kind of thing.'

'And this is Ros,' he said, introducing a striking young Black woman with large brown eyes. 'She's our trainee stroke helper. You know, diversity and all that.'

187

Ros rolled her eyes. Will decided to get it over with straightaway and smiled back at her, locking on to her gaze. He was relieved to see an old woman in bed in what looked like her own bedroom in the dead of night. Dying in her sleep. The best possible way, and in 55 years' time.

'Don't mind Zar,' said Ros. 'He thinks he's a right little joker.'

'Don't worry. I'm used to Zar's little ways,' said Will.

'Ah, you're bonding. How nice,' said Zar with a grin.

Dexter butted in. 'Ok folks, time to concentrate. Our main job now is to find this man.' He gestured at a picture of number two up on a screen.

'You'll tell me his name now, surely,' said Will.

'Naqi Pirani, aged twenty, Pakistani origin. Comes from Isleworth, from an apparently respectable family. No sign of radicalisation. Yet he turns up this morning as one of the attackers intent on knifing an old lady to death.'

And will be shot by the police in two days' time, thought Will. Would Will's closer involvement make that more or less likely? Could he save Naqi, or was he just setting him on the path to that police bullet?

'If there was no sign of radicalisation, why did you bring him in the other day?' asked Will.

'We had a tip-off,' said Dexter.

'But you had nothing else on him,' said Will.

'He was connected,' said Dexter. 'Why don't you read the file and we can talk later? Ros will get it up for you. Get up to speed on the other killings today, too. Naqi connects both sides of this puzzle and we need to find out how.'

Will swallowed all his other questions and sat down at the desk Dexter had pointed to. It was a start to be on the inside. He gazed around the busy room and then back to the team he had officially joined. Javanshir had his eyes fixed on his screen.

He decided to clear the air. 'You don't have to let me see,' he said. 'I quite understand.'

Javanshir kept his eyes on the screen. There was a silence, then finally he offered. 'I have nothing to hide. I just don't want to know. The idea freaks me out.' He looked embarrassed.

'That's perfectly alright,' said Will. 'Most people feel like that. I will do my best not to let it happen by accident.'

'I guess it's a primitive feeling,' said Javanshir. 'Like those South Sea islanders who refuse to be photographed because they think you're taking a piece of their soul.'

Will smiled. 'How you die should be a private thing. Unfortunately, with me around, it isn't.'

'You'll understand if I never look at you directly?' said Javanshir.

'Fine by me.'

Will went back to flicking between the news reports on the screen in front of him. Three old women attacked in broad daylight on busy London streets. Clearly designed to sow the maximum terror. Innocent defenceless old ladies against implacable young men with very sharp knives. It could happen to you at any moment.

The news reports had captured that febrile tone. 'On a tranquil spring morning, an old lady out shopping met her killer.' 'They showed no mercy.' 'It was a brutal, frenzied killing.'

Every phrase achieving what the terrorists wanted, thought Will. Sowing fear and despair. If you couldn't even walk down a famous London shopping street without risking violent death, what could you do?

Ros returned with a thin file. 'Have you logged on yet?' she asked.

'I don't have a username or password. First day,' said Will with an apologetic shrug.

'First day working for Five?' asked Ros, surprised.

'First day in an office where I need one.'

Ros gave him a knowing look. 'I'll get you set up then. Move over.'

Will sat at the next desk and picked up the file. There was a black-and-white photo of Naqi Pirani and two sheets of paper, a biography and a summary of the interview.

The biography was straightforward, an unremarkable suburban childhood in Isleworth, attended the local secondary, a worshipper at the local mosque but no sign of any radicalisation. Parents Labib and Hadiya, a respectable immigrant couple. Younger brother of sixteen equally straight.

Will turned to the interview notes with more interest. He hadn't been able to hear at the interrogation in the warehouse. Maybe this would reveal more. But it turned out to be a series of dead bat denials to every question. He didn't know any of the names put to him. Didn't have any radical connections. He behaved like a confused and fearful

190

innocent. So how did he get from that to trying to kill an old lady in the street a few days later?

Will turned to Ros in frustration. 'There's nothing in here.'

'I've got you on. Try the file online,' she said. But the online version was precisely the same apart from one file that was hidden behind a firewall.

'That's classified,' she said, peering over his shoulder. 'That's strange for someone with such an apparently innocent background.'

Will scanned the room for Dexter, but he was nowhere to be seen. Zar was talking to Javanshir again, and he seemed pleased, pointing at something on the screen. Will came up behind him and peered over his shoulder. The ticker strapline at the bottom of the news screen grabbed Will's attention. 'Leading industrialist Jeremy Brenton killed in helicopter crash.'

Will remembered looking into the man's eyes. So that had happened today. He'd forgotten it was due in all the furore. Mr Brenton had paid the price for his desire to save a few minutes' travel time.

Zar turned and saw him. 'Well done, Will,' he said, gesturing at the screen. 'Spot on again.'

Javanshir shook his head. 'It's all a bit creepy,' he said, yet again avoiding Will's gaze.

Zar laughed. 'And the timing could hardly be worse. The attacks have already driven the stock market down. This will push them through the floor.'

'And that's a good thing?' asked Will.

191

'It is if you were trying to short the market. You could have made a fortune.' Zar clapped him on the shoulder. 'Except that thanks to you, we could suggest to the Bank of England that it should put a few contingency plans in place, so it should all be contained. Bonuses all round, eh?'

Will smiled weakly. Another death, another apparent boost to his reputation. But they hadn't told the industrialist to take a different route, to keep off the helicopter. He was expendable. It was the knowledge that was important. Being ahead of the game.

'We're going for a drink after work tonight. The Three Tuns,' said Zar. 'Now you're part of the team, why don't you join us?'

Will was surprised. 'Surely I can't be seen outside this building?'

'Don't worry. We have the use of a private room there with its own back entrance. Patrick can smuggle you in. No-one will see you.'

Will's first instinct was to say no. He was so unused to being sociable. Besides, he wanted to be alone with Alice. But he was on the inside at last. He might as well be friendly. 'Sure,' he said. Why not?'

He noticed a look of panic flit across Javanshir's face, but Javanshir replaced it with a forced smile. 'That would be great,' he said.

By the end of the afternoon, the police had issued the names of the three women who had been killed. Mary Baker, seventy-four, from Orpington, Emily Hebblewhite, seventy-two, from Richmond, Yorkshire on a two-day trip to London, Jennifer Walton, sixty-seven, from Esher in Surrey. There was much pontificating on the tragedy and a lot of speculation on this new ruthless terrorist strategy in targeting elder women. Al-Qaeda sinking to new depths, a rogue Isis cell. The chatter went on and on, but no-one actually knew anything.

Ros got the CCTV for Will to watch. It made for grisly viewing. In each case, the attacker had come up behind the woman and the first thing they would have known was when the knife bit into their neck. One blow, two, a raking cut across the throat, and it was over. All the attackers had kept their heads down under baseball caps, shielding their faces from any cameras. From the little he could see, he did not recognise any of them. They all ran off with passers-by getting quickly out of their way. There would be witnesses, of course, but he would have to wait for their statements.

It was a dispiriting afternoon. He collared Dexter briefly. 'Why was there so little in the file on Naqi?' he asked.

'We really had nothing on him,' said Dexter.

'And the classified document I can't see?'

'That's just your assessment. We don't want that to get out, do we?'

'Can I see the files on the others?'

'Others?'

'Numbers one, three, four and five,' said Will impatiently.

'We need to concentrate on finding two,' said Dexter.

'And you don't think the others might be related?'

Dexter spread his hands. 'Okay, you can see them tomorrow.'

And with that, he was gone. Why tomorrow, thought Will? Why not now? Where was the bomb maker right now, or number one, or the other young men, numbers three and four, that Will had been sure were innocent? Were they even now planning another atrocity, or were they being lined up for a quiet death?

It was half past seven before they finally left the office. Patrick picked him up in the Thames House basement and drove him to a back alley behind the pub. Will was wearing a hoodie and dark glasses although that just made him feel even more conspicuous. But he needn't have worried. There was no-one in the alley and he was inside in a flash.

The pub room turned out to be a rather dull wood-panelled private dining room and Zar, Javanshir and Ros were there already, holding glasses of wine, and making small talk. This did not look like it was going to be fun.

There were some bottles and cans on a table in the corner. Will turned to Patrick.

'What can I get you?'

'Can't drink. On duty,' said Patrick, who was looking at his watch. A rather nice watch, Will registered.

'Is that a Rolex?' he asked. 'I haven't seen one with a green face before.'

'They're quite rare. It was my dad's,' said Patrick, showing it to Will. 'I wear it in his memory.'

Sentimental, too, thought Will. Whatever next. 'What do you want?' he asked again.

'Just a Coke, please.'

Will fetched one for Patrick and got a Coke for himself too. No alcohol, he thought. Not now, maybe not ever.

They joined the others. There was some desultory chat about football and how Arsenal's chances of even being in the top four were evaporating again.

Then Javanshir surprised Will by asking, 'What was it like in the Army?' He still wasn't looking at Will's face. Will was stumped. Was this an innocent inquiry? He must know Will's chequered past.

'Too much time hanging around in Afghanistan, and when there was fighting too many casualties,' said Will shortly.

'I wanted to join the Army,' said Javanshir, surprising Will. 'Eyesight was too bad.'

'Well, you got a much better job,' said Will.

Will noticed Zar was listening in on their conversation. 'By the way,' Will said. 'Thanks for the tip to pack warm clothing the other day. Really useful.'

Zar laughed. 'I hear it can be parky out there in Iraq, particularly at nights.'

'Hilarious,' said Will. He was watching Zar's face carefully and saw the humorous grin change to alarm. Something behind Will had clearly worried him.

'Excuse me,' said Zar, brushing past. Will turned to see an exotic-looking woman wearing what Will thought was a Hermes scarf as a hijab. She had flawless make-up and deep-red lipstick. Will saw Zar whisper something to her, and she reached into her handbag and brought out a pair of dark glasses which she put on.

Zar led her over. 'This is my wife, Rash,' he said. 'She brings me out in one,' he added laughing. 'This is Will.'

She shook Will's hand and smiled. 'It's Rasha, actually. Nice to meet you,' she said. The sunglasses were impenetrable. Zar clearly wasn't going to have Will look into his wife's eyes. That was interesting.

'This is Ros. She's joined us recently as a trainee,' said Zar, and the two women shook hands.

'Bad luck, getting Zar as your first boss,' said Rasha.

'Oh, I think his bark is worse than his bite,' said Ros.

'And Bean, you know,' said Zar, gesturing at Javanshir. Will flinched again at the racist nickname, but Javanshir just smiled at Zar and his wife.

'Hi, good to see you again,' he said.

There was no doubt that Rasha lit up the room and Will could see Zar admiring her fondly. But after half an hour Zar brought it to a close. 'Well, we must be going. Early start tomorrow. Killers to catch.'

After they'd gone, Will asked Javanshir. You really don't mind him calling you Bean?'

'He means well,' said Javanshir, keeping his eyes averted. 'Look, he's got a Muslim wife. It's just a front, the racist chatter. His heart is in the right place.'

Will couldn't help wondering whether it was the racist nicknames that were a front or the Muslim wife. Either way, Zar didn't ring true.

***

When Will got back to the flat, Alice gave him a silent kiss and then they moved apart. They had agreed not to say anything in the flat that might give away their newfound relationship. The place was undoubtedly bugged.

'How was the drink?' Alice asked.

'All very convivial. I met Rasha.'

'She's something, isn't she?' said Alice. 'A walking advert for multi-culturalism.'

'If that comes with a Hermes scarf and Laboutins. I'm going to turn in. It's been a long day.'

Will mouthed the word 'Bathroom' and Alice nodded. Then he mouthed 'ten minutes' and she nodded again.

'Good night then,' she said out loud. 'See you in the morning.'

Will made a show of drawing the curtains in his bedroom, stripping down to his underpants, sliding under the covers and turning the light off.

He counted to ten minutes in his head and then slipped out of bed. He tiptoed to the door and down the corridor to the bathroom. The shower was full on, and the room was already steaming up.

Alice was just wearing a loose T-shirt and pants again. As soon as Will saw her, all thought of the conversation he needed to have went out of his mind and he pulled her to him and kissed her deeply.

Alice certainly seemed to enjoy it too, pushing her body against him, but after a few seconds she broke away.

'Whoa. Work first or we'll never get to that,' she said.

Will reluctantly agreed. 'Alright. Two points. Dexter seemed very reluctant to let me see the other files besides number two. In the end he said I could see them tomorrow.'

'I've looked at them already,' said Alice. 'They've all been cleaned up. There's no mention of Dexter re-interviewing number three which is worrying. He's clearly keeping that off the radar.'

'Who told you?'

'I have my sources,' said Alice with a smile.

'Can you double-check he hasn't seen number four again too.'

Alice nodded. 'And the other point?'

'Zar and Javanshir were crowing over the death today of the industrialist Jeremy Brenton in a helicopter crash. One of those I predicted. And then Zar said someone could have made a fortune shorting the market if they'd known in advance.'

'And?'

'It just made me wonder if anyone did that. Short the market.'

'You think Zar's a cheap fraudster now? After money on the side?'

Will looked sheepish. He didn't know what Zar was. He thought about telling Alice that Zar was going to kill himself, but that seemed too big a conversation for right now, and he wanted to find out more first.

'I don't know. It might just be useful to check. Do you have any City contacts that could see if there are rumours of insider trading?'

Alice nodded. 'Alright,' she said. 'I'll try. Is that it?'

They looked at each other. The bathroom was a haze of condensation, and Alice's T-shirt was clinging damply to her breasts. Will could barely contain himself.

'It seems a shame to waste a good shower,' Alice said with a grin. So they didn't.

Chapter Twenty-Three

Alice came into Will's bedroom the next morning and woke him. She handed him her laptop.

'You should see this.'

There was a feed on X with a picture of Will kneeling outside Thames House with the knife he had knocked out of Naqi Pirani's hand next to him on the ground.

He scanned the caption with a sinking feeling. 'This is the hero who disarmed a terrorist attacker on Millbank yesterday morning. Does anyone know who he is?' The hashtag just said #Findthisman.

'How did this get out? I thought your people were going to confiscate all the footage and photos taken then.'

'They were supposed to.'

'And weren't the papers warned off?'

'It's not in the papers, just on X.'

'Not yet. Who's Public Defender?' asked Will, looking at the account name.

'He's an investigative journalist called David Leonard. It's curious that he's got it, and even more curious that he's making a public appeal.'

Will scanned down the responses. So far there were no positive hits but one or two with an ominous 'I think I've seen him somewhere before.'

Will checked when it was posted. An hour ago. They were bound to get an ID soon and then all hell would break loose.

'Do you think the papers will stick to the line if my identity is all over X?'

'I doubt it,' said Alice. 'We put out a DSMA alert. What they used to call the old D notice system. But the papers will just say that's unenforceable once your name is out in the public domain. We'd better get in as quickly as possible.'

Alice rang and demanded a different car with heavily tinted rear windows, and they were soon driving into a back entrance of Thames House.

Zar was unhelpful, as usual. 'The conquering hero comes,' he said jovially. 'Although round here, we try to stay below the radar. You know, spies, and all that.'

'Very amusing,' said Will. 'What happens when they make the connection?'

'You lie very low and keep silent,' said Zar. 'Be a church mouse.'

Will found that Ros had pulled out the other files for him. The ones on number three and four were as slim as Naqi's had been, and as Alice had said, looked like they'd been tidied up, but one and five were reassuringly thick.

He sat down to read them, but Zar immediately interrupted him by tapping him on the shoulder.

'Church mouse time,' he said, shoving his phone into Will's line of vision.

'It's the guy who caused the bus crash a few weeks back,' said one line on X.

'Fuck me,' said another. 'From Zero to Hero.'

'What's the odds?' said a third.

They were flooding in now. Opinions on X from all over. Will could see the way it was going.

'How come he's at a bus crash and the terrorist incident within a few weeks? Do you think it's a set-up?'

The next one quickly took up the conspiracy theory. 'It's the Government. They're behind it all.'

'They probably set up the terrorist attack.'

'You do realise, guys, that this happened outside MI5. The spooks must be involved.'

In the middle of it the originator, Public Defender, tweeted, 'Anyone know where he is now? I want to find him.'

And as if that wasn't bad enough, the next one chilled Will's blood. 'I want to find him, too. He killed my wife and daughter, and I'm going to kill him.'

Will knew immediately. The guy with the brick. The guy in court, radiating hatred, and now thanks to X Will had been served up on a plate.

Will scanned the tag. Dead Dad, it said and underneath, 'Bereaved husband and father looking for justice.'

'Do you know how we can find this guy?' he said, pointing out the threatening message to Zar.

'Phew,' Zar whistled. 'He's got your number.' He looked at the moniker. 'Dead Dad, I love it. Bean, this one's for you.' Javanshir appeared at his side. 'Find this lunatic, please.'

Javanshir looked at the screen, raised his eyebrows and went back to his desk.

Zar turned away. Will sat down, feeling rather empty and alone. Where had Alice got to?

Ros stood in front of him, smiling sympathetically. 'Would you like a tea?'

'Thanks,' Will said, looking her full in the face and seeing her peaceful death again. 'I appreciate it.'

He turned his attention back to the files. Must pull myself together, he said to himself. After all, where could be safer than inside MI5, surrounded by all this security with identity card locking systems on all the doors?

He opened number one's file. Real name, Mahfez Ashkani, thirty-eight, entrepreneur, financier, owned a company in Isleworth. His picture exuded poise and wealth. He didn't look like a terrorist at all. And as Will read further, it was clear no-one had pinned anything on him. A lot of dubious financial deals, one or two distant cousins, but nothing definite. He was big in the community, donated to local charities, sponsored a boys' club, the picture of rectitude.

The bomb maker was called Ghanni Mansoor. Again, a long history of possible connections, a lot of movement into Pakistan and out, but nothing absolutely definite. The only thing they had in common was Isleworth.

Will flicked through the other two files. Number three was nineteen-year-old Saabir Baksh and number four was twenty-one-year-old Taahir Morad, both young men with no track record of radicalisation. And no connection to the others beyond living in Isleworth. There was the transcript of the interviews he had witnessed, no mention of the second interview with number three.

So why had Dexter rounded them all up? A tip-off, he said, but anonymous or from a known source? Will might be sitting inside the MI5 building, but he felt he was still being kept out.

Alice interrupted his reverie. 'Dexter wants a word.'

She led him to a side room where Dexter was sitting brooding over a photo. He pushed it across the table to Will.

'This is Dead Dad. Recognise him?'

'Of course. He tried to attack me at the court appearance,' said Will.

'We think he's a credible threat,' said Dexter.

'What, you mean he really wants to kill me? Get away,' said Will sarcastically.

'We're going to increase security around you.'

'I'm buried already. How could he possibly attack me?'

'I don't want to take any chances,' said Dexter.

Will looked at the photo, staring into the man's manic eyes and remembering the sour breath washing over him as they struggled on the floor of the courtroom.

'He's Colin Maynard. His daughter Lucy died in the bus crash, along with his wife Margaret.'

'I know, I know. It was in the papers,' said Will.

'I guess he has a double reason for wanting you dead.'

A wave of sadness washed over Will. So much pain because he'd intervened, and now he was doing it daily. 'Well, you'd better keep me safe then,' he said flatly.

Dexter's mouth tightened. 'He won't get near you. What did you think of the files?'

'Uninformative. There doesn't seem to be a connection apart from the fact that they all live in Isleworth. The tip-off you got. Was it anonymous or a source?'

'A source. Why?'

'Well, you might ask him or her why they were all lumped together. If the one dead cert was the bomb maker, Ghanni Mansoor, then the question is surely, how are the others connected to him?'

'I'll ask,' said Dexter, getting up to leave.

'And the newspapers? Will you be able to shut them down?

'We'll try. But now your identity is out on X, maybe not. From their point of view, it's too good a story.'

'But not from mine,' said Will.

Dexter gave him a small smile and was gone.

***

Back in the office, Alice appeared, clutching her laptop. She seemed very wound up. 'I need a word,' she said, gesticulating at a vacant office.

As soon as they were inside, Alice closed the blinds and put down her laptop in front of him. 'Here's the Pavel interview. Just press this,' she said, indicating the return button.

Will had almost forgotten about Alice's internal predicament. Was now the right time to be looking at this? But he could see from Alice's face that she needed to know. 'Ok,' he said. 'I'll take a quick look.'

'I'll wait outside,' she said and left.

205

Will pushed play and the figure on the screen burst into life. Pavel was a forty-something Russian, thin face and big eyebrows. He was also a mess of nervous tics and wide staring eyes shooting round the interrogation room.

'You've got to calm down,' said a voice off-camera, which Will recognised with a start. It was Dexter. Why was he doing the interrogation himself?

Pavel took a deep breath, but when he spoke his voice was high and panicky. 'You must believe me. They will kill me. They will find a way.'

'Then you'd better tell us all you know. Patrick here will look after you. If you co-operate,' said Dexter crisply. The implication was clear. If you don't co-operate, you won't be looked after.

Pavel gave Dexter a startled glance at the implicit threat. 'You must look after me first. Get me away from here,' he said.

'You're in one of our safe houses. No-one can get at you. Tell me about Myakov. When did he first contact the President?'

Pavel eyes widened further. 'No, nothing. Not till I am safe,' he said obstinately.

Dexter lost patience. 'If you don't give us anything, I can't protect you.' He carried on returning repeatedly to the point for nearly ten minutes, but Pavel would not budge, and he was getting more and more agitated. His eyes were roving the room as if he was looking for a way out, and just for a second, he looked straight at the camera.

Will was overcome by a strange feeling, like a premonition of one of his visions, but blurred and fuzzy. He couldn't see what was happening, but he had a strong feeling that Pavel hadn't committed suicide.

Finally, Dexter said, 'I'm leaving you with Patrick. You have twenty-four hours. Co-operate or you're on your own.'

Pavel started shaking. 'You would not do that.'

'Try me,' said Dexter, and then the tape went to black.

Will sat there for a few minutes, turning the interview over in his mind. On the one hand, it could be a standard hard-ball interview technique to get the subject to cough up. On the other, Pavel looked genuinely terrified, and Dexter sounded ruthless and careless of the man's safety. But did he sound as if he might have Pavel killed?

And what was the vision about? Was he beginning to see through a camera, too? Maybe the more he used his terrible gift, the more he tuned in. But if that was what was happening, it was an alarming development. He wouldn't be able to watch television for fear of people spilling their secrets.

Still, one thing was clear. It hadn't felt as if Pavel had committed suicide.

Will went and found Alice. 'Is that the only recording?' he asked.

'All I can find.'

'No second interview?' She shook her head. 'And when did he die?'

'The next night.'

'It's all a bit convenient, isn't it?' said Will. 'In the light of what happened Dexter's threats have a pretty ominous tone.'

'I know. But like I said, the forensics boys were certain it was suicide.'

Will decided he wouldn't mention his mini vision yet. It all felt rather flaky, but it had given him an idea on how to get to the truth.

'I'm interested in Patrick's role. I still haven't looked into his eyes yet. It might be useful to find out what's in store for him.'

'But that's the future,' said Alice. 'It won't tell you anything about the past.'

'You never know. Leave it with me,' Will said, squeezing her arm. 'I'll figure this out.'

***

Will went back to poring over the files on the five Muslim suspects, searching for a connection. The three young men, Naqi and Saabir and Taahir most probably know each other from something in Isleworth. But they didn't go to school together, and didn't belong to the same mosque, although of course they could have met there. One of them was a Chelsea fan, but there was nothing recorded for the others. They could have football in common, or maybe they literally met on a street corner.

Then he remembered Ashkani sponsored a boys' club. Maybe the youngsters had met there, but frustratingly, there was no reference to that in their files.

Will searched for a way to use his skills to figure it out, but he'd already looked into their eyes, and all he knew was that Naqi was due to die tomorrow at 8.24 a.m. It couldn't be a random incident with CO19 involved. They must be going to track him down beforehand.

He wondered about sneaking out down to Isleworth and trying to see Naqi's parents, but would their deaths have any bearing on this? Unlikely, and surely MI5 had already been through all this.

In the end, Will concluded that he would have to wait for the intelligence on Naqi's whereabouts to come in, and then make sure he was there. When he saw Dexter in the distance across the office, he decided to collar him.

'Can I have a word?'

Dexter looked faintly irritated, but eventually smiled. 'Of course.'

'Naqi is going to die at 8.24 a.m. tomorrow. And yet you have no lead on his whereabouts at all?' Dexter nodded. 'Okay, that means he's going to get identified tonight or early tomorrow morning. It will be a tip-off or a member of the public.'

'So?'

'I want to be told, and I want to be there when you catch up with him. I want to see this necessary step for myself.'

'Impossible,' said Dexter, his mouth set.

'Make it possible,' Will snapped. 'Or you won't get any co-operation from me again. Ever.'

Dexter looked surprised, then angry. 'You can't do that. You have a duty.'

Will glared back. 'Try me. It works like this. I close my mouth, and I don't open it again.'

'Why does this one man matter so much to you?'

'I want to be sure he's not being eliminated. Not just conveniently shot in the back. I want to see it for myself.'

'You think we'd do that?'

Will said nothing. Dexter looked around for a second, as if seeking support from elsewhere, then he decided.

'Alright. I doubt it will convince you. We have nothing to hide. I'll make sure you're there, but don't interfere in any way whatever. Understand.'

'You have my word,' said Will, although he had absolutely no intention of abiding by that.

Chapter Twenty-Four

The call came at quarter to six. Will and Alice had prepared the night before and they were out and in the car in fifteen minutes heading for the Isle of Dogs.

A security guard had seen Naqi down near the City Airport. He had pulled out a knife and threatened the guard but then run off when a second guard had appeared. Because of the knife they had phoned it in and quickly identified a photo.

When Will and Alice arrived, they found Naqi had been tracked to an enormous construction site where yet another collection of expensive flats and homes was being built. Dexter had set up a command post on the entrance to the main road and the police had the entire area surrounded.

As they entered the control van, Will could see feeds from all the site's CCTV cameras and local roads displayed on a wall of monitors.

Dexter looked irritated at their arrival. 'We've been waiting. We're going to start a sweep through the site to try to establish exactly where he is.'

'I want to join the sweep,' said Will.

'You'll stay here. You can watch it on the monitors. If there is a chance, we'll move you closer when we find him. Not till then,' said Dexter curtly and left.

Will studied the screens. Almost all the cameras were on the perimeter, with only a couple covering the central area of the site. He would see nothing from here.

He put his coat over a chair, then said to Alice. 'Just going to find a loo.'

Alice nodded but said nothing. It was what they'd agreed. Will did a quick scan around the entrance to the site checking out a collection of cabins that were presumably offices and changing rooms. He could see Dexter in the distance, conferring with a police officer with a peaked cap who must be the head of the police operation. Near them were ranks of armed police milling around waiting for instructions.

They were clearly going to start the sweep here and move towards the far end searching as they went. Will scanned the area. There were three small tower blocks and half-a dozen streets of low-rise. It was going to be slow progress moving through all that.

Will ducked into one of the cabins. Desks, chairs, blueprints over the wall. The main planning office. The next cabin was more profitable. Yellow hard-hats and hi-vis vests. Not exactly camouflage, but at least he would look like he belonged.

Will pulled a set on and slipped back out of the door between two of the cabins. He would keep them between him and the police line. He needed to get further into the site and trust he could find Naqi before the police did.

He had just one advantage, knowing where the killing ground would be. Will cast his mind back to the vision when he had first looked into Naqi's eyes. The young man was running down an alley between a taller building and the back

212

gardens of a street of low-rise. So, assuming that Naqi was moving away from the police, that meant he was going to be on the right-hand side of one of the three skeleton tower blocks Will was looking at.

Will racked his memory for any other clue. There had been a pile of plywood under a blue tarpaulin and then open ground beyond. He would surely recognise it when he got close. The challenge was to find the location before the police.

Will set off down the right perimeter fence, keeping close to the walls of the nearest tower block. It was completely quiet on this side of the building site. There was a wooden fence separating the site from open ground beyond, and in the distance, another new development was rising.

Will quickly realised that this tower block on the right was not a candidate. There were no low-rise houses on the right-hand side, just a bare patch of ground and the perimeter fence. He would have to move left towards the centre of the site, and it would be better if he had the tower blocks between him and the advancing police. He turned at the end of the block and looked left. There was a grid of low-rise housing between his block and the next and open ground on the right that was probably intended to be a green space where the residents could relax but now was just an expanse of rutted bare earth full of rain-filled holes.

He was about to move down towards the next block when he heard the noise of a car. There was a chain-link gate in the perimeter fence and beyond it a police car drawing to a halt. Fortunately, the gate was locked. A police officer jumped out and shouted. 'You. Stop.'

Will ignored him and ran down the side of the tower block into the first available entrance. He stood there panting until he regained his breath. There was no further sound of pursuit. The police officer couldn't get through the gate, but he must have radioed it in. Time was running out for Will and Naqi. He checked his watch. 8.04 a.m. Just twenty minutes left.

The inside of the tower block was a mess of machinery and rough concrete floors and rainwater. Will hurried through, heading across the site next to the back road. He reached the end of the tower block and scanned the road leading back towards the advancing police. No-one visible yet.

He hurried through two rows of low-rise houses till he came to the last one before the middle tower block. If luck was on his side, he would look round the corner and recognise the scene. There was empty ground to his right. All he needed to see was that pile of plywood under a blue tarpaulin.

But when he carefully edged his head round the corner, he found an empty street. No plywood, no nothing.

That meant it must be at the base of the third tower. Will looked at his watch. Seventeen minutes. He had to hurry. He ran across the road and behind the second tower block. Its bulk would shield him from the police cordon, so he put his head down and pounded on, dodging the potholes full of water, gasping for breath.

Then he was out on the far side with the last grid of houses to cross and the third tower block barely two hundred yards away. He glanced to the left and could see movement at the far end of the street. Armed police were ducking from house to house. He hoped Naqi was already down the end of the third block nearest to him.

Will ran across the street and into the small houses. Soon he was at the back of the house nearest the last block and to his relief, when he poked his head round the corner, he saw the distinctive blue tarpaulin covering a large stack of plywood. This was it. This was the killing ground.

He scanned the street. No sign of Naqi, but down the far end he caught another glimpse of a police helmet and a police rifle poking round the end. Naqi must be inside the tower block and the police were approaching fast.

Will propelled himself across the street and through a doorway into another mess of machinery and stacks of wood and steel rods. He flopped down behind a small concrete mixer and looked at his watch. Five minutes to go. There was no time for subtlety.

'Naqi,' he shouted. 'Naqi Pirani. I'm not armed. We need to talk. Your time is running out.'

Will stood up and walked out into the middle of the floor. 'Look, you can see I'm not armed.' There was a silence. 'Naqi, you need to talk to me.'

There was a scrape behind him. Will turned and there was Naqi. His face was badly bruised where Will had head-butted him. His eyes were wild-eyed and staring. There was a sheen of sweat glistening on his forehead and a machete in his hand.

'You were the one outside the spook place,' said Naqi, his eyes widening further.

'You must listen to me,' said Will. 'You're going to die.'

'No, you're going to die,' he said, raising the machete.

215

It would have been almost funny, but Will knew the seconds were ticking away. 'No, I'm not going to kill you. I mean, the police will shoot you if you don't do as I say. In precisely....' He glanced at his watch. 'Four minutes.'

Naqi licked his lips. 'You're not making sense, man. They're going to shoot me, anyway.'

'Not if you let me help you.'

'You're just one of them,' he said, glancing around.

This was all going too slowly, Will decided. 'Why did you try to kill the old lady? When I saw you the week before, I was sure you weren't a killer.'

Naqi looked confused. 'When did you see me before? Where?'

'At the police station when you were being interrogated. I was watching behind two-way glass.'

'You are one of them,' Naqi said again, hefting the blade.

'What made you decide to become a jihadi?'

Naqi was looking round wildly now, his eyes flicking from left to right. Will glanced at his watch. Two minutes.

'They killed my friend,' said Naqi, through bared teeth. 'He was nothing to do with anything and they killed him.'

'Who? Who did they kill?'

'Saabir, my oldest friend.'

Will went cold. Number three. 'How did he die?'

'They had him in for interrogation twice and then they said he hanged himself when he got home. But he wasn't like that. He wasn't involved at all.'

Will's head was spinning. Saabir wasn't supposed to have died like that. Why had Will not seen him killing himself?

216

And why wasn't his death in the file? Or indeed the second interrogation?

'He died after the interrogations?' asked Will.

Naqi was crying now, the tears falling down his cheeks. 'They said he killed himself. It was a lie.'

Naqi advanced towards Will, raising the machete. 'You were there. You were responsible.'

'I didn't know. I can still help you.'

'Too late. Much too late,' Naqi said, and he raised the machete to bring it down on Will's head. Suddenly, there was the whip-crack of a shot and a bullet thudded into the concrete just by Naqi's head.

Naqi spun round, dropping the machete. He looked wildly at Will, then turned and ran for the doorway to the street.

'Stop. They'll shoot you,' shouted Will, but Naqi was past hearing. Will ran after him and just reached the doorway in time to see Naqi sprinting away down the street past the tarpaulin-covered plywood towards the open area. It was the killing ground, and it was time.

Will flinched as shots rang out, hitting Naqi in the back and throwing him down on the ground. Will dropped into a crouch and stared at the dirt. He'd failed. He didn't need to see Naqi die. He'd seen it once already.

***

Dexter was furious, the light dancing in his eyes. 'You disobeyed me, and you nearly got yourself killed. You couldn't have been more wrong about him being innocent.'

217

Will bit back on his reply. 'He was still shot when he was unarmed and running away,' he said.

Dexter bridled. 'He'd just threatened you with a knife. It was a perfectly reasonable response.'

'Your rules of engagement seem rather different to the Army,' said Will.

'We're fighting an undercover war,' said Dexter.

Alice motioned to Will to back off. They were standing in the control gallery. One monitor showed Naqi's body being loaded into an ambulance, although he was past helping. The sight made Will's stomach turn. Another death, more blood on his conscience. He was getting people killed whether he intervened or not.

'What did you say to him?' Dexter asked.

Will decided to be economical. There was no way he was going to tell Dexter the truth.

'I just told him he would die if he didn't give himself up,' said Will.

'Well, he didn't listen, did he? Anything else.'

'I asked him why.'

Dexter raised a sceptical eyebrow. 'And?'

'The usual jihadi rant. He said he'd been dreaming about it for years.' Will looked away. Perhaps best not to embroider it too far. 'Is that all? I think I'd like to go home and take a shower. I feel dirty.'

Dexter grunted, then made a shooing motion. 'Go, go. But I want to talk back in the office later,' he said.

***

On the journey back Will stared out of the window blankly. Alice was beside him, but they couldn't talk about it all because of the driver.

Will's mind was going round and round. Had Saabir been killed, and it made to look like suicide? That would surely have to be the work of his colleagues in Five, wouldn't it? And someone high up must have sanctioned it. Dexter was the obvious candidate.

The resemblance to what had happened to Pavel was worrying, too. And why wasn't it in the file? Had it been omitted deliberately?

Will couldn't understand why he hadn't seen it in Saabir's eyes. The only plausible conclusion was that the decision to do it was taken after Will had done the assessment, and taken by someone who knew how Saabir was supposed to die.

Will knew now from Grantley and the patrol that it didn't have to be him intervening. So, who knew and could then take such a decision? The only other candidate was Zar and Will couldn't believe he would have acted without authorisation, which brought it back to Dexter again.

Will felt the pace was quickening. The death of the bomb maker was only four days away. If Saabir had been killed, but it had been made to look accidental, what was likely to happen to number four, Taahir? It could be the same, if he wasn't dead already. Will needed to find him, and fast.

Back at the flat, Will had a shower and was drying himself off when Alice came in. 'Are you alright?' she asked.

Will embraced her, kissed her, then whispered in her ear. 'We need to talk.'

Alice looked at him and nodded, then changed the subject. 'Have you seen this?' she said, proffering her phone. Will took it and saw it was open on X and there was a message from Public Defender next to a picture of Will outside Thames House.

'Thanks everyone for helping to identify Will Gray. So now we know who he is, but we don't know where he is. Keep your eyes open. #Findthisman.'

'Persistent, isn't he? How long before that hits the papers?'

'Tomorrow morning is my guess,' said Alice. 'You'll have to stay away from public areas.' Alice spread her hands in a gesture that said to Will, 'Where can we go?'

Will grabbed a pen and wrote 'BASEMENT'.

Alice nodded and said out loud. 'I'll call a car. The one with the heavily tinted windows. In the basement. Fifteen minutes.'

'Ok,' said Will, pulling on his clothes.

They left a few minutes later, taking the lift to the basement.

'We've got ten minutes before the car arrives, 'Alice said, leading him over to a far corner of the underground car park.

'You don't think this area is bugged,' asked Will. Alice shook her head. 'Ok, Naqi told me something before he was shot. He said that his friend, Saabir, number three, was dead. Hanged himself. Suicide supposedly, although Naqi didn't believe it and was convinced Saabir had been killed.'

Alice gasped, 'That's not possible.'

'He was sure we were to blame, and that's what led him to take part in the attack three days ago.' Will couldn't help thinking about the parallels with the Pavel case. Too many people apparently hanging themselves. He looked straight at Alice. 'Do you think Dexter had Saabir killed?'

'But he wasn't supposed to die that way. That wasn't what you saw.'

'No, but that means someone intervened after I looked into his eyes. Someone who knew the result, and that's just a handful of people.'

'What about the others?' asked Alice.

'Well, my guess is that they'll let the bomb maker, number five, play out, just as they did with Naqi. If he blows himself up in three days, that's a PR win, plus they must be tracking him, hoping for more info.'

'That leaves one and four both at risk. I'm most worried about four, Taahir. He's young. I thought he looked innocent and his friends Naqi and Saabir are dead. I think we need to find him quickly.'

'How?' asked Alice.

'Go to Isleworth. Knock on his parents' door. Track him down.'

'But you could be spotted?'

'If I'm in the papers tomorrow, then getting around will be far harder. Anyway, I don't think I've got that much time.'

The sound of an approaching vehicle interrupted them. The barrier at the far end raised and the car that Alice had ordered rolled into view.

'Send them away. Tell them I'm sick,' said Will, and he turned away and stuck his fingers down his throat. The

221

timing was just right. As the car pulled up, Will vomited a splatter of bile over the garage floor that quickly gave off a pungently sour stink.

'Sorry, guys,' said Alice to Patrick, who was driving. 'Won't be needing you now. Will's not very well.' She gestured at the spreading pool and Will coughed up a bit more for effect.

'I'll take him back to the flat. We won't be going anywhere else today.' Patrick nodded, and the car reversed and left the garage.

'Thanks,' said Will.

'My pleasure,' said Alice. 'Though I could have done without the technicolour effects.'

'Can you pretend you're putting me to bed? I'm going to leave from here.'

'Ok, good luck.' She said, kissing him on the cheek. 'Yuk,' she added as she caught the smell of sick. 'You'd better find some mints or no-one will talk to you.'

Will smiled. He sketched a wave as he left the car park.

Chapter Twenty-Five

Taahir's parents lived in a small Victorian terrace on a tidy road in Isleworth. The front gardens were all well-kept, the windowsills painted, the roof tiles clean and neat. It all spoke of modest means but respectability.

Will knocked on the green door and it was answered by a diminutive, middle-aged Pakistani woman wearing a traditional sari and shawl. She had a pallid, careworn face and Will noticed an oxygen canister on wheels in the hall. She eyed him fearfully.

'Is Taahir home?' asked Will.

The woman's anxiety increased. 'No. Why do you want him? Are you the police again?'

'No,' said Will. 'I just want to talk to him. It's very urgent.'

The woman's eyes darted about. She looked like a trapped animal. 'He's out with friends. He won't be back till late. Is he in trouble again?'

'Are you his mother?'

The woman nodded miserably. Then suddenly she looked straight at Will. 'Don't hurt him again. Please.'

Will looked into her eyes and saw she was close to tears. Then he saw her in a brightly lit white room with steel cabinets from floor to ceiling, looking down on a body in front of her. Her face was a mask of misery that was suddenly contorted with pain. She gasped for breath, her eyes rolled up and she fell to the floor. Will knew straightaway it was a heart attack and worse still, it was tomorrow morning at 9.02 a.m. The place looked like a morgue and Will had a sinking feeling that the body on the steel tray in front of her would be Taahir.

He blinked. Taahir's mother was saying something.

'He's been really upset. His friend Saabir died the other day,' she said. 'Killed himself, and I'm afraid Taahir will do the same.' Her eyes implored Will, but all he could see was the morgue and the knowledge that her time was running out, too.

'When did his friend kill himself?'

'Three days ago. They were arrested by the police, and they didn't know why. I don't know why. He's never done anything wrong.'

'Can you think where he might be?' asked Will. 'I need to warn him.'

The woman gave a small sob. 'He's in trouble, isn't he?' She wrung her hands. 'You might find him in a pub off the High Street, the Green Man. He doesn't drink. Just orange juice. But it's a place to meet his friends.'

'Ok. Thank you.'

'Tell him to come home. Tell him I'm worried,' she said forlornly.

Will could only think she had good reason to be worried and if he didn't find Taahir quickly, there would be two more deaths on his conscience.

Will hurried to the High Street and found the Green Man, a rundown pub with grubby floors and hardly less grubby clientele. Worse, the drinkers were almost all white. Will went up to the one Pakistani guy and got a blankly hostile response when he asked if he knew Taahir Morad.

'What's it to you, mate?'

'I need to find him.'

'Well, you won't find him here, will you,' said the man, looking around. 'Why don't you piss off, copper?'

'I'm not a policeman,' said Will, but the man just turned his back.

Will retreated to the High Street. Where now? He tried the local mosque, but the doors were shut and barred. It was too late to go to Taahir's old school, then Will remembered the boys' club mentioned in the files. A quick check on his phone and he discovered it was only 500 yards away. It was getting dark now and raining.

Will broke into a run, his thoughts harried by the images of Taahir's mother in the morgue tomorrow morning. He couldn't be too late for this one.

As he approached, he could see a group of young men on the pavement, then one broke away and started to cross the road. Immediately a black car pulled out of a parking place fifty yards further down and accelerated towards him.

'Taahir,' Will screamed and the young man turned his head towards him, oblivious to the car behind. Will knew straightaway that he was too late, and the car ploughed into the back of Taahir and sent him flying.

There was a moment of unnatural silence as the body cartwheeled, then it hit the kerb with a sickening crunch. The car's engines revved, and it was coming straight for Will. He dived sideways, catching only a fleeting glimpse of the driver, who had a baseball cap pulled low over his eyes and was wearing dark glasses.

Then the car was past, and Will was rolling in the gutter, cursing his stupidity. A few seconds earlier and he might have saved Taahir.

Now all he had was the certainty that Taahir had been deliberately killed and that meant Saabir's suicide was probably staged, too. He had seen the driver only briefly, but he had at least got the car, a VW Passat with the registration number EA47 KJD.

Will hauled himself to his feet, feeling sick. There was a crowd gathered round Taahir's body and several of the youths were looking at him. Time to leave.

Will put his head down, but even as he moved away, a flashlight turned the air white. He looked up and there was a youngster pointing a mobile phone at him, and then the flash went off again. Will ran. There were several half-hearted shouts of 'Stop', but Will had no intention of hanging around and after a few hundred yards he had left them behind.

He jogged back to the High Street still feeling sick and as he emerged on to the main road, it all became too much and he threw up in the gutter.

'Disgusting drunk,' said a woman walking past, and he remembered again Melanie's mother issuing the same condemnation as she dragged her daughter away. How long ago was that? Just a few weeks, yet it seemed like an age. And he was in a far worse position now.

Back then, he hadn't caused the bus crash, hadn't got involved with too many shady people and seen the deaths of so many more. He hadn't been tied up in some labyrinthine

226

plot that was getting murkier by the second, with the bodies piling up around him.

Will wiped the bile from his face and hailed a cab. A car stopped and the driver said, 'You don't look so well. You're not going to puke in here, are you?'

'Don't worry. I already have,' said Will.

When the cabbie hesitated, Will said, 'Joke, Joke,' and climbed in. Soon Isleworth was miles behind.

***

Will and Alice played out the same pantomime at bedtime and met in the bathroom shortly afterwards. But this time, sex wasn't on their minds. Will told Alice the whole grisly tale of Taahir's death.

'He was run down deliberately right in front of my eyes,' Will said. 'Saabir was probably deliberately killed, then dressed up as suicide. It looks like someone's eliminating all the Muslims I vetted, and my bet's Dexter.'

'Did you get the registration number of the car,' asked Alice.

'It was a VW Passat, number EA47 KJD.'

'I'll get that run through the system tomorrow.'

'Dexter told me they wouldn't go after the others. He's a lying little shit,' said Will.

'To be fair, one of them died as you predicted,' said Alice.

'Yes, shot in the back. Much better.'

Alice grabbed Will by the shoulders. 'You've got to stand back. Think clearly,' she said. 'Naqi was allowed to die in the way you predicted, right? And the bomb maker is going to blow himself up when?'

'The day after tomorrow.'

'They'll let that play out. They must be keeping very close tabs on the bomb maker, gathering information on him, seeing if anyone visits,' said Alice.

'You're right. It would be really useful to see that log.'

'I'll try and get that. What about number one?' asked Alice.

'He was supposed to die in a swimming pool. Forty odd years from now. So, either he gets away or if they want a clean sweep they get him too. My bet is, by the end of the week they'll all be dead.'

'Maybe,' said Alice. 'He was older and wilier, and if he is involved, he must be in touch with the bomb maker. I bet they're following him, too.'

'We absolutely must get those logs.'

Alice nodded. 'Anything else I should know?'

Will grimaced. 'Yes, someone photographed me. One of Taahir's friends.'

'Great. When that comes out, the shit really will hit the fan. There's already Public Defender on your trail and I heard yesterday that *The Sun* were sniffing round,' said Alice.

'What do you think they'll do at Five if that comes out?'

'Lock you down even more. Keep you in a hole somewhere.'

'Get rid of me?' said Will.

'Not yet. Dexter thinks you can still be useful.'

'Not yet is not very reassuring,' said Will.

'Welcome to spook land,' said Alice, kissing him. 'Don't worry, I'll protect you. We'll find a way out of this.'

Will hesitated. It didn't feel like the right time on top of all the other bad news, but he needed to tell Alice about Zar. It had been playing on his mind. Surely that was an important piece of the puzzle. He took a deep breath.

'I've got something else to tell you. You won't like it.'

Alice smiled. 'More bad news? Is there no end to your gifts?'

Will tried to smile back, but he knew she was going to be angry. Very angry. 'You know I said I had another wild card.' Alice looked quizzical. 'When I told you about Grantley.'

'I'd forgotten in all this fun. What is it?'

Will swallowed. There was no easy way to say this. 'Zar is going to shoot himself. The day after the bombing.'

Alice looked thunderstruck. 'What? You said he died in a car accident.'

'I'm sorry, I was lying. I didn't know you well enough then.'

'You didn't trust me,' said Alice bitterly. 'Why didn't you tell me back at my flat?' Her eyes flashed. 'After we'd fucked.'

'It didn't seem the right moment.'

'Or the next night? Or last night?'

'I wanted to, but there was so much happening. Look, I know you're angry. But to be honest, I don't know how important it is. Could he be killing himself because the bomb goes off, or because it doesn't go off? Is it because he's in disgrace over that, or something else altogether that we know nothing about yet? I just don't know.'

Alice was still rigidly furious. 'We could have worked on that together.'

'We can now, and we will. The fact is, it happens after the bombing, so it's probably a consequence of that.'

'Was that why you wanted the insider trading checked? You think he's corrupt, and he kills himself out of remorse?' said Alice.

'It's a possibility.'

'Not much of one. That's not Zar at all. He doesn't do remorse. The world revolves around him.'

Will laid a hand on her shoulder, and she shrugged him off. 'I'm sorry. The last couple of days have been so full of fresh developments and setbacks. They seemed like a bigger priority.'

'But it could be the key to everything,' said Alice.

'It could be, but I can't figure out how. As it is Naqi is dead, Saabir is dead, now Taahir is dead and his mother will die in the morning. Dexter is the driving force behind all this. I can't see how Zar could do something, and Dexter have not given the go-ahead.'

'They could fall out, I suppose,' said Alice. 'But over what, and why?'

'The only clue we have is the hit-and-run car, so I think we should concentrate on that. Agreed?'

Alice nodded, but she wouldn't look at Will, and when he tried to kiss her, she ducked away. Will's bed felt cold and lonely when he returned there.

Chapter Twenty-Six

Will had a terrible night, racked by regret over Alice and guilt over Taahir and his mother. He thought about trying to stop Taahir's mother from going to the morgue, but would that prevent her from dying? She must have a weak heart anyway, and the strain of her son's death could bring on a heart attack at any time.

Besides, someone had already taken a photo of him out there. To go back only increased the chances of him being identified, which would make it far worse.

In the morning Alice was cold and business-like. They sat silently in the car to Thames House. As they crossed Lambeth Bridge, Will looked towards the Houses of Parliament and Big Ben and saw that it was 9.02 a.m. Taahir's mother was dying right now, and he shivered as despair and guilt settled in his stomach.

When they got to the office, Zar looked up. 'Feeling better?' he asked. Will looked blank. 'You were sick yesterday, weren't you?' asked Zar, with an amused grin.

He looked so in control Will found it hard to imagine that in a few days' time he would shoot himself.

'Just something I ate,' said Will.

'A little novichok, perhaps,' said Zar with a laugh.

'Very funny. Anything happening?'

'There's a flap about the security for the G7 meeting and the State Opening of Parliament. If they can get to the Home Secretary, can they get to that?'

'Has the Home Secretary's event been officially cancelled yet?'

'Patience, patience. Of course, it would be terrible PR to let that bomb go off with so many dignitaries in town.'

'You're worried it would look bad,' said Will sarcastically.

'That's realpolitik,' said Zar. 'But I'm sure you can see it would be better not to cancel till the last minute so that the terrorists don't switch their attention to the G7.'

'Surely they'd be going for that anyway if they could.'

'Well, we need to make sure they don't.'

'What do you want me to do?'

'We're going to have you vet the security team for the summit just in case it shows anything.'

Will laughed. 'It will only show something if they're going to fail. Dramatically.'

'Exactly,' said Zar. 'Anyway, that's being set up now.'

Will found Alice. 'I'm going to be out this afternoon. More vetting. Any news on that car?'

'They've traced it. Stolen in Isleworth a few hours before.' She still wouldn't look him in the eye.

Will grimaced. 'And the owner?'

'A Mr Stephen Bartlett.'

'Any connections?'

'Not obviously, but they'll keep looking,' said Alice.

'No further forward?'

'Well, it looks more like it was deliberate. If you were going to run someone over, you'd steal a car, wouldn't you? Less chance of it being traced back to you.'

And with that, Alice turned and left. Cold War still going on then, Will thought to himself. No prisoners.

***

By mid-afternoon, Will was ensconced in the safe house in Pimlico while a stream of security experts and officials paraded past. This was a production line, but apart from a drug death and a suicide, both some years away, there was nothing of any interest at all. It was laborious stuff, one after another, and by the end of the afternoon, Will was exhausted.

'Not much learnt from that,' said Will.

'Just reassurance,' Zar replied.

'Maybe they're all so incompetent that they won't be around when it goes badly wrong.'

'Pessimist,' said Zar with a laugh. Javanshir smiled. 'Want a refresher?' asked Zar casually.

Will nodded. A few moments' release would be nice, maybe lift the pervasive sense of guilt he felt about Taahir and Taahir's mother. When he woke, Will felt more relaxed. Zar was busying himself at a computer.

'Alright for you?' he said, without looking round.

'Great, thanks,' said Will. Javanshir seemed to have disappeared. 'Can I go now?'

'Sure,' said Zar. 'There may be more of these tomorrow, but I suspect we've learnt all we can from this.'

233

Zar remained gazing at the computer and gave Will an airy wave goodbye.

'See you,' said Will, and wondered what Zar was finding so absorbing. Or did he just not want to look at Will?

***

Will and Alice had a tense evening, a pasta dinner, and then watching a mindless TV programme. Will was consumed by regret. He should have told her earlier about Zar, and he recognised how much he needed her now to discuss the endless questions that were ricocheting around in his brain.

Will was also distracted by her body, so close to him and yet so far away. He could smell her subtle lavender fragrance. He was conscious of her breasts under her T-shirt, the nipples making small peaks. Below the T-shirt was a line of skin visible above her belted jeans. Her stomach was so flat and muscled that there was a gap down the front of her jeans where her hips held the belt line higher. He wanted to put his hand down that gap and he could feel himself get aroused. This was not good.

'I'm knackered. Time for an early night?' he said.

Will held up his hand and signalled ten minutes again. Alice shook her head emphatically, but Will mouthed, 'We need to talk.'

He wasn't sure that she had agreed, and he was relieved when she finally entered the bathroom.

'I'm still angry with you,' Alice said.

'I get it,' said Will. 'But you must remember how disorientating this all has been for me. The bus crash, the court appearance. Dexter's rescue act. Then I'm stuck in the middle of MI5, their secret weapon to be manipulated by everyone. And just to top it off I find out there's a plot to blow up the Home Secretary, and the man that I'm given as my trusted boss is going to kill himself.'

'I guess when you put it like that,' said Alice.

'It's all been a nightmare, and it seems to be getting worse. I need your support, I need your advice, and most of all, I need you.'

Alice finally looked directly at him. He saw the old people's home again and the curious stranger sitting at her bedside. Then a thought struck him. The man must be a relative. The eyes seemed a bit like Alice, but the angle of the jaw and the set of the face was also familiar.

And then it hit him. That was because the man looked a bit like Will himself. Could he be their child? Will felt a warmth spread through his chest. His son.

When he zoned back in Alice's blue eyes were alive with a teasing amusement. 'Ok. Truce.'

'How much of a truce?' Will said. 'No-man's-land, or a new treaty of co-operation?' He reached for her, and she let him pull her close.

Alice leaned forward and kissed him, her tongue flicking into his mouth. 'Full merger,' she said.

Will felt an overwhelming relief as they kissed more deeply. He wondered if he should share his revelation now but then he thought that what they were surely about to do might lead to the conception of their child. He could tell her afterwards. A wonderful bonus, or at least he hoped she would see it that way too.

Now he was conscious of the slimness of her smooth, neat body and the firmness of her breasts and the heat that was already radiating off her, but it was her face framed by her fine black hair that he wanted to study, her full lips turned up in an anticipatory grin, the strong tilt of her chin and yet the delicacy of the skin underneath on her neck when he touched it. Most of all he wanted to lose himself in her deep blue eyes and see his son again.

Eventually, Will broke away from their kiss, took all the towels and lay them down on the spacious bathroom floor. 'My boudoir,' he said, gesturing, and Alice laughed.

'This time, I want to look into your eyes the whole time. No hiding,' said Will.

'And it won't get in the way. Being reminded of my death?'

'I can cope. I want to see the whole story.'

As he moved into her, he lost himself in her gaze. They took it slowly, and it felt as though with every movement he was more immersed in her. Her eyes never left his, even when they turned glassy with desire, and he knew part of her was concentrating on her own building sensations.

This was a closeness that he'd never had before and as they moved towards their climax, he was locked into the depths of her pupils, the light shifting and reflecting every urgent movement. This was going to be amazing.

Then suddenly the picture flickered and broke and Will realised with a jolt that the image behind her eyes had changed, and even as he felt his own climax overtake him he was at the same time watching in horror as he saw Alice's face surrounded by crowds against a London skyline, and then an enormous explosion ripped through the image and him, a bigger flash of light and fire than he had ever experienced before. It coursed through his body, lifting him up and throwing him to the side, where he emptied his guts on the bathroom floor.

Alice let out an involuntary cry. 'Christ, Will,' she said 'That was revolting. What's got into you?'

Will lay prostrate, his chest torn by spasms of pain. Maybe this is a heart attack, he thought. If only. It would have felt like a welcome release. But he knew the pain was a reaction to the enormity of what he'd seen and felt, and his grief at the loss of his son's future. He'd only known he was going to be a father for a few minutes and then it had been ripped so cruelly away.

He tried to piece together the new images. The size of the explosion had been huge and a fair proportion of the thousands of people milling around in the background must have died, too. There was also something strange about the explosion. It didn't feel like the clean blast he was used to. It felt worse, contaminated somehow.

And then there was the date imprinted on his mind. May 10th. The same day as the Home Secretary's bomb but instead of a mosque, the target was the Houses of Parliament and the state re-opening. All the G7 leaders, the Cabinet, the King and thousands of members of the public.

'Will, what's happening? You're frightening me,' said Alice, touching his shoulder.

'Your death date. It's just changed,' he whispered in Alice's ear.

Alice went white. 'How can that be?'

'I don't know. I don't know,' said Will, his mind whirling. It could only be because someone was intervening, someone who knew what was supposed to happen.

'When is it now?' asked Alice.

Will could hardly bring himself to say it. 'May 10th,' he whispered.

'This May 10th,' said Alice. 'But that's just four days away.' She wrapped her arms round herself as if seeking comfort. 'Jesus. Where?'

'It looks like the state re-opening of Parliament.'

'The same day as the Home Secretary's bomb. They've switched from the soft target to the biggest. Or could it be both?'

'I don't know. I think it must be a switch. They must have found out that the Home Secretary's event isn't going ahead and changed tack.'

'We need to warn Dexter,' said Alice. 'As soon as possible.'

'There's something else,' said Will, but when he took in Alice's pinched, frightened face he baulked at telling her about the baby. It might be a figment of his imagination; it might well not have been conceived yet. Better to keep that to himself for the time being. If he didn't stop this bomb then possible parenthood was irrelevant. And besides there was something more pressing.

'The bomb explosion was strange, different somehow from any I've experienced before.'

'What do you mean?'

'I don't know. The air felt contaminated.' Will struggled to articulate what he was feeling. Then finally he knew. 'It was radioactive.'

Alice let out an involuntary gasp. 'Jesus Christ. A dirty bomb?'

'That's what it felt like.'

'But that's appalling. It could contaminate the whole of Westminster. Take out the whole of Government and make the place unusable for years. We must warn Dexter. Now'

'What if it's him?' said Will. 'He could have done this whole thing. He wouldn't change the Home Secretary's event. Now he's going to, and the terrorists have changed their plans too.'

'Don't be ridiculous. We must tell him.'

'Wait. Let me think.' He flopped onto the toilet. What on earth was going on? It looked like there were thousands who could be caught up in this blast. If it had changed for Alice, it must have changed for all of them surely. He propped himself against the sink and splashed handfuls of water into his face until he was numb with the cold.

He could see Alice watching him. Finally, reluctantly, with a growing sense of doom, he raised his eyes to the mirror. He knew what he would find, but the force of it still ripped through him. Same explosion, same setting, confirmed with a flash of Big Ben in the background. Same date.

He sagged into her arms. That was it. Both he and Alice were due now to die in four days' time. How was he going to save them, their future baby, and the thousands who were going to perish on May 10th too?

Chapter Twenty-Seven

They argued for most of the night.

'We have to find out more,' said Will. 'Give me today to check it out.'

'What's to check out?' said Alice. 'We've just three days to prevent this, and the sooner that everyone's on to it, the better.'

'We need to find out what's happened in the last few days to make the terrorists change their target,' said Will.

'Maybe they found out we knew about the mosque bomb. Maybe it's a knock-on from what happened to Naqi and Saabir and Taahir.'

Will stopped and stared at her. 'Yes, you're right. But if that's the case, then someone's reacting, and it's got to include the bomb maker.'

'But doesn't he die tomorrow?' said Alice.

'That was what I saw, but who knows now? If it's changing for us, it might be changing for him. We need to know more. Dexter said the bomb maker was being watched. We must find out where.'

'Alright,' said Alice. 'But as far as I'm concerned, we need to tell Dexter by lunchtime.'

Will decided not to press Alice any further. Once they were in the office at Thames House, Will went in search of MI5 members of the security team for the State Opening of

Parliament, who he had vetted the day before. He wanted to look into their eyes and get confirmation that their future had changed too, and the bombing really was going to take place.

It was, he knew, searching for the proverbial needle in a haystack. He didn't have names. He'd just been told that they were members of the security task force, so some must have been from the police and the Home Office as well as MI5. There might only be a couple of them in the building.

Will patrolled the building systematically floor by floor, but he soon encountered entire areas he didn't have clearance for. The security monitor bleeped, and the doors remained firmly closed. Will was sure that a record would be kept of refused entries, so he was forced to stick to the public areas.

After half an hour he had exhausted the obvious possibilities without success and was attracting curious glances. Dispirited, he ducked into a Gents and stood next to a thirty-something in a sharp suit and tie. When Will glanced in the mirror, he was shocked to see a familiar face. It was one of the security team from yesterday, but there was no way the guy was going to meet his eye in a mirror over the urinals. For a second, he contemplated deliberately splashing the man, but that was as likely to end in a fight as anything. In the end he made sure that they both washed their hands and then as the man was leaving, he said. 'I'm sorry. Have we met before?' forcing the man to turn back towards him and look at him full on.

'I don't think so,' said the man with a puzzled expression, but Will was already locked on to the man's gaze, and seeing beyond. Hospital bed, drips. Parkinson's. Twenty years away. Although that probably meant the guy had already got it. Will wondered if he knew.

'My mistake,' said Will. 'You look like a friend.'

Did it mean anything that the explosion did not catch him? Not necessarily. If he was co-ordinating security, he wouldn't have to be at the site. He could be in an operations room well away from the scene.

Will made his way disconsolately back to his desk. There must be another way. Who else was going to be among the casualties? Certainly, Cabinet ministers, maybe some senior MPs of all parties. It was the state re-opening of Parliament, so surely most MPs of any standing would attend, though how many would be on the main podium was another matter. Of course, if the bomb was big enough, it might take them all out.

'How do I get outside TV again please?' he asked Ros, who gave him a sunny smile.

'What do you want? Entertainment, reality show, my favourite is the Kardashians.'

'Ha ha. Just the news channels, please. All of them.'

'You can cruise between all the satellite channels here, and we have a few you won't get on your TV at home. Like this.' A picture appeared of a middle-aged woman sitting in a dated TV studio reading the news in front of a picture of Kim Jong Un. North Korean TV.

'Very entertaining. I think I'll stick with the main ones.'

Will flicked around. He stopped on the BBC's Parliament channel, which was showing PM's questions. The Prime Minister was doggedly batting off criticisms about the G7 and the security costs. Very appropriate, thought Will.

Will scanned the faces in the Chamber. The Foreign Secretary was there with the Home Secretary and many of those on the front bench who were likely to be in the stands at the state re-opening. He couldn't just barge into the House of Commons and demand to look into their eyes. He was going to have to try to find one of them on the street outside Parliament later. While he was pondering what to do, Alice came back.

'More bad news, I'm afraid,' she said. She proffered her phone and nodded at it. There was a tweet from Public Defender with a picture of Will in the road in Isleworth. Will groaned, but the caption was worse. 'First, he saves someone from a killer, then he watches someone die. Is this man the Angel of Life or the Angel of Death?' It was followed by the same ominous hashtag #Findthisman.

'Christ, doesn't he ever stop?' said Will.

'Well, he certainly won't now. He'll whip up a storm and the tabloid headlines can't be far behind.'

'Can't they reinforce that DSMA notice?'

'They already have, but this is getting too juicy for the newspapers to ignore.'

'I'm surprised Dexter's not at my desk already.'

'You're lucky. He's out of the building, but he'll be back in a couple of hours.'

Will looked at his watch. 'PM's questions must be over soon. I'm going to see if I can get some other confirmation before I see Dexter.'

'Let me know if you do.'

Will spent half an hour surfing the news channels, searching for any clue to the movements of a senior MP who might be at the Parliament Square ceremony. Then he saw an MP being interviewed in Victoria Gardens. That was just down at Millbank. Maybe he should go over there and ambush an MP after an interview. He would have to take the risk that he was recognised.

He was mulling this over when he flicked across Sky News and there was Barbra Dent being interviewed. Will caught the presenter saying. 'Thank you for coming into our Westminster studio, Home Secretary.'

Will remembered that all the TV studios were in Millbank House, just three hundred yards up the road from where he was. The interviews were often pretty short, but they must last three or four minutes, surely. If he was quick, maybe he could catch her on the way out.

Will leapt into action, ran down the stairs, through the front lobby, ignoring the curious stares and out on to Millbank. He sprinted up to the Lambeth Bridge roundabout, nearly got hit by a black Ministerial limousine as he shot across Horseferry Road, and then he was pounding the pavement opposite Victoria Gardens. As he forced himself on, he wondered how he could be sure to get her attention. The TV entrance was less than a hundred yards away. He would have to pretend to be a journalist, ask an offensive question.

He came to a halt, breathing heavily, noticing another black ministerial limousine idling at the kerb. Just in time. As if on cue, the double doors of the main entrance swung open and a couple of young women, sharp-looking political aides, came out and looked around to check the way was clear. Then Barbra Dent emerged heading purposefully to her car.

This was not the moment for subtlety, Will decided. 'Home Secretary,' he called out. 'Why is your immigration policy such an abject failure?'

Barbra Dent's head spun round, and she glared at him. The minute he locked onto her eyes he could see her future had changed. There was no 'I'm on display' smile of a political animal about to perform on the podium, as there had been at the mosque. Instead, she looked bored sitting in a crowd of politicians and dignitaries, clearly not the centre of attention at that moment.

Suddenly, something caught her eye off to the right. There was a flicker of alarm on her face, then the blast of the explosion ripped through, smoke and fire and pain and blackness, and then as the smoke cleared, he could see her body spread-eagled on the floor, blood across her face from her mangled skull, her sightless eyes gazing upwards. And the time and date were the same as he had seen in Alice's eyes the night before.

He felt the explosion rip through him, and he doubled up, but avoided vomiting on the pavement in front of her. By the time he looked up, she was being hustled into the car and all he saw was her puzzled expression as she glanced back at him.

He took a few deep breaths as the car moved off into the traffic. It was clear that what he had seen in Alice's eyes was right, and poor Barbra had been saved from one bomb only to be blown up by another. Interestingly, she had not been close enough to be obliterated. Whatever she had seen to the right must have been some commotion just before the bomb exploded.

There was no doubt now, but should he tell Dexter? And if he had to because of Alice, just how much should he reveal? Will pondered his options as he trudged back to Thames House, breathing deeply, trying to settle his roiling stomach.

Dexter had always been reluctant to spell out when the mosque event would be cancelled. Had he decided to do that now and the bombers had moved on to the state re-opening? Would Dexter just say I told you so? We should have cancelled at the very last minute.

And what was Dexter's involvement in the gang's elimination of cell members? He'd let Naqi be shot. He'd always argued that a dead terrorist was the best option. Had he ordered the supposed suicide of Saabir and the hit and run on Taahir? If MI5 was behind any of those deaths, it was hard to believe that Dexter wouldn't know.

Will entered the building and made his way back to the office, lost in thought. Now that the target had changed, surely Dexter would have to act decisively. The bombing of the ceremony at Parliament put at risk the G7 leaders, the King and the senior members of the Government. How could he let that happen?

His reverie was broken by someone clearing their throat behind him. He turned and there was Dexter, looking as angry as Will had ever seen him.

'A word please,' said Dexter with icy control. He headed towards an empty office, clearly expecting Will to follow.

Will saw Alice on the other side of the room and gestured for her to follow.

When Dexter saw Alice approaching, he tried to close the door, but she just barged in.

'I want to talk to Will alone.'

'No, you don't. You want to tell me off, too. We're in this together.'

There was a pause, then Dexter gave in. 'Very well, since you both deserve a bollocking. What on earth were you playing at? You were supposed to stay guarded, and you,' he said to Alice, 'were supposed to keep him safe, and yet Will trucked off to Isleworth, got involved in a fatal hit-and-run and worse still got himself photographed.'

Will decided to meet fire with fire. 'I was investigating you. What are you up to? Because to be honest, I no longer believe a word you say. You've been lying to me all the time.'

'What do you mean?' said Dexter haughtily.

'The fatal hit-and-run, as you so charmingly call it, was Taahir, number four in our little vetting parade from hell.'

'What's that got to do with me?'

'It doesn't bother you, he just got run over.'

Dexter grimaced. 'It's obviously a tragedy, but it has nothing to do with me. You told me he was going to live for years.'

'Yes, and what that says to me is that someone who knew about that intervened.'

'It could be a coincidence.'

'There are too many coincidences in this. Number four is dead but curiously so are number two and number three.'

'What are you talking about?' said Dexter. His anger had gone, and he looked shaken, but was he shaken because he didn't know about it, or because Will was on the right track?

'What happened to number three?' Dexter asked.

'Well, he supposedly committed suicide after his interrogation at MI5's hands.'

'And you think it wasn't suicide?'

'Curiously he died before number two, and it was his death that tipped number two into becoming a proper jihadi.'

'That's speculation.'

'No. That's what number two told me before he was shot,' said Will flatly. 'And now number four's gone too.' Will ticked them off on his fingers. 'Naqi, Saabir and Taahir.'

'You didn't tell me that before,' said Dexter. 'Anyway, we don't fake suicides, and we don't organise hit-and-runs,' said Dexter.

'You'll forgive me if I don't believe you,' said Will coldly. 'I feel I've been manipulated from beginning to end. I can only assume that number one is heading for a similar fate and number five is due to blow himself up tomorrow, so by tomorrow night you may have a full house.'

Dexter was silent for a while. Finally, he met Will's eye. 'I'll look into what you've said, although I'm sure we aren't involved.'

Will would have made a dismissive snort, but his attention was caught by the scene playing out in Dexter's eyes. No longer a car crash. There was a blue sky and crowds of people behind Dexter who looked tense. Then there was the blackness and the flames and the smoke, and when it cleared nothing but a hole in the ground. And the date inevitably was the 10th of May, the same as Alice and the Home Secretary.

The explosion ripped through his body again, even more intensely. Will couldn't stop himself. He leaned forward and vomited over Dexter's glossy brogues. It would have been sweet revenge, but all Will could think about was that Dexter was going to die there too, and even closer to the centre of the blast. He would hardly kill himself in his own plot, would he? Or maybe his plot had unwittingly set in motion the new bombing and he would be one of the victims. That would be a rich irony.

Dexter surveyed his splashed shoes and said with icy control, 'Tell me.'

Will wiped his mouth and raised his eyes. 'New bomb. May 10th, Parliament Square.'

'And I die?'

'You and I suspect hundreds of others. They're going to blow up the state re-opening of Parliament.'

'How do you know it's hundreds of others?'

'Well, so far I've found you.' He looked at Alice and she nodded. 'Alice, me and the Home Secretary.'

Dexter looked surprised. 'The Home Secretary? You said she would die in the mosque bombing.'

'Yes, well, you must have cancelled the mosque event, and the terrorists have changed tack. Was the mosque event at the same time as the State Opening?'

'It was.'

'You've cancelled the mosque. She's free to go to Parliament Square, and she dies there,' said Will.

'Hang on,' said Dexter. 'I can see how you discovered about Alice and yourself and me. But how did you get close enough to the Home Secretary to see her?'

Will couldn't be bothered to lie. 'She was leaving Millbank after a TV interview and I doorstepped her. Just now. I had to know if she was still going to die in the mosque bomb.'

'You did what? That was another breach of security,' said Dexter angrily. He glared at Alice, who just shrugged.

'If you don't keep me in the loop, then I'm going to take my own actions. What are you going to do about this? Cancel the State Opening?' asked Will.

'Don't be silly. It's the culmination of the G7. We'd look like fools in the eyes of the world.'

'Not half as foolish as if you let all the world's leaders get blown up.'

Dexter glared at him. 'Forget it. Not going to happen.'

'Not even if I tell you it's a dirty bomb. There's some kind of radioactivity mixed up in the explosion. You could end up with the world's leaders irradiated and a no-go zone at the heart of Whitehall.'

This time Will had to concede Dexter looked seriously shocked. 'Are you sure?' he said with a catch in his voice.

'Sure as I can be. We'd better stop it somehow, hadn't we?' said Will. 'Maybe it would be a good idea to bring the bomb maker in and question him, rather than letting him die.'

'But if he dies, then that's the end of it,' said Dexter.

'I'm afraid not. He was supposed to die and still the mosque bomb went off. Either he's built another bomb already or there's another bomb maker out there. He's the best lead you've got now. Him and number one. I'd bring them both in if I were you.'

Dexter looked like he had a fly stuck in his throat. He clearly hated Will telling him what to do.

'We've lost track of number one. He's disappeared,' Dexter admitted.

'Great. Now the bomb maker really is the only option we've got.'

Dexter glared at him. 'I must consult. Stay here,' he said peremptorily.

'If you decide to pick him up, then I want to be there. And Alice. No more keeping us out.'

Alice nodded and smiled. Maybe they could find a way through this together.

'Oh, and you might want to check whether there's any nuclear material missing. It would only take a tiny amount to contaminate the area.'

Dexter glared at Will then turned and left without saying another word. He was clearly pissed. Fine, so be it. Will wasn't prepared to clear Dexter yet. There were still too many unanswered questions.

Chapter Twenty-Eight

Zar appeared in the doorway, like a predator sniffing prey. 'What's going on? Dexter went off at speed. I sense bad news.'

Will felt irritated. As far as he was concerned Zar was in the same mould as Dexter. Another ambitious opportunist with no morals.

'There's going to be a new bomb,' said Will shortly. 'Three days' time.'

Zar whistled appreciatively. 'As well as the mosque bomb?'

Will saw Alice raise her eyebrows and shake her head. So Zar didn't know.

'Instead of,' said Will.

'And the target?'

Alice shook her head again, and Will realised she was telling him to shut up.

'What's the target?' asked Zar again.

'Let's wait till Dexter gets back, shall we?' said Will, and he was pleased to see Zar look taken aback. Good. He wasn't going to jump to their commands any more.

Zar drifted back to his desk.

'You don't think I should tell him,' Will said to Alice.

'Let's wait and see. He'll just pass anything on to Dexter, and at the moment I don't trust anyone either.'

Will glanced across at Zar who was talking animatedly on a mobile.

253

Then Dexter returned. 'Alright,' he said crisply, 'We'll pick up number five now.'

'We?' said Will.

'You're going to tell me you're coming I'm sure, so let's assume that.'

'And Alice?'

Dexter sighed. Then Zar appeared at his elbow. 'I'm coming too. Where are we going?'

Dexter grimaced. 'I may as well hire a charabanc. We're going to pick up number five.'

Will noticed a flash of something in Zar's eyes. Was it shock, or irritation? He wasn't sure.

'I thought we'd agreed he was going to be left to blow himself up,' said Zar.

'Will argued that he was our best possibility of information on the new bomb, and I agree,' said Dexter.

'That's a shame. All that preparation for nothing,' Zar muttered.

'Let's get going. I've got CO19 on the way, and we'll meet them there,' said Dexter.

***

After a high-speed drive across London, they turned off the main road at Becton in the East End and into a seedy, run-down industrial estate. They stopped behind an anonymous grey saloon and a man in a leather jacket and jeans got out and came back to their car.

Dexter lowered the side window. 'Anything? Any movement, Sean?'

'Not a dicky bird,' said Sean.

Dexter picked up the radio headset. 'Ok everyone. In we go.'

Suddenly vans of armed police drove quickly past and turned the corner ahead. They followed and saw a dozen police pile out and the lead officer with a mini-battering ram take down the door of a small nondescript lock-up, one of a line of roughly twenty along the road.

The waiting police officers filed quickly in, guns at the ready. There were a series of crashes from inside that sounded like doors being kicked open or knocked down, and then silence. It didn't look good. Will glanced at Alice who gave him a tense half-smile. Dexter was looking ready to explode with frustration, but Zar seemed calm.

'Not our lucky day then,' Zar said quietly, as Sean came across to them.

'He's gone,' Sean said. 'No idea how, but there's no-one there. You'd better come and see.'

They trooped after him. Inside was a grubby little workshop with a couple of workbenches littered with pieces of wire and soldering irons, a discarded blue nylon rucksack, and some rolls of duct tape, but no bomb or bombs.

Beyond there was a filthy toilet and stained washbasin, and a small room with a dirty single mattress and blanket. A metal standing wardrobe stood at an angle against the wall. Will peered behind the wardrobe and saw a shadow and when he pulled the wardrobe away, there was a hole in the wall.

'For God's sake,' said Dexter exasperatedly. 'See where it goes.' He waved to Sean, who disappeared into the gap and returned a few moments later.

'It goes into the next lock-up, but there's a corridor behind that leads all the way back up the row, so he could have got out right at the end.'

'Never have a bolthole without a way out,' said Zar.

'However,' Sean said, 'He might have dropped this.' Sean held up a cheap burner phone.

'I'll take that,' said Zar, grabbing it. 'I'll get Bean to run all the checks on it. At least we might find out who tipped him off.' Will swallowed his irritation at Zar calling Javanshir Bean again. The man was a closet racist, surely, but now was not the time.

'Why do you think someone tipped him off?'' asked Will.

'Pretty curious that he should do a runner just moments before we arrive, wouldn't you say?' Zar looked Will straight in the eyes and Will saw again the gun at Zar's head and the man himself pulling the trigger. Interesting, thought Will. He's not caught up in the Parliament bomb and he's still dying the same way he was before. What does that mean?

They went back into the workshop. There was something very wrong here, Will felt. Not only had the bomb maker been tipped off, but he'd also had time to clear the workbenches of anything really incriminating.

Then Will noticed a pile of rubbish in the corner. Discarded takeaway boxes, pizza cartons, Chinese, and underneath something plastic and green. He bent down and turned it over. It was a circuit board. Why would the bomb maker leave that behind? Will glanced round. Dexter and Zar were in a huddle with their backs turned, so Will slipped it into his pocket. Then he gestured to Alice, and they went outside.

'This doesn't make sense,' said Will. 'Who would he get a tip-off from? We only decided to come here and pick him up three-quarters of an hour ago. First Saabir dies, then Taahir is killed. Now this. Someone's pulling the strings.'

'Dexter?' said Alice.

'Well, he's got to be my favourite candidate,' said Will. 'He's playing the whole thing like a game he can't bear to lose.'

'Or Zar, maybe?' said Alice.

'I guess it's possible, but could he really do it without Dexter knowing?'

'It could be someone else in MI5,' said Alice. 'Maybe even higher.'

'And what about Public Defender? It's funny the way he's on my tail,' said Will. 'Do you think it's just members of the public or is someone feeding him info?'

'Why don't we ask him?' said Alice. 'I could set up a meeting.'

'Good idea,' said Will, squeezing her shoulder. 'It's time we got a lot more pro-active.'

He looked around, checking they were unobserved. 'By the way, I found this,' he said, sliding the circuit board out of his pocket so that Alice could see and then pushing it hurriedly back.

'What on earth are you doing? That's evidence. Dexter will fry you,' said Alice.

257

'We need to get ahead of the game,' said Will. 'I'd like to get our own analysis of this, and not just the official version.'

'You'll never get it in past security,' said Alice. 'Leave it under your seat in the car, and I'll fetch it later.'

Will nodded. Then Dexter and Zar came striding out of the lock-up, both grim-faced. 'Come,' said Dexter imperiously, and they piled into the waiting car and headed back to Thames House.

***

By the time they arrived back at the office, Alice had already had a reply from Public Defender.

'He wants to meet in Pimlico. Some tapas bar, in an hour,' Alice whispered to Will in the lobby. 'I should go and find out if a meeting with you is possible later.'

Will nodded. 'Take care. I want to look in his eye. There's got to be a connection.'

Will went back to their desk area. Javanshir was hunched over his computer as usual and waved without looking up.

'He'd gone,' said Will. 'Someone must have tipped him off.'

'Zar said,' Javanshir replied. 'I'm just looking at that phone you found.' Will noticed it was on Javanshir's desk with a lead into his laptop.

'Anything?'

'Not much. A succession of calls from what I think will be similar disposable phones.'

'Anything this morning that could have been the tip-off?'

'Don't think so. I should have it cracked in half an hour,' said Javanshir.

Will went back to his desk, puzzling over their bad luck. At every turn, they seemed to be behind the pace. Who could it be? Will was still inclined to think it was Dexter pulling all the strings.

Ros interrupted his reverie, leaning over his desk.

'Can I borrow you for a second, Will?' she asked.

'Sure,' said Will, following her across the office to where a young Black man was waiting, looking nervous.

'This is Jeff,' said Ros. 'He works in IT. He's the one who keeps our computers up to speed.'

Puzzled, Will shook the man's hand and smiled. 'Nice to meet you. Great job,' he added lamely.

Then Will was shocked to see Ros standing behind Jeff, point to her eyes and then to Will and then Jeff. Will gaped, then finally it clicked. She wanted him to look into Jeff's eyes. She knew about Will's ability, and she wanted it used on this guy.

Without thinking, Will obliged, locking eyes with a hesitantly smiling Jeff. There was a bed in a homely bedroom, a wizened version of Jeff lying under the covers and a much older version of Ros holding his hand with tears in her eyes. Fifty-five years away, heart failure, but really just old age.

Will broke his contact and said 'Nice to meet you,' again. Then he turned to Ros and mouthed 'what the fuck', although he'd already worked it out. He went back to his desk and Ros joined him shortly.

'You know?' said Will. Ros nodded and smiled, then after a second she added, 'Well?'

'I'm guessing he's your boyfriend,' said Will.

'Fiancé, to be accurate. Have I picked wisely?'

There was a smile in her eyes, but she looked apprehensive.

'Don't worry. Pretty good choice. I would say you're going to have fifty-five years together and you'll be at his bedside when he dies. You looked sad, so I guess you kept on loving him, but he will die first.'

Ros blinked back a tear. 'Always the way, the bloke goes first, but I could hardly complain after more than half a century.'

She suddenly stepped forward and hugged Will.

'How did you find out?' said Will.

'What do you think I am? Deaf, blind and stupid?' she said with a laugh.

'Ok. Glad to be of service,' said Will. 'But if you notice anything else, let me know. We have a rather more pressing problem. Someone on the inside who's sabotaging our operations.'

Ros's eyes opened wide. 'Tell me about it,' she said, so Will did.

Chapter Twenty-Nine

When Zar returned, Will went straight over. 'Can I have a copy of the list of calls from that phone?' he asked.

Zar raised an eyebrow. 'Why? We're looking into it.'

'I have an idea,' said Will.

'An idea about what?' There weren't any tip-off calls and they're all burner phones.'

'I'll tell you if it works.'

Zar looked at Javanshir, who nodded. 'Ok,' he said reluctantly. A few minutes later, Javanshir handed Will a list.

Will scanned it carefully. No calls that morning, but why would you leave in such a hurry that you dropped your phone if there had been no tip-off? That felt odd for a start, and then there had been the discarded circuit board.

Still, there was information to be had from this. Will scanned the night before. There were two calls, one at 8.05 a.m. and one at 10.40 a.m.. The later one chimed better with the time that he and Alice had been making love. Could that have been when someone decided on the Parliament Square bombing? He should concentrate on that call.

Will went over to Ros. 'Can you run a number through the system please,' he whispered.

'Isn't Javanshir already doing that?' asked Ros.

'I'd like an independent check. I'm particularly interested in this call last night,' he said, pointing.

'Ok, Captain,' Ros said with a wink.

Will went back to thinking how odd it was that the bomb maker had got out in time, and why Dexter and Zar had seemed so pleased when they discovered the bomb maker was going to blow himself up. Will thought back to the vetting session. There had been a definite moment before the bomb went off when the bomb maker had looked surprised. Was that a premonition, or had he found something wrong with the circuit board?

Alice returned after lunch. 'Creepy guy,' she said. 'It took a while to talk him round. He's very full of himself. Claimed he was a defender of the public's right to know, hence the name tag. Asked point-blank if you were an MI5 agent. I said no, of course. He claims he's been getting a lot of help from the public, but in the end it came down to two regular sources. One of them passed him the Isleworth photo.'

'Well, that's something,' said Will.

'But he won't tell me who they are. He wants to meet you.'

'Do you trust him?'

'Not as far as I could spit him,' said Alice crisply. 'But if we want to pursue this, we haven't really got a choice.'

'Where and when then?'

'This evening. Same tapas bar, seven o'clock.'

'Isn't that a bit public?'

'It may be better than some darkened alleyway.'

***

Ros came back to Will mid-afternoon with more bad news.

'I'm afraid that phone was a cheap burner. That's been confirmed. Could have been bought by anyone.'

'Bugger,' said Will. Then a thought occurred to him. 'Can they track down the calls that burners make?'

'It's possible,' said Ros. 'Rather a long shot.'

'It might give us a lead. Let's work backwards. See if there are any calls that we can find made by that phone that rang the bomb maker. If we throw the net wide enough, maybe it will throw up a call to someone we can trace.'

'Sounds desperate.'

'I am desperate,' said Will. 'Can you give it a shot?'

Ros nodded and went. Will was left to ponder why every new trail seemed to peter out so frustratingly.

He looked up and saw Patrick across the office. Will was suddenly conscious that he had done nothing about Alice's Pavel problem. He'd promised, but there had been so much going on. Well, this was a chance. He may as well seize it.

He went up and tapped Patrick on the shoulder. Patrick turned round with a lazy smile. 'Hello, mate,' he said, although Will noticed Patrick kept his eyes slightly averted. Had he always done that, and Will hadn't spotted it?

'Could I borrow you for a second, Patrick? I've got a favour to ask.'

'Sure, no problem,' said Patrick with another amiable smile.

He followed Will into a side office and looked at him quizzically. Will decided aggression was the best option.

'I need you to look into my eyes,' Will barked. 'Right now.'

The change of tone clearly startled Patrick. His eyes flicked up involuntarily and Will locked on.

And there Patrick was, the light fading in his eyes. His head canted at an unnatural angle as the noose bit into the folds of his neck and choked the life out of him.

A hanging. Another hanging. Will felt his own breath knocked out of him. Pavel, Saabir, and now Patrick. There were a few too many apparent suicides around this operation. And the date was just two months away.

Will doubled over, trying to breathe.

'You alright, mate,' said Patrick with a solicitous touch on the arm. But there was an edge to Patrick's voice. He knew what had just happened. 'You read me, didn't you? What did you see?' Patrick demanded.

Will decided to keep him dangling for now. 'I wanted to ask you about Pavel,' said Will sharply. He thought he saw a flicker of unease cross Patrick's face.

'What about him? You're not supposed to know about that.'

'Didn't it seem strange to you? You go out and as soon as your back is turned, he hangs himself.'

'Yeah, well, Alice was supposed to be looking after him, wasn't she? She fucked up and now she's been whining to you.' There was no pretence now. Patrick looked and sounded harsh and hard.

'And you didn't smell a rat that she fell asleep just then? Or maybe you knew why, because you'd just drugged her?'

'You little fucker,' said Patrick angrily, but Will could see that he was off balance, uncertain whether to hit Will or storm out.

264

Will decided it was time to go for the jugular. 'There seem to be an awful lot of hangings connected to you recently. Three, by my reckoning.'

'What are you talking about?'

'Well. There was Pavel and then Saabir.' At the mention of Saabir's name, Will definitely saw Patrick flinch.

'My guess is that you killed Saabir and made it look like a suicide. Just like you did with Pavel.'

Patrick sneered at Will. 'You're losing it, mate. They were both suicides, just like it says on the tin.' He took a deep breath, trying to control himself. 'Anyway, you said three. Who's the third?'

'You are,' said Will, staring Patrick in the eye and seeing his body swinging from the rope. 'You are.'

Will made sure Patrick could see the absolute certainty in his eyes. Suddenly Patrick deflated, all the anger gone, and he groped for a chair behind him and sat down shakily.

'I'm going to get hung,' he said.

'You are, in two months' time,' said Will remorselessly. 'And I'm guessing from your reaction that you don't think you're going to kill yourself out of remorse. You think it'll be made to look like suicide. Just like the others.'

He could see Patrick's lips moving. He knew what the answer was now, and he marvelled at the treachery involved, but he wanted Patrick to confirm it.

Finally Patrick muttered, 'The bastard.'

'Let me guess,' said Will harshly. 'You're talking about the bastard who's going to kill you, or the bastard that ordered you to kill Pavel and Saabir. Or maybe they're the same.'

Patrick glanced at Will, and he knew he had been right.

'Dexter,' said Patrick softly. 'It was Dexter.'

'He told you to kill Pavel and set up Alice to take the blame.'

Patrick stared ahead, his lips still working, the muscles in his shoulders and arms shifting and contracting with the tension. Finally, he nodded.

'And Saabir?' He nodded again.

Will sat down, drained. 'He is a bastard, isn't he?'

***

Will found Alice and took her to the side room. The implication of so much betrayal was still ricocheting around in his mind. He wondered how Alice would react.

'What is it?' she demanded.

'I've got some news about Pavel,' he said.

Alice looked at him uncertainly. 'That's great, but we don't have time for it now.'

'I think you'll want to hear this. It'll affect what we do next.'

Alice looked at him curiously. 'Go on then.'

'Pavel didn't kill himself. He was eliminated,' said Will.

Alice sat stock still, then a smile crept across her face. 'I knew it. I knew it all along. Was it the Russians?'

'I'm afraid not,' said Will. 'Closer to home.'

'MI5? How do you know?'

'I've just had a very interesting conversation with the killer.'

'But you were talking to Patrick. I saw you.' Alice clapped her hands to her mouth. Finally, she whispered, 'Patrick? Really?'

Will nodded. He could see the rising fury in Alice's eyes.

'Patrick set me up. He must have drugged me. The utter fucking bastard,' she said, clenching her fists as if she wanted to hit him right now. 'And Dexter must have masterminded the whole thing. They were worried that Pavel was a plant. They must have decided they were better off without him. And it suited them for me to get the blame.'

'He ordered Patrick to kill Saabir, too.'

Will watched the anger and then the resolution on her face. God, she was a tough one, and he knew then that he loved her. She stood up and came over and kissed Will hard.

'Thank you, you're my saviour. I won't forget this. Ever,' she said.

'It does, of course, raise a few questions. If Dexter is capable of that sort of double-dealing with a colleague, what else is he capable of?' Will wondered. 'Stabbing you in the back. Playing fast and loose with the Home Secretary bombing. Interrogating suspects and keeping it off the record, and to cap it all, he's arranged the killing of two innocents. He doesn't seem to have any limits. What are you going to do?'

'He's going to pay,' Alice said. Will could see the fire in her eyes. 'When the time is right, I'll make him squirm.'

***

The more Will sat at his desk and thought about the depths

267

of Dexter's betrayal of Alice, the more worried and angry he became. If Dexter was happy to sanction a murder and ruin a colleague's career in passing, then ruthless hardly covered it. Will cursed. He should have asked Patrick about Taahir. If he could get Pavel and Saabir hung and make their deaths look like suicide, then surely he could have arranged the hit-and-run on Taahir too.

Now Dexter wouldn't cancel Parliament Square, and by the time he had agreed to pick up the one lead they had left, the bomb maker, it had been too late. He seemed to get in the way of every chance they had of stopping the bomb. Yet he was due to die there too. It didn't make sense.

He went to find Alice. 'I need to see Hillyer,' he said. 'Without Dexter around.'

'Impossible,' Alice said. 'You wouldn't get in.' Then she hesitated. 'There is an end-of-the-afternoon wrap-up meeting in the operations room at half past five that she attends if she can. Likes to be seen with the troops. You might grab her as she's leaving that. I'll find out if she's going to be there.'

Alice came back with a grin. 'She'll be there. You don't want to go to the meeting. Dexter and Zar may well be attending. You'll need to ambush her in a corridor as she's leaving this floor.'

They scouted a suitable site with an empty office nearby and Will was in position at six o'clock when the meeting was supposed to end.

Will was thinking about Alice's parting shot. 'Don't tell her about Pavel. That's between me and Dexter, and anyway, we have no proof.' She was probably right, and yet it was one of the strongest indicators they had of Dexter's manoeuvrings.

Will heard approaching footsteps and then Hillyer appeared round the corner with just a junior assistant in tow. His luck was in.

'Ms Hillyer, I need to have a quick word, please.'

Hillyer gave him a withering look. 'Get Dexter to make an appointment, Mr Gray.' Will saw the assistant give him a look of surprised recognition. Well, he would be more surprised shortly.

'This won't wait. I need to talk to you now,' Will said, planting himself firmly in the way.

'You are trying my patience,' Hillyer said.

'Of course, I could just tell you this in front of your charming assistant and whoever else might wander along, but given it concerns your personal security, you might prefer it in private.' Will gestured at the empty office.

Hillyer looked as if she was ready to shout, but then two more people came round the corner at the end of the corridor. 'Don't let anyone in,' she said to the assistant sharply. 'Absolutely no-one.'

She stomped into the office and Will followed and shut the door. She was staring at him aggressively and Will saw again the tubes and wires and the heart monitor. Could her poisoning have anything to do with Dexter's plotting, he wondered?

'Well?' she said icily.

'I'm not sure if you're aware how much Dexter is frustrating efforts to stop the bomb in Parliament Square,' said Will. Hillyer said nothing. 'We are in danger of losing the only lead we currently have, the bomb maker, who will die tomorrow if we don't find him.'

'Forgive me, Mr Gray, but if he blows himself up, then that may be the bomb they were going to use in Parliament Square. If that is indeed going to happen.'

'You don't believe me.'

Hillyer gave an irritated shrug. 'Your prophecies are coming thick and fast, like your accusations about my staff.'

'You wanted me to help you,' said Will.

'No, Mr Gray, I let Dexter persuade me, but now I'm wondering if you aren't more trouble than you're worth. You are destabilising the entire operation.'

Will was open-mouthed. 'An operation that has so far cost the lives of three elderly shoppers and three young Muslim men, one goaded and entrapped into jihadi activity, and the other two killed but made to look like accidents.'

Hillyer didn't blink. 'As I said to you before, there is no way of knowing whether those women would have died anyway, and as for the others, there are always casualties in war.'

It was like listening to Dexter or Zar. The same justification, the same evasion. Will felt sick. She would never listen; they would never listen.

'At present, you are promising both mass carnage in two days and a Russian nerve agent plot in twelve months. Maybe you are over-egging the pudding,' said Hillyer.

'You don't know the half of it,' Will retorted.

'What does that mean?'

'Zar is going to shoot himself in three days' time.'

'What?' Hillyer was clearly horrified. 'Why?'

'That's the problem. I don't know.'

Hillyer glared at Will. 'Enough, Mr Gray. You will tell no-one. Especially Dexter or Zar himself. Crazy accusations like that, and we'll all be at each other's throats. No more, do you understand me, or I may well be tempted to lock you up and throw away the key.'

And with that, she was gone, leaving Will to contemplate another dead end.

Chapter Thirty

Alice and Will left the building at 6.45 p.m., saying they were going home, but then they diverted the car to Pimlico and the rendezvous with Public Defender. Will had summarised the meeting with Hillyer. 'We're on our own,' he said at the end. 'Let's hope this gets us somewhere. It's our last chance.'

At seven o'clock they entered the tapas bar. Will thought it was a terrible place to have a clandestine meeting. It had wide bay windows looking out on to the street. Anyone could see in, and you couldn't leave undetected. But it was too late to worry about that.

Alice led him to a corner table where a thin young man with a mop of unruly brown hair was sitting. The man rose and held out a hand, which Will reluctantly shook.

'Hi. I'm Public Defender. Pub for short,' he said with a cracked laugh. Will didn't reply. 'Do sit,' he said, gesturing to a free chair opposite the window.

Will saw he would be in a clear line of sight for anyone passing outside. 'No thanks. I'll have your seat,' he said assertively.

Pub looked put out, but held his hands up in a gesture of surrender and moved so that Will could sit in the corner seat. As Pub sat back down, Will noticed how jumpy he was, how all his movements seemed like little muscular jerks. Will waited for him to raise his head, then locked onto his eyes.

A filthy room, a bed with dirty sheets and a pock-marked scabbed arm lying over the edge. A needle in the folds. Staring vacant eyes and a final twitch. Heroin overdose. Fifteen months away.

Will shook his head. The man had clearly asked him something and was looking at him expectantly.

'Sorry. What did you say?'

'Drink?'

'Just a Diet Coke, if that's okay?'

'You can have whatever you like. You're paying,' said Pub.

'I'll have the same,' said Alice, smiling sweetly and proffering a twenty-pound note.

Pub returned with the drinks, plonked them down and took a swig from a pint of lager.

'Change?' said Alice, but Pub ignored her.

'You seem to get mixed up in a lot of very unusual things,' said Pub, looking at Will. 'The bus crash, a jihadi attack, a hit-and-run.'

'Just bad luck,' said Will.

'Remarkably bad luck,' said Pub with a secret little smile.

'I want to know who's tipping you off about all this.'

Pub looked at him as if weighing up his options. 'First things first, you help me understand what's really going on and I might help you.'

'You promised to help if I bought Will here,' said Alice.

'I promise lots of things,' said Pub lazily. 'But I only deliver if I get something in return. Now I heard there might be a reason you were present at all these little incidents.'

'A reason?' said Will with a sinking feeling.

'I heard you know the future somehow,' said Pub with a leery smile. 'You knew they were going to happen.'

'Who told you that?' asked Will.

'A little birdie. So, is it true or not?'

'Sounds far-fetched to me.'

'It's just coincidence you turned up there?'

Will wondered how Pub had found out and just how much he really knew. If it was from the bus crash, then Slater might have talked about the premonition line, and it had leaked. But if Pub really knew what Will could do, then that could only have come from inside MI5.

'What do you mean, tell the future? Like a fortune teller?' said Will with a smile.

'Bit more specific,' said Pub. 'You knew the bus crash was going to happen.'

So, it probably was Slater, thought Will. Blabbing to one of his mates down the police station, who then accepted a casual bribe for the information.

'Oh that,' said Will. 'I think I just said I'd had a premonition.'

Pub laughed. 'Tea leaves, is it?' He nodded at Alice. 'I hardly think the big boys and girls at MI5 would be so welcoming if it were just party tricks.'

'Who told you all this?' said Will.

'I have my sources, but I'll need more from you before I give them up.'

'Very honourable, but aren't they anonymous tip-offs? You don't know who they actually are?'

'I have tracker friends. They can trace them back to the source.' Pub smiled at Will. 'Do you want to know or not?'

Alice butted in. 'If you help us, we can be very helpful to you in the future.'

Pub laughed. 'I'm not sure a spook's promise is worth the paper it isn't written on.'

Time to shake things up, Will thought. 'Call it a premonition if you like, but you're going to die on August 22nd next year of a heroin overdose.'

Pub was suddenly very still, and the colour drained from his face. There was a silence. 'How do you know that?' he said, eventually. 'How can you possibly know that?'

'Like I said, it's a premonition. The name of your source?'

Pub was gaping now. 'Bartlett, Wendover Avenue, Isleworth,' he muttered.

Bartlett. The man who claimed his car had been stolen. The car that was used in the hit-and-run. Will's brain clicked through the options. That wasn't Slater, that had to be someone in Five.

He looked at Alice, who had clearly come to the same conclusion. 'We should get out of here,' she said. But even as they made to move, Will saw a black-jacketed figure come into the bar with unmistakable purpose, raise a camera and then there was a blinding white light as the flash went off time and time again.

Shit. They were being doorstepped. Will grabbed Alice's hand and pulled her past the photographer, but Alice

275

wrenched free and kicked at the photographer's knee. There was a crunching sound, and the man screamed in pain and fell to the floor. Alice bent down and grabbed his camera.

They ran through the entrance hall and out of the front door of the bar, only to be met by a barrage of photo lights again. The intensity of the flashes blinded Will and then he glimpsed a dark figure running towards him.

'You bastard, I'll kill you,' said the man, throwing himself at Will and knocking him to the ground. Will struggled to get away from the man's flailing fists and then he smelt again the man's sour breath and felt the hatred that rolled off his attacker, and he knew it was the father whose wife and daughter had died in the bus crash.

The flashes stopped for a second and he saw the man's eyes fixed on him with feverish intensity and felt the man's hands closing round his throat. His fingers were digging deep into Will's neck. They had a manic strength that promised a terrible ending indeed if Will didn't do something. Will brought his knee up ramming it between the man's legs and there was an exclamation of pain, and the hands loosened fractionally. Will seized the opportunity and punched the man in the face.

Then, suddenly, Alice was there barging into the man and pushing him aside. 'Time to go,' she said. 'Run.'

Will leapt to his feet and sprinted away with Alice next to him, followed by a cacophony of cameras going off and lights flashing. They fled into the darkness.

***

276

'Well, that's definitely the shit hitting the fan,' said Alice. Will grunted. He was still catching his breath. 'You're guaranteed a prominent place in the tabloids tomorrow. Maybe even the front page.'

'I guess they'll ignore the DSMA notice then,' Will finally managed.

'You just punched a bereaved parent in the face. I guarantee it.'

'I was trying to stop him throttling me. But I see your point. We'd better get a move on.'

They made their way back to Thames House. It was late, but with the G7 and the terrorist threat looming, there was still a hum of activity. Fortunately, there was no sign of Dexter or Zar but Ros was there.

'You're working late,' said Will.

'Thought I could be of help,' Ros replied.

'Can you run that search on Bartlett again? There must be something we missed the first time.' He gave Ros the address.

'On to it.'

'What about the circuit board?' he asked Alice.

'I'll ring my man. He hasn't had long, but who knows.'

Will sat back in his seat. He could still feel those hands around his throat and the barrage of camera flashes. That would not look good, and it would be hard to operate if his identity was all over the tabloids.

Time was running out. The bomb maker was due to die tomorrow, and they would lose that lead. The Parliament Square bombing was only two days away. For every step they made forward, another obstacle appeared. There was something he was missing, he was sure, but he couldn't figure out what.

He heard Alice say, 'You're kidding?' loudly on the phone. He watched her listening intently, then she finished the call with, 'Thanks, you're an angel. I owe you.'

Alice came over, grinning. 'Well, we know now why Dexter and Zar didn't want to save the bomb maker. Someone had rigged the circuit board.'

'How?' asked Will.

'There was a hidden connection so that as soon as the explosive was attached and the circuit tested, it would go off.'

Will thought back to the vetting session. 'That was why he looked surprised. He knew it wasn't reacting the way it should.'

'I reckon Dexter and Zar planned this. Get a booby-trapped circuit board into the bomb maker's supply chain. One less terrorist to bring to court.'

'Now we've got that circuit board, the bomb maker might not die tomorrow,' said Will.

'Or there might be more than one that's been tampered with,' said Alice grimly. 'We should keep this to ourselves.'

Will nodded. Just then Ros came over with a smile of her face.

'I think it's been cleaned up,' she said.

'What do you mean?'

'There's so little there you wonder why he has an active file at all. There's nothing in his past to show why we would be aware of him. Someone must have doctored it.'

'Why not just erase it altogether?' asked Will.

'Because that would leave a gap, the computer equivalent of a big flashing red light. Whoever did it decided it was better to just censor it.'

'Is there any way of finding who did it, or at least who looked at the file last?'

'Sure. I'll ask my friend in IT,' said Ros, winking at Will.

'Just tell Jeff he owes me one.'

Will was tempted to go straight out to Isleworth and knock on Bartlett's door. It was getting harder for him to move around, and it might be impossible if the story broke in the tabloids. But it was past ten o'clock. It would be difficult to turn up on someone's doorstep with an innocent story and expect to be believed.

He was just wondering whether to go for it anyway when Alice returned with a grim face.

'More bad news, I'm afraid,' she said.

'Let me guess. The bereaved father has filed for assault.'

'Well, that may be a possibility, but this is a bit more serious. That flag I put on Randall. He's just re-entered the country.'

Will let out a mirthless laugh. 'Great. Now I've got a trained SAS killer who wants me dead on my tail. This just gets better and better.'

Chapter Thirty-One

In the end, they decided on a few hours' sleep and an early start. But the phone ringing interrupted them at quarter to six. Alice took the call.

'It's Dexter,' she said. 'The story's in *The Sun*. Front page. He wants us to sit tight, and he'll be over soon.'

'We won't tell him I talked to Hillyer yesterday, OK?' Alice nodded. 'Let's see if he brings it up.'

Alice fetched her iPad from her bag, and they pulled up the front page of *The Sun*.

'Bloody hell,' said Will.

The splash was uncompromising. In big bold type, the banner headline screamed, 'The Angel of Death'. Underneath were two photos, a mugshot of Will from his Army days and a messy flash shot of his rolling round on the pavement last night with Colin Maynard. They'd caught the shot of him punching the man perfectly.

There was a strapline. 'We track down the mysterious former squaddie linked to so many violent deaths,' read Will. And the caption on last night's struggle read, 'The out-of-control soldier attacks a bereaved father.'

'I didn't attack him. He attacked me,' said Will.

'Bit academic now,' said Alice.

The more they read, the worse it sounded. Will was portrayed as a soldier psycho, disgraced in Afghanistan, and then causing the bus crash by trying to abduct Melanie

Burton. They even made the fight with Naqi on the pavement outside Thames House sound as if Will was the aggressor and glossed over whether he had saved the old woman's life. 'Put the public needlessly at risk' was the phrase that stood out.

And by the time they dealt with Taahir's hit and run, it sounded as if Will had arranged that too.

Finally, there was a tub-thumping leader. 'This man was in a British court just three weeks ago accused of child abduction and causing multiple deaths. How was he allowed to go free and carry on his reign of killings? The Government seems to have recruited him to MI5, and then had the nerve to try to use a DSMA notice to hide what they have done. Well, we will not be cowed. We say they have a lot of questions to answer. We say they have a lot of blood on their hands.'

'Wow, that's what I call an assassination piece,' said Will.

'It's going to make sorting this out a lot harder,' said Alice.

They switched on the TV news and found Will was the top story. There were the same old pictures of the bus crash, grainy footage from phone cams in Isleworth and outside Thames House, and tickertape headlines hinting at his guilt. Several rent-a-gob MPs had been drafted in to say what a disgrace it all was.

The right-winger couldn't believe that the Government had been foolish enough to re-employ a disgraced former soldier, and whatever happened to the rule of law. Will was supposed to be in prison, awaiting trial, wasn't he?

281

For the left-winger, it was another example of MI5 spying on ordinary citizens, although she wasn't clear exactly who was being spied on.

Will flicked news channels with more shots of the wrecked bus and explanations of the tragedy of Mr Maynard who lost his wife and child in the crash, which was either a tragic accident or deliberately caused violence not far short of murder, depending on the channel.

The sound of the front door banging open interrupted his reverie, and then Dexter barrelled into the room with Zar following.

'What the fuck's going on?' he shouted at Will. 'You go off piste again and get yourself splashed all over the tabloids. Can't you follow a single instruction?'

'And what are you doing?' Will shouted back. 'Fiddling while Rome burns. The bomb is going to go off tomorrow and where are you? You still haven't found the bomb maker, have you?'

Zar clearly couldn't resist butting in. From the gleam in his eyes, he was enjoying this. 'That won't matter soon,' he said.

'What do you mean?' said Alice.

'The bomb maker is due to die in…' Zar consulted what looked like an expensive watch. 'In four minutes.'

Will was shocked to remember that the bomb was about to go off. 'We'll have lost the best lead we have,' he said. 'And you don't seem worried at all.'

'We knew this was going to happen. We decided it was a worthwhile trade-off,' said Dexter.

'Who's we?' said Will. 'You and him?' He indicated Zar. 'Hillyer? The Government? I have no idea.'

'You don't need to know,' said Dexter huffily.

Will figured that Hillyer had said nothing about their meeting or Dexter would have included it in the list of Will's transgressions. He had been wondering whether to tell Dexter about the link between Public Defender and the Taahir hit-and-run. Or even that he knew about the circuit board, but Dexter's comment was the final straw.

'Well then, you don't get to know anything more from me,' said Will. 'Game over.'

'Don't be childish,' said Dexter. 'Why were you meeting that journalist? That was incredibly stupid.'

Will said nothing. 'Alice?' said Dexter threateningly.

'We thought he might lead us to whoever was tipping him off. But it was a set-up,' she said. Will looked at her. He could see the fury at Dexter in her eyes. No more, he tried to convey. No more.

'It was a massive mistake,' said Dexter. 'Now we've got a big PR issue to deal with as well.'

'Hardly as big as the PM and the cabinet, the G7 leaders and maybe even the King getting blown up by a dirty bomb,' said Will.

'I've told you,' said Dexter. 'That will not happen. The security is completely watertight. We'll catch them.'

'You don't believe my visions any more then?'

Dexter grimaced. 'I think we can prevent it from happening.'

'And yet the bomb maker will die in…' He looked at Zar.

'One minute,' said Zar.

'And you'll be back to square one,' added Will.

'There are other lines of inquiry,' said Dexter.

'But you won't tell me what they are?' Dexter remained silent.

'What about the radioactive substance. Anything missing from Government stocks?'

Again Dexter stared at Will, saying nothing. 'Stalemate then.'

Will turned to Zar. 'I know I don't trust Dexter. Can I still trust you?'

'Absolutely,' said Zar. 'I believe in you.'

'And yet you don't seem terribly worried.'

'Oh, I am, but it's all under the surface,' said Zar with a smile. 'Keep calm and carry on.'

'What are you going to do?'

Just then, Zar's phone beeped. He gazed down at the message and there was the trace of a smile.

'Bomb's gone off. By the river at Deptford,' he said flatly. 'Could be our man?'

Will glanced at his watch. Spot on time, but how would they know so quickly? They must have had surveillance in place. In which case, they had deceived him again. They had always meant to let the bomb maker die.

'We'd better get down there,' Dexter said to Zar.

'I'm coming,' said Will.

'Not a chance,' said Dexter. 'We can't risk you being seen in public. We're going to move you to another safe house in the country later today. Till then you stay here.' He turned to Alice. 'And you make sure he does,' he said with a steely smile.

'Yes, sir. I always do what I'm told,' said Alice sarcastically, but Dexter didn't seem to notice.

'We may want you to do some more vetting as well,' he added to Will.

'I told you. No co-operation,' said Will.

'Think about it. There is always the possibility of resurrecting those criminal charges. Along with a whole host of fresh ones.'

Dexter left, and Zar gave Will an apologetic shrug and followed him.

Will slumped down on the sofa. This was not going well. He gazed blankly at the TV, which was still reporting silently on his story.

Suddenly, Will saw a shot of Melanie that mixed through to live footage of Melanie's mother being interviewed on a sofa. He flicked up the sound.

'He's an evil man,' she said. 'If he hadn't tried to snatch my daughter, none of it would have happened. He should be locked away for life.'

Will grimaced, but then he saw a leg on the couch behind the woman and Melanie's face peeped round her shoulder.

'And this is the daughter you nearly lost?' asked the interviewer, ratcheting up the emotion. Melanie's mother pulled the little girl on to her lap and glared defiantly at the camera. 'I couldn't have survived without my Melanie, and I'm heartbroken for the other parents who lost their kids,' she said, with a tear rolling down her cheek.

Will looked at Melanie. She was the beginning of it all, and just three weeks ago. His urge, his compulsion to save this child had set him on a bitter road, and now Will wanted re-assurance. She looked alright, despite everything she'd been through. He was hoping she would have a long life, die an old woman, at least make some sense of everything that had happened, of all the deaths he had been forced to witness.

Will hoped that she would look at the camera, and as if on cue, Melanie turned her head and looked straight down the lens. Will stared into those cornflower blue eyes again and experienced the same strange feeling he'd had with the footage of Pavel. It was like a distorted, impenetrable vision, but he had an overwhelming feeling of doom.

Then the interviewer's voice butted in, suddenly unctuous. 'And we understand Melanie has a special treat lined up for tomorrow?'

Melanie's mother hesitated, as if unsure what he was talking about, then she cottoned on. 'Oh yes, she's going to that big shindig in Westminster. The re-opening of the Houses of Parliament.'

'That'll be nice for you, won't it, Melanie? A special day out,' said the interviewer.

Will let out an involuntary howl of misery and despair. How could this be? The Gods were playing with him now. Every way he turned led back to this bombing. He had a sudden image of Melanie's little body lying on the ground broken, her cornflower blue eyes staring into the void.

Alice came running. 'What's wrong?'

Will just pointed at the screen and Alice saw Melanie, and the camera pulled back to a two-shot of her and her mother.

'That's the girl from the bus,' she said.

'And she's going to be at Parliament Square tomorrow,' said Will.

'You're joking,' said Alice.

'I wish I was.'

'But why? That's ridiculous' said Alice, looking shocked.

'Can you find out?' said Will. 'I'm not sure I can bear much more of this.'

Alice nodded and left Will staring mutely at the screen as the coverage moved on. All he could think about was the growing death toll, not just politicians and world leaders, but the few people he cared about. Alice and maybe now even Melanie.

He went to the bathroom and doused his face in cold water. Think, think. What should he do?

He was still lost in the horror of it when Alice came into the bathroom. She nodded grimly. 'They have invited a group of children from that school. Melanie's one of them. It's described as an act of healing.'

'Some healing,' said Will. Suddenly, he knew he had to act. He turned on the shower to cover what he was about to say.

'Well, fuck this. I'm not sitting around waiting for Dexter to lock me up in some safe house while nothing gets done. The only way now is to sort it out myself.'

'I'm coming with you,' said Alice.

'It might be better if you're still apparently on their side. My eyes and ears on the inside.'

'They'll never trust me if I let you go.'

'We'll have to take that chance. Say I forced you. Stay away from Dexter and Zar. They'll be stuck down in Deptford for a while,' said Will. 'I need you to find out if

Ros has any more on Bartlett and that other phone number. Bartlett is our only lead at present. I'm going to stick to him.'

'Ok. Get a burner phone and ring me. If I don't answer, wait an hour and ring again.'

Will nodded. A final thought occurred to him.

'Find where Randall is. I may need you to direct him to me. He's got a part to play in this somehow.'

Chapter Thirty-Two

In the car park Will hesitated. How to get to Isleworth when his face was all over the media? The Tube would be a nightmare, a taxi gave the driver far too long to look at his face and figure out the connection. None of the obvious options looked good, but then another way presented itself. The barrier opened and a motorbike drove in and stopped on the other side of the car park. Will watched the rider take off his helmet and lock it in the back carrier. He saw the rider pocket the keys and walk away.

Time for action. He needed those keys, and he was going to have to get them by trickery or by force. So, try the trickery first. Will pulled an old receipt from his pocket.

'Oi, mate,' he called, advancing on the rider. 'You dropped something.'

The rider turned to find Will almost on top of him. He tried to move back, and Will pretended to trip and went sprawling into the rider, knocking him to the floor.

'Sorry, mate. Sorry,' said Will, trying to help the rider to his feet and sliding his fingers into the man's pocket and pulling out the keys.

'Clumsy idiot,' said the rider, a stubbled, dark-haired man in his thirties. The man's eyes glinted with anger, but Will ducked past, avoiding the direct contact.

'I thought you dropped this,' he said, proffering the crumpled piece of paper.

'It's not mine. Just go away,' the rider said and turned angrily to the lift. Will held his breath until the lift door shut and the man was gone.

Time to get a move on. He might discover he'd lost his keys straightaway, or he might not miss them for hours. There was no way of knowing.

Will retrieved the helmet from the pannier. It was tight but it would have to do and then he was riding out of the car park on to the street, giving thanks that his Army service had given him some motorbike experience.

The journey to Isleworth passed uneventfully. Will felt safe behind the tinted glass of the visor. The bike purred along easily, and for a second, Will was tempted to just keep driving, head out into the country and lose himself. If he went somewhere remote, grew a beard, lived rough, he would be unrecognisable pretty quickly. And yet he knew he couldn't. So many people were going to die tomorrow. He couldn't let it happen. Not to Alice, not to Melanie, not to any of them.

He stopped and bought a burner phone from a garage, flicking his visor up for the minimum time so they could see his eyes. There was no immediate hullabaloo, but he knew that the bike's number plate could already be on the police tracking system.

He reached the address without a problem and stopped just down the road. It turned out to be a new gated development of flats and houses on a rather desolate turn of the Thames where the river split in two round a large island and the lesser branch was full of rusting hulls including a large floating warehouse that must have once been used to repair boats. It was a strange view for luxury flats, but Will

290

guessed being this close to the river increased the price even if it wasn't a salubrious sight.

Will watched the entry gate. He couldn't wait on the outside; he was too conspicuous. And he needed to know whether Bartlett was in, rather than just hang around.

Fortunately, the solution presented itself almost straightaway. A delivery van drove up and pressed the buzzer. Will leapt back on his bike and drove towards the gate. As the van passed through, he followed it in, keeping the bulk of the van between him and the intercom and camera.

Will soon found the address, an anonymous town house in a row of ten with their backs facing the river. He rode slowly past. There was no sign of life. He would have to knock on the door and see if Bartlett was in. It wasn't a good idea to hang around in a place like this. He stood out too much.

He parked the bike at the end of the row and risked a call to Alice. It would just look like he was checking in with his control.

Alice answered straightaway. 'Where are you?'

'Outside Bartlett's house.'

'Ros has found out the last person who went into Bartlett's file was Zar. He must have done the clean-up.'

'It is an MI5 operation then,' said Will. 'I knew it.'

'There's just one oddity. That check on suspicious trading in Brenton's company at the time of his death has thrown up an unexpected name. Number one, Ashkani,' said Alice.

Will was shocked. 'How on earth did he get that information? And what's the connection to this? I don't get it.'

'There's only one place he could have got it from. Inside MI5,' said Alice. 'We're missing some vital pieces here. Be careful.'

'Did you find Randall?' asked Will.

'I've got his phone.'

'Point him in this direction. Give him this address. I think he's part of the endgame,' Will said and then shut the call down.

Will scanned the doorways of the string of townhouses and saw what he was looking for three houses down from Bartlett. An Amazon parcel.

He picked it up and returned to Bartlett's house, ringing the doorbell. The front door opened and there he was. Six feet tall, built like a rugby player and with an extremely suspicious look on his face. And rather surprisingly olive skin and distinctly Middle Eastern features.

'Parcel,' said Will.

'I haven't ordered anything,' said Bartlett.

Will pretended to consult the package. 'Oh no, it's for a few doors down. My mistake.'

'Aren't you supposed to lift your visor?' said Bartlett irritably.

'Sorry, sir. Got a cold. Didn't want to transmit all my germs. I won't trouble you further.'

Will turned away, but almost immediately he felt cold metal on the back of his neck.

'Stop right there,' said Bartlett.

Will did as he was told, and when he turned, Bartlett was holding a pistol with a suppressor pointed at his face. 'I think you should come inside, and we'll have a friendly chat. Cold or no cold,' Bartlett said.

Bartlett gestured with his gun, and Will went into the house with Bartlett following and covering him. Will knew he'd been stupid to blunder in, but maybe he would find out at last who was behind it all, and how far up the tree it went at MI5. At what cost? Will had no illusions left now. If they could kill Pavel, Saabir and Taahir, then they wouldn't have much compunction about dispatching him.

Bartlett pushed Will through a small hallway and into the main room, which had a view of the industrial junk on the river. Will noticed there was a footpath and a woman walking a chocolate-coloured spaniel. Ordinary life barely fifty yards away.

'Off with your helmet,' Bartlett ordered, smiling as Will's face was revealed. 'Now sit down,' he added, pointing at a wooden armchair.

He kept a wary eye and the barrel of the gun aimed at Will while he closed the heavy curtains. Then he came and fixed Will's hands to the arms of the chair with plastic ties and his feet to the chair legs. Will was surprised to see a prayer mat on the floor facing what he guessed was east.

'You are a nuisance, aren't you?' Bartlett said. 'Never do what you're told.'

'And you always do what you're told, I suppose,' said Will. 'Drive over an innocent in the street, tip off a journalist about me.'

293

Bartlett pursed his lips. 'He wasn't an innocent, he was jihadi.'

'Who deserved to die?' asked Will. 'Who are you working for? Dexter? Or someone higher?'

Bartlett laughed. 'You may be good at visions, but you're not much good at intelligence. What's my future looking like?' He moved closer to Will and stared into his eyes.

Will saw Bartlett standing in a room that he recognised was the very room they were in. A hand appeared round his neck, and then a vicious little knife came in from the other side and slashed him across the throat. There was a shocked expression in Bartlett's eyes and then the blood spouted, and his eyes rolled up in his head and he fell to the floor. Will didn't see the killer's face, but he had a powerful impression of who it might be. And the date was today, the time 8.22 p.m.

Will swallowed. 'Nothing very interesting. An old people's home. Forty-five years away.'

Bartlett regarded him coolly. 'I don't think so. Doesn't ring true, somehow, in this business. Ah well. Time to call in the reinforcements.'

He picked up a mobile and punched a button. 'He's here,' Bartlett said and then 'Will do.'

He put the phone down. 'We're going to have a bit of a wait, so I suggest you make yourself comfortable.'

Will prodded. 'You're not officially on Five's books, so who are you? Someone they hire for their dirty work?'

Bartlett said nothing.

'What I don't understand is why they're doing this? What do they gain? Kill a few jihadis? There will always be more.

294

Or do they really want the bomb to go off? Some right-wing plot, so there'll be a crackdown. More money, more power for the security services.'

'You couldn't be further from the truth,' said Bartlett. 'Why don't we just sit in silence, eh?'

Will sat for a while, weighing up the alternatives. He could wait till the reinforcements turned up. But if it was Dexter, he'd be hauled off to a safe house at best. And if he continued to refuse to co-operate, they could send him back to jail. Or terminate him. His best chance of learning something was now.

'I was lying about you living to a ripe old age,' he said. 'Didn't want to upset you. But in fact, you're going to die tonight.'

Bartlett bristled. 'Really, how?' he said challengingly.

'Someone's going to cut your throat.

'Bartlett's eyes widened. 'Oh yeah. 'Would that be you?'

Will shook his head. 'Sorry. I can't oblige. I can't see precisely who, but I think he's SAS. Trained killer.'

Bartlett looked shaken. 'Shut your mouth. No more,' he said.

Will lapsed into silence. Of course, he could have got this completely wrong in some way he couldn't fathom. But it looked like MI5 was behind the deaths of all of them. He still couldn't understand their involvement in the bombing, though. And how had the tip-off about Brenton's death got to Ashkani? Was someone in MI5 helping the bombers? The prayer mat in the corner kept drawing his eye.

The day wore on until finally, as the sun was setting, the bell rang. 'It's on the latch,' Bartlett called. There was a scrape from the front door, and then Zar walked in. He flashed Will an ironic smile.

'Well, hello. Causing trouble again,' he said.

So Zar really was in on it, too. 'Do you think you and Dexter can get away with this private killing spree? That the end justifies the means,' Will said.

'My dear boy,' said Zar. 'As my namesake, Zarathustra would undoubtedly have said, the end always justifies the means.'

'And what's that in this case? Some conspiracy theory that if the bomb goes off, it will mean more funding and power for MI5?'

'As ever, Will, realpolitik eludes you.'

Will was about to snap back a retort when there was a noise from the corridor, the door opened and in walked Zar's wife, Rasha, dressed as if she was off to a cocktail party in her dark glasses and black coat over a silk wraparound dress, except she was holding a pistol with a suppressor on the end, and holding it with purpose and familiarity.

'I told you to wait in the car,' said Zar.

'You don't give me orders, remember,' said Rasha. 'Besides, I wanted to make sure you two got a move on.'

Will's mind was racing. If Rasha was in on it too, then could it really be MI5? Had he misjudged the whole thing, and it really was a terrorist plot? Rasha looked remarkably comfortable despite the charged atmosphere. And there could only be one reason she was wearing dark glasses indoors. She still didn't want Will to see into her eyes. What would he find, he wondered?

'We should kill him now,' she said.

'Not here,' said Bartlett. 'Too messy. Too hard to cover up.'

'Besides, we need to discover exactly what he knows,' said Zar.

'Looks like you're coming with us,' said Rasha, pointing the gun at Will's chest. 'Nothing to say?'

Will shook his head. No point in saying more till he had a better grasp of what was going on. If Rasha wanted him dead, then it seemed more likely they were jihadis, and they were behind the bombing. And Zar was helping them. Will felt an icy pool form in his stomach. If Zar was a traitor, then anything was possible. Could Dexter be involved, too?

'Cut him free and bind his wrists behind his back,' Rasha ordered Bartlett. When it was done she jammed the pistol into his back. 'Get up, walk where I tell you and say nothing.'

Will got to his feet and she pushed him towards the door, with Zar following.

'You're not leaving me here,' said Bartlett. There was fear in his voice.

'What's the problem? You didn't want him killed here.'

'He said.' Bartlett swallowed. 'He said I would die tonight. In this room.'

'He was just winding you up,' said Zar.

'He said an SAS killer would cut my throat.'

'Time to grow some cojones, son,' said Zar brutally.

'Well, I'm not staying here,' said Bartlett.

'Leave if you must, but wait until we're clear,' said Zar. 'Understood?'

Then they pushed Will out of the house. Will looked around. Was Randall here and watching? Would he kill

Bartlett? That was no use to Will, because Randall wouldn't know where they'd gone. Will thought he heard a rustle in the bushes bordering the road, but nothing happened.

They arrived at an anonymous black Audi. Rasha opened the door and pushed Will in. 'Climb over to the other side. Any trouble and I'll shoot you,' she said.

Then she got into the back seat next to Will and Zar got into the driving seat. No black-clad avenger leapt from the shadows. Will would almost have welcomed Randall coming to kill him now. It would be a risk worth taking, because otherwise he was stuck with two traitors apparently set on bombing Parliament and no way out.

But nothing happened. Zar started the engine, engaged gear and the car glided off.

Chapter Thirty-Three

They drove back towards the centre of town, winding their way through Chiswick to Shepherd's Bush, but then they turned back out on to the A40 to Park Royal and a drab area of warehouses and run-down terraces. Zar turned into a beaten-up industrial estate with a similar row of lock-ups to the bomb-maker's base in the East End. By the time they arrived it was dark and the area was quiet. Zar pressed an electronic fob and a garage door raised. They drove in and it shut behind them.

Not good, thought Will. Trapped in this garage and no-one close enough to hear anything. Not good that they hadn't blindfolded him, either. They clearly didn't intend for him to leave. But then, given he knew the extent of their treachery, that was hardly surprising.

Rasha climbed out carefully, keeping the gun trained on him as he followed. She indicated a chair bolted into the garage floor, just ahead of where the Audi had stopped. 'Sit there,' she said.

Will hesitated.

'Don't worry, I will shoot you,' said Rasha. 'Sit.' She still had her dark glasses on. Still taking no chance of Will seeing anything, even now.

When Will sat down, Zar moved behind him and tied his bound hands to the back of the chair and then put restrainers round Will's legs.

'We should kill him now,' said Rasha, with no trace of doubt.

'Soon, my love, soon,' said Zar. 'I just want to find out exactly how much he knows.' Zar took a leather pack out of his coat pocket and unfolded it. There was a syringe and several ampoules of clear liquid.

'Time for a little relaxation,' he said to Will. 'You know the drill.'

Will realised with a sinking feeling that this had been the routine all along. Not relaxation, but some kind of truth drug to discover what he knew. And there he had it, plain as day. That was how they had known about the Colonel. Could they have found out about Hillyer's poisoning, too?

And if they put him out now, then they would discover everything he knew about the bomb attack and maybe about Randall too. His options were narrowing fast.

Zar approached with the needle and, without ceremony, shoved it through Will's shirt and into his arm. Within a few seconds, Will was feeling woozy, and as the world slipped away, he had time only to consider just how badly this would turn out.

He dreamt of Alice. There was something he had to tell her, and she was there, but she was just out of reach and drifting away. He was overcome with an immense feeling of regret at all the missed opportunities. Tears were streaming down his face. He thought his heart would break for the sorrow of it all.

Gradually the fog cleared, and when he opened his eyes, Zar was staring at him. Will was surprised to see a trace of sadness in Zar's expression.

'You were crying,' said Zar. 'Never seen that before. Never mind, it will all be over soon.'

Will coughed and cleared his throat. 'Did you get what you wanted?'

'Fine, thank you. Interesting about the journalist. Bartlett was a fool to use an IP address that could be traced so easily.'

'I just told you everything, then?'

'I ask a question. You speak,' said Zar. 'It's very straightforward.'

Maybe they didn't know about Randall though. That was Will's only wild card, although it was just as likely that Randall would try to kill Will.

'And that's how you found out about Colonel Grantley?' Will asked, trying to keep the conversation going. Zar nodded. 'And you told Dexter? So why did you get me sent out there? Did you want me to get killed?'

'It was Dexter who wanted you to go. I was curious to see how it played out. But I was happy you survived. You were more use to me back here.'

'I was useful?'

'All your digging around kept the pressure on Dexter and the spotlight away from me. He thought it was all about our little plot, the tampered circuit board, blowing up the bomb maker, eliminating the jihadi suspects. He thought we were working together to strike a blow against terrorism, breaking the law for a good reason, but I always had other plans.'

'What about the women stabbed in the street?'

'Just a diversion to keep you and Dexter under pressure and looking in the wrong direction.'

'But you killed Saabir and Taahir?'

'They were necessary sacrifices. To be accurate, Dexter agreed to have Saabir killed, and I said I would arrange Taahir. My one mistake was getting Bartlett to do it too quickly, but you were closing in.'

'All those deaths were just camouflage?' said Will bitterly.

'You've got to admit it worked. You thought it was a right-wing plot. He thought it was part of our covert game. It stopped you trusting each other and paying enough attention to me, to what I was really doing,' said Zar with a satisfied smile.

'And number one, Ashkani, has he been sacrificed too?'

'No, he's much too valuable. He's far away.'

'With the money from the insider trading deal?'

'Oh, you know about that, do you? All funds to benefit the cause. Why miss a golden opportunity?' said Zar with a grin.

Will was stumped. He had let himself be outmanoeuvred at every turn. He had kept on blaming Dexter when the real danger was right in front of him.

'You're a jihadi?' asked Will.

'I'm a convert. My wife showed me I could strike a real blow in the holy war.'

Rasha looked at her watch and moved decisively between Will and Zar. 'Enough. It's past three in the morning. We've taken too long on this. You need to be going,' she said to Zar.

'He'll wait,' Zar replied.

'We can't risk that. He's our only chance now. Go.'

Will wondered who was the only chance? Did they have another bomb maker, or was the bomb maker not dead at all?

Zar could have rigged the explosion for the right time, set the whole thing up. It fitted the pattern.

'Goodbye, Will,' said Zar. 'I'm sorry you must die. You have such a unique skill. Dexter will be so upset.'

'Really?'

'He understood your potential, but I made sure he never really used it. A nudge here, a word there. You're both remarkably gullible.'

Will grimaced. He had been a complete fool. Nothing to lose now then.

'Since you're so clever and you know all my secrets, I guess you know that you're going to kill yourself,' he said.

Rasha whirled round. 'What?' She stared at Zar. 'Why would you do that?'

'It's what he says will happen,' said Zar. For once he looked ruffled, but only, Will thought, because Rasha was upset. 'Sometimes fate can't be avoided,' he said.

'When?'

'Tomorrow.'

'That means we must fail,' said Rasha.

Zar came over to her and hugged her. 'Have courage, my love,' he said. 'The bomb will still go off.'

'How do you know?'

'That's what he's seen everywhere. He's desperate to stop it but we're going to kill him, so he can't.'

'Why would you want to kill yourself?' asked Rasha.

'I don't know. Dexter finds out. Something else goes wrong. We can only play this game one step at a time. I may avoid it yet. But in the end, our fate is in Allah's hands.'

Rasha looked torn and for once vulnerable, but she took a deep breath. 'Very well. We must be strong,' she said. 'You go. I'll just tidy up and I'll follow you.'

Will didn't like the idea of being tidied up. He would have to delay this as long as possible.

There was a silence after Zar's departure. Rasha was studying him as if he were an insect she was about to crush. She looked imperious in her designer coat and boots, completely out of place in the dingy garage. And she was still wearing her dark glasses, which added to the air of unreality. How could he get her to take the glasses off?

'You never wanted me to look into your eyes, did you?' he said.

'I prefer to keep my secrets to myself,' she replied.

'And all the gloss? The designer clothes?'

'Hide in plain sight,' she said simply.

'What are you, a jihadi, a suicide bomber? Are you going to deliver the bomb? Is that what I'd see?'

Rasha laughed. 'You think I would tell you?'

'What does it matter? You're going to kill me.'

'You will never know,' she said, standing in front of him, pointing the gun at his chest. 'It is not for you to know my fate. Only Allah knows our allotted span. Not some blasphemer.'

'Don't you even want to know how your husband dies? Where the bullet hits him?'

Rasha leaned forward and brought her face close to his. 'Stop trying to mess with my head, unbeliever.'

304

Will could see himself reflected in the lenses of her dark glasses. It was enough. He drove his forehead into her face, catching her just above the bridge of her nose.

Rasha staggered back, cursing, as her glasses went flying. Will found himself staring into her amber eyes, flushed with anger as she put her hand up to try to stem the blood flowing out of her nose and splashing her designer coat.

'Kafir bastard,' she screamed, but Will was locked on to her eyes. Like Bartlett, the picture hardly changed. She was in this garage, she was glaring at him, raising her gun to shoot when a knife hit her in the neck and blood cascaded. Her amber eyes widened in shock, then they rolled upwards, and she slumped to the ground, blood pooling around her.

Will felt the double jolt of her death and the realisation that it was imminent, just seconds away. She was about to die in front of him.

Chapter Thirty-Four

Will shook his head, and looked up to see Rasha glaring at him, raising the gun to shoot him once and for all. Almost instantaneously, the knife hit the side of her neck. Those golden eyes were staring with shock and disbelief, and then she let out a desperate gurgling sound, dropped the gun, and fell to the floor.

Will watched her blood flow out over the concrete. He gagged and retched, then he tried to swallow. He couldn't afford to throw up right now.

'Still having trouble with your stomach, Mr Thomas,' said an icy voice, and Randall appeared out of the shadows, standing before Will, looking at him with utter contempt. His eyes had a feverish quality, and he looked wound tight, ready to snap.

'Death seems to follow you around, doesn't it?' he said, bending down and pulling the bloody knife from Rasha's neck and wiping it on his trousers.

'I'm glad to see you,' said Will.

'Really,' said Randall. 'You want to die?'

'She was going to kill me. And you saved me.'

'Only because I intend to kill you myself.'

'You will not kill me.'

'I have the memory of four colleagues to avenge,' said Randall. 'You have to die.'

'You're not listening to me,' said Will. 'You are not going to kill me. I know. Didn't Colonel Grantley tell you about my gift?'

Randall looked at Will with loathing. 'He told me some gibberish about how you could tell when people were going to die. How you knew he was going to die that day.'

'And he did,' said Will.

Randall closed his eyes. There was a silence, then he said, 'That's nonsense. If he knew, why didn't he avoid it? It was a roadside IED. He could just have taken a different route.'

Will knew he was talking for his life here. Every word had to count, or he would be the next one getting a knife through his neck.

'He wanted to avoid it. He'd thought about it, but he'd just had a terrible example of what can happen if you try to change the future.'

Randall glared at Will. 'What was the example?'

'You.'

Randall let out a little groan.

'The Colonel asked me to vet your patrol, as you know. You were going to die, and the others would escape. It looked like you were all caught in an ambush, and you saved the others by giving them the time to get out.'

Randall wiped away some moisture from his eye. 'At least that would have been a good death, saving my mates. Not this misery.'

Will pressed on. 'The trouble was Grantley didn't want to lose you, so he made up an excuse to get you off the patrol.'

Randall's eyes widened. 'And they got ambushed without me, and they all died.'

'I tried to warn him. There was no way of knowing what the outcome would be. As it turned out, it was worse. Much worse.'

Randall strode across the gap between them and put his knife against Will's throat. Will could feel the icy edge pressing against his skin.

'You could have stopped it. You could have told him what was going to happen.'

'Only if I'd vetted you all again. He didn't want to know. In his view, he was the commanding officer in a combat situation. He would take responsibility for the decision.'

Randall pressed the knife harder. Will felt the metal nick his skin.

'You didn't do enough,' Randall said.

Will pressed on. 'That's why the Colonel didn't avoid his own death. He knew if he tried, anything could happen. Someone else could have died instead, blown up by the same IED a little later. He didn't want more deaths on his conscience.'

Randall let out a little wail. 'What use is it knowing, then?'

Will could feel the pressure of the knife lessen. 'It's a curse,' he said. 'But it does at least give you a choice. Nothing will bring back your colleagues and believe me, I'm truly sorry for that. But you could help save a lot of lives right now.'

Randall lowered the knife. 'Go on,' he said.

Will gestured to Rasha's body. 'Her jihadi friends are going to blow up a big ceremony in Parliament Square in a few hours with a dirty bomb. And I'm trying to stop them.'

'What's that got to do with me?' said Randall fiercely, looking straight into Will's eyes. Will met his gaze and saw again the alleyway and Randall shooting, and the man running away behind Randall as two bullets hit him in the chest and he went down. Two hours away.

Will was certain now that he was the man running away, and that Randall was saving his life. 'I need your help to stop the bomb, but it will cost you your life.'

Randall shrugged. 'I'm used to that. But how do you know if you stop the bomb something worse won't happen?'

'I don't,' said Will bluntly, 'but that's a risk I'm going to have to take. If I don't the whole of the Cabinet, all the G7 leaders and maybe even the King will die, along with hundreds of innocent members of the public and the area will be contaminated with radioactive dust for years.'

'How are they going to get the bomb in there? Surely the security's going to be watertight.'

'I don't know how at the moment, but given the plot involves a senior MI5 man, I've got to assume they'll find a way. I'll just have to get close enough to stop it if there's a chance.'

'Sounds like a suicide mission,' said Randall.

'Probably.'

'And you would do that?'

'I must try. That's my responsibility.' Will watched Randall's face. 'By the way, how did you find me here?'

Randall looked surprised, then suspicious at Will's change of tack. 'I've been receiving odd messages on my phone. This address and the previous place.'

'The townhouse by the river?' Randall nodded. 'That would be my colleague, Alice. I asked her to point you in the right direction. What happened there?'

Randall shrugged. 'He wouldn't tell me where you'd gone. It got messy.'

'But you persuaded him?' asked Will.

'No. I just got another text with this address.'

Will wondered at that. How had Alice got the location? 'Where's your phone?'

Randall pulled it out.

'Dial the number of the texts you got,' said Will.

Randall looked reluctant, but after giving Will a glare, he pressed the buttons. He held the phone to his ear and after a brief pause said, 'Are you Alice?'

He listened some more, then held the phone towards Will. 'She wants to talk to you.'

'I can't hold the phone,' said Will. 'Can you put it to my ear?' Randall looked as if he wanted to say no, but after a pause he walked over and pressed the phone to the side of Will's face.

'Are you OK?' said Alice.

'Still in one piece, just,' said Will. 'Alice, listen. It's Zar and his wife. She is, or was, a jihadi.'

'Was?'

She's dead on the floor. She was about to kill me, but our friend arrived in the nick of time.

'And Zar?'

'He left for a meeting with someone. I'd bet the bomb maker.'

'But he's dead,' said Alice.

'Maybe not. If Zar is behind it all, he could easily have staged the explosion. We have to find Zar. He's our only way in.'

'Will our friend help you?'

'He's coming round, but I'm still tied up. Can you talk to him? I've told him the outline. Just tell him the truth.'

'Ok.'

Will leaned away. 'She wants to speak to you. Ask her anything. She'll tell you.'

Randall took the phone and listened. Will was praying he would be persuaded. There wasn't any other way out of this. Eventually Randall put the phone down.

'Will you untie me now?' said Will. Randall hesitated, but then he took the knife and cut the ties binding Will to the chair. It felt good to be free. Will picked up the phone.

'Are you still there? He's cut me loose.'

'Good. So how do we find Zar and the bomb maker, if it is him? And how are they going to deliver it?'

'Zar knows the security inside out. It won't be hard for him to get it inside the cordon.'

'But he can't deliver it himself. Surely too risky. Besides, he's supposed to shoot himself the day after. He doesn't die there.'

'How did you find me, by the way? I thought I was a goner when they brought me here.'

'Tracker. In your coat collar.'

'Well, thank God for that. Can you find out where the explosion was and if they've any more on the supposed body? It's our only lead right now.'

'Ok. I'll get straight back.'

311

Will put down the phone and turned to Randall. 'Thanks,' he said.

'What shall we do with the body?' said Randall, gesturing at Rasha.

'Leave it,' said Will. 'No time.'

Then he realised he hadn't done the most obvious thing. He bent down and searched the pockets of her coat and trousers. Nothing except car keys. The Audi's car keys. Will looked at the car. Zar hadn't taken it. He must have had another car there. It must be Rasha's, and she was going to drive it after she'd killed him. Drive it to wherever she was meeting the bomb maker and the deliverer. Will looked at his watch. It was nearly five a.m. Time was running out.

Will climbed into the driver's seat of the Audi and looked around. It was scrupulously clean. He opened the glove compartment. She wouldn't have left any obvious clues. He switched on the ignition and turned on the sat nav. Surely, she wouldn't have made the elementary mistake of putting in a rendezvous with the bomb maker. Anyway, there was nothing in the last few days. He saw Home and punched that. Thirty-four Alexandra Mews EC1. Somewhere on the edge of the City. Must cost a bit.

And then a small light clicked on in Will's brain. If you were in an alley near that address, what would you see? Maybe it wasn't an alley, maybe it was the end of a mews.

Will got out of the car. Randall was sitting on a chair idly stripping down Rasha's gun and re-assembling it as though he were doing an exercise.

'Look at me,' said Will.

'What?'

'I need to look into your eyes.'

Randall stared defiantly at Will and he locked on. The same scene, but this time Will wasn't looking at Randall being shot. He was looking behind him. The alleyway could easily be a walkway out of the far end of the mews. And above it, Will could see the sky was lighter as dawn approached. And there was a giant building emerging in the background, a rather familiar building. The Gherkin. That would work.

Will shook himself from the image of Randall collapsing to the ground, fatally wounded. He jumped back into the car and looked at the sat nav. Alexandra Mews was a small development in a courtyard near Aldgate. It ran east-west, so if you were looking along it back to the west, what would you see? The Gherkin. Bingo.

'I know where they've gone,' Will said to himself, then louder to Randall. 'I know where they've gone. Get in.'

Randall got in the passenger seat, still holding the gun.

'They've gone to their home. It's in a mews just to the east of the City.'

'How do you know that?'

Will hesitated. 'It's in the background of what I just saw in your eyes. A City landmark.'

'The place I'm going to die,' said Randall flatly. 'No maybes or buts?'

'I'm sorry.'

'And these are definitely jihadis?' Will nodded. 'Ah well. Maybe I'm avenging my colleagues differently. Let's go.'

They found the switch for the garage door, opened it and drove out.

'Do you want to take your car?' Will said without thinking.

Randall gave a ghost of a smile. 'I won't be needing it, will I? Anyway, this is a nicer ride.'

Will couldn't think of anything further to say. The man beside him would be dead shortly. Arguably his fault again. He could save Randall by stopping now, but then he might never find out who was going to carry the bomb, and he might die at Zar's house without Randall's protection. There was no way out of this conundrum. He just had to concentrate on trying to prevent the bomb from going off.

He drove in silence for a few minutes. Then he remembered Alice didn't know where they were going.

'Can you call Alice again?' he said to Randall. 'Put it on speakerphone.'

Randall hit the re-dial button and held the phone up. Will could hear the ringing tone, but there was no answer. 'Come on, come on,' he muttered, but it eventually went through to messages.

'Alice, I know where they are. Zar's house, Thirty-four Alexandra Mews, Aldgate. Get there with back up as soon as you can. Give me a ring when you get this.'

Randall grunted and took the phone away. 'What's your plan for getting me killed?' he said.

Will hesitated, but really, there was no choice. He might as well be honest. 'It's a mews house with a walkway out of the street at the far end. You need to cover me getting away down the walkway.'

'And in the process, I get shot?'

'That's what I see.'

'Not a very enticing prospect, is it? No chance I survive?'

'Sorry.'

Randall was silent for a moment. Finally, he said, 'If I wait on the spot, then I'd definitely be ready.'

'True,' said Will, 'but I might need some help getting into and out of the house. No use waiting outside if I can't get back to you.'

'And you can't see that part at all?'

'No,' said Will. 'The only way forward is to do what seems best at the beginning and assume it's going to work round to what I've seen by the end. And the logical thing is for you to come in with me.'

They were driving through the empty streets of the City past the Stock Exchange building and the looming presence of the Walkie-Talkie and the Cheese Grater. Silly titles for vast impersonal skyscrapers, as if a few bizarre shapes and a handy nickname really made a difference.

Will saw the distant outline of The Gherkin. 'We're getting close,' he said.

Will let the sat nav guide him to the mews. He parked on a road next to the end where the walkway came out. That way, they could go past the killing ground and case it out, and when he ran towards the car, it would take them back past the right spot.

He parked up, turned off the engine, and looked at his watch. 5.40 a.m. They would need to move. Randall was due to die in just nineteen minutes.

Then the phone rang. Randall listened and handed it to Will.

'Where are you?' asked Alice.

'Outside Zar's house. I recognised the location from the background I could see in Randall's eyes.'

'The bomb maker explosion was less than a mile from you, but there's no word on the body yet.'

'I think we have to assume he's still alive,' said Will.

'Ros came back on that phone number. That phone made another call to the bomb maker the next morning, just before we arrived.'

'To warn him,' said Will. 'But it wasn't on the list Zar gave us. He must have made that call, and then deliberately left it off the list. He's kept one step ahead of us the whole way.'

'There's another thing you should know. The nuclear research centre at Harwell have just admitted there's a capsule of caesium-137 that's gone missing in their decommissioning process. It looks very much like an inside job.'

'That's where they got the dirty part. It's all coming true.'

'Dexter wants you to come in,' said Alice. 'He won't accept it's Zar. He wants proof.'

'And that phone call isn't proof? Forget that. Anyway, there's no time left. We're going now.'

'Wait for me,' said Alice. 'I can be there in twenty minutes.'

Will glanced at his watch again. 5.44 a.m. Down to fifteen minutes. 'Sorry, got to go. There's a deadline.'

Randall looked at him with a hard smile. 'My. Dead. Line.'

'I'll see you outside here after,' Will said to Alice and shut off the call.

Randall held up Rasha's gun. 'You're not armed?' Will shook his head. 'Take this,' said Randall, handing him the knife with its wicked serrated edge.

They climbed out of the car and headed through the entrance to the walkway that led to the mews.

Will took a careful look round as they passed the spot where Randall was going to die. The mews ahead comprised of two sets of terraces with doors opening directly on to the cobbled street. No hiding places at all, so whoever was going to shoot Randall was either in a doorway or in the middle of the street. Will glanced back. There was the skyline and there was The Gherkin, getting more distinct in the lightening sky. This was it.

'Head on?' asked Randall.

'There's no way round the back, and we're running out of time. Head on,' agreed Will.

They marched up to the front door and rang the bell. Randall positioned himself close to the door frame, the pistol with its suppressor raised and almost touching the door knocker.

There was a silence. Will glanced at his watch. Three minutes.

Then the door opened and Zar appeared, urbane as ever, with a slight smile. He saw Randall and the gun. 'I was expecting you,' he said. But then he saw Will step out from behind Randall, and his face fell. 'But not you.'

Will realised he must have told Zar about Randall when he was drugged, but not about his suspicion that he was there too, running away.

Randall moved forward through the doorway, his gun aimed firmly at Zar's chest. Will followed with the knife raised, although he wasn't sure what he would do with it. Zar backed off into the hallway. He was staring at Will with barely restrained anger.

'I'm guessing that if you're here, Rasha didn't make it. Did you kill her?'

Will nodded at Randall. 'He did.'

'She wouldn't believe me,' said Zar. 'She thought it was all superstitious nonsense. But you've been right all along, haven't you Will? If you'd looked into her eyes, you'd have seen her die.'

Will said nothing. Zar laughed, although his voice cracked. 'I know I'm going to shoot myself tomorrow. I understand why now that my darling Rasha has gone. And our friend here will die in….' He glanced at his watch. 'One minute.'

'Why not give up now and stop all this unnecessary death?' said Will.

'I have to keep my promise to Rasha and there's nothing you can do to stop me,' said Zar. 'You've predicted every death. Nothing's going to change now or in a few hours' time. The bomb will go off in Parliament Square and we will win. Besides, you know the consequences of stopping it could be far, far worse.'

Will noticed Zar's eyes flick to the side, and he suddenly knew they were about to be surprised.

'It's a trap,' he shouted, grabbing Randall's arm and moving sideways. A figure appeared briefly in a doorway. It was the bomb maker, Mansoor. He wasn't dead after all.

318

There was a loud bang as Mansoor loosed off a shot and ducked back inside. Will felt a sharp pain in his left arm, and instinctively reached up towards it, dropping the knife.

Randall fired at the doorway where Mansoor had been, and splinters of wood flew off the side of the door frame. Then there was another bang, and the wall exploded behind Randall.

Zar ducked back towards another doorway and disappeared.

'Run,' said Randall. 'Now.'

Will pulled open the front door and threw himself out. He hesitated for a second over which way to go, but he knew he had to turn right towards the car. This was heading to the inevitable conclusion.

He could hear Randall behind. 'There were two of them in that room,' he shouted to Will.

Will turned as he passed the killing spot. Randall was five yards behind and there was Mansoor emerging into the street and two loud cracks as he fired at them.

Randall stopped on the precise spot, turned, and fired. Mansoor was thrown backwards by the force of the shots. But then very distinctly, there were two more shots. Will couldn't see where they came from. He carried on running. They must have hit Randall just as predicted, but he didn't look back because the figure in Randall's eyes hadn't. He just had to run and ignore the sick feeling in the pit of his stomach and the sharp pain in his arm.

It was all such a waste. Randall was dead, and all he had learned was that Mansoor had been alive but was now dead, and that they had another jihadi back there too, the one who would probably carry the bomb.

Will ran round the corner and almost bumped into Alice, who was crouched waiting with a gun at the ready.

'You're hit,' she said, reaching towards Will's arm.

'I was lucky it wasn't worse.'

'And Randall?' asked Alice.

'He saved me right on cue. There was Zar and two others. Mansoor was one of them, and Randall shot him, but the other one killed Randall.'

'Who was it?'

'I don't know. I never saw him.'

Will was overcome by the pointlessness of it all. Two more people were dead. When would this carnage ever stop?

Alice helped him over to her car. 'Get in and wait for me,' she said. 'I'm just going to check.'

'Careful. The police will surely get here any minute.'

Alice disappeared round the corner. Will stripped off his jacket and shirt and examined the wound as best he could. It looked clean. The bullet had gone straight through. He tore off the sleeve of his shirt and used it as a bandage to stem the blood, then put his jacket back on. The bullet hole wasn't too noticeable. The pain was manageable. It would have to do.

He felt sick and ashamed. He had just stormed in there, relying on Randall to save him and then to die. And what had been achieved? Well, the bomb maker had been alive, so they surely had another bomb. Zar had escaped with another jihadi, so the bombing was clearly going to happen. Maybe Zar was right. Will's visions were accurate, so the bomb would go off, too.

320

He was lost in guilt and misery when Alice slid into the driving seat.

'It was the bomb maker, Mansoor, so the explosion was just a ruse. No sign of Zar or the other one.' They heard approaching sirens. 'We should get out of here,' she said, and started the car.

As they reached the main road, a police car, blue lights flashing, passed in front of them.

'We've got a choice now,' said Alice. 'Dexter refuses to believe Zar is behind it all. He wants me to bring you in so he can talk to you himself. He says if you can convince him, he'll take action, but I don't think he really means it.'

'If we go to Thames House and we're not arrested, we get trapped in an endless discussion till the bomb goes off. Not much of a choice,' said Will. 'Let's head straight for Parliament Square. The question is, how will we get through the security cordon?'

'I can get through. We'll have to bluff you,' said Alice.

'How about Ros? She'll have a bright idea,' said Will. He rang her, and she picked up straightaway.

'Boy, are you in trouble round here. The shit is absolutely hitting the fan,' she said with an uncertain laugh.

'You may not want to help us then.'

'Tell me what you want,' she said, and when Will spelled it out she just replied, 'On to it,' and rang off.

'She's a gem,' said Will.

Alice nodded. She was driving through the City traffic towards Westminster. 'I brought those,' she said, gesturing at the back seat.

Will turned and looked. 'Do we really need them?'

'Better to be on the safe side.'

'They won't stop a bomb.'

Alice touched his knee. 'For me,' she said. Will relented, pulled the bulletproof vest from the back seat, and put it on.

'There's one other thing I wanted to tell you. In case it all goes wrong.'

Alice flicked him a worried glance. 'Yes?'

'I worked out who the man was, sitting at your bedside when you die.' Will stopped and swallowed. He could hardly bear the thought that their future together would be erased if the bomb went off.

'Don't keep me in suspense,' said Alice with a catch in her voice.

Will placed a hand on her arm. 'He's you and me. Our son.'

Alice let out a small sob. 'Really? I'm pregnant?'

'You may be already. You certainly will be in the future.'

'But that's gone, hasn't it? It's no longer there.'

'Not if we stop this bomb.'

'Well, we'd better fucking well make sure we do then,' said Alice fiercely, putting her foot on the accelerator and weaving through the rush hour traffic.

Chapter Thirty-Five

By the time they reached the Embankment the sun was shining, and it was promising to be a hot spring day. There were already crowds of people on the pavements heading towards Parliament Square.

Will recalled that because of security everyone had been told to be in place early, and the bomb was due to go off at 9.55 a.m., just before official proceedings began. He looked at his watch 9.05 a.m. Just fifty minutes away.

There was a line of traffic being forced to turn up towards Trafalgar Square as the last stretch of the Embankment was blocked to traffic. Alice suddenly angled the car into a space against the pavement.

'We should walk from here,' she said.

'You'll get towed away,' said Will.

'Least of my problems,' said Alice. 'Come on.'

They joined the crowds surging down the pavement towards the looming tower of Big Ben.

How would they get through all these people in time? And even if they did, he was no nearer to working out who the bomber was.

On impulse, he stopped a man walking next to him. 'Excuse me, is this the right way to Parliament Square?' he asked.

The man looked at Will as if he was a moron, but he stared straight at him. 'Just follow the crowds,' the man said. But Will wasn't listening. He was focussed on the man's eyes.

Blue sky, an expectant look on the man's face. Will knew it already. Then the man turned to the left, looked surprised. There was the flash and the smoke and the man was crumpled on the ground. But no clue to the perpetrator.

Will tried hard not to gag. Less than forty minutes and this man and so many of those walking with them on the Embankment would be dead. He had to do something.

Then a thought struck him. The Home Secretary had looked right just before the blast. This man had looked left. Something had disturbed them. Could he use triangulation to figure out where the bomber would be?

He grabbed the man again. 'Where are you sitting?' he demanded.

'What's it got to do with you?' the man said irritably.

'Please, it's very important.'

'South stand, now leave us alone,' the man said and turned his back. Will tried to remember the layout. Three stands in a C-shape facing the Houses of Parliament. South, West and North. The VIPs were in the west stand. He needed to see exactly where the Home Secretary was to be certain, but it looked as if the bomber would be between the West and South stands.

They were hemmed in now by the crowd that was funnelling down towards security checks at the corner of the Embankment and Westminster Bridge.

'This is no good,' said Alice. 'We'll be trapped in the queue and then they'll probably arrest us when we get to the front.'

Just then, her phone rang. 'Ros,' she said briefly. 'Thank God. Any solutions?' Alice listened intently, her hand pressed over her ear to block out the sound of the crowd.

'You're a Godsend,' she finished, and then Alice grabbed Will's hand and said, 'This way.' She pulled him back against the crowd towards the buildings looking out over the river. There were irritated cries and exclamations. People shot them furious glances. And every time Will looked into their eyes, all he saw was imminent death bearing down on them.

Alice pulled him into an alleyway with a gated entrance twenty yards down. A police officer with a sub-machine gun stared at them aggressively, but beyond the gate was a nervous-looking young man who leaned up against the bars and whispered something in the guard's ear.

As they came up to him, Will heard the police officer say, 'You're sure?' and the young man nodded. Alice flashed her MI5 pass at him, and that seemed to mollify him further. He waved them through.

'Tom?' said Alice, and the young man nodded. 'Thank you so much.'

'Ros said it was incredibly important. Life and death,' he said. 'I hope she's right because I could get fired for this, or worse.'

'You're doing the right thing.'

'Where is this?' said Will.

'It's a side entrance to Portcullis House where the MPs have their offices.'

'And what use is that?'

'We go through to the front entrance, and it gets us beyond the main security into the square,' said Alice. 'Lead the way, Tom.'

They quickly passed through a side corridor into a huge central atrium that was completely empty.

'The building's been closed down today for better security. Anyway, lots of MPs are going to be in the Square,' said Tom.

'Don't we know it,' said Alice.

'Is it true that someone's trying to detonate a bomb?' asked Tom.

'It certainly is,' said Alice. 'And it's due to explode in….' She looked at Will, who glanced at his watch again.

'Eighteen minutes,' he said flatly.

Tom blanched. 'What should I do?'

'Get us out of the front entrance, and you'll have done everything we could ask. Then if you can, leave by the Embankment entrance and get as far away as possible.'

They approached the main entrance, which had a row of armed police officers standing outside and the crowds streaming past on their way to the square.

There were two policemen on the inside who turned at their arrival and looked surprised. 'We're not allowed to let anyone out,' said one of them.

Alice showed her security pass. 'This is an emergency. We're tracing a bombing suspect. This man is the only one who can identify him. You can search us. We're not carrying anything.'

The policeman looked reluctant. Tom weighed in. 'I'll vouch for them,' he said, but the policeman was unimpressed.

'You've been shot,' said the other officer, looking at Will's shoulder.

'We had a firefight with them,' said Will. 'There's one left and he's inside the security cordon.'

'I'll have to call it in,' the first officer said.

'Fine. But let us through now. We're losing time and the suspect could get away,' said Alice.

Will could see the policeman weighing it up. 'He's there,' Will said suddenly, pointing at the passing crowds.

Alice cottoned on straightaway. 'Come on,' she said impatiently. 'That man is trying to blow up the whole ceremony, and he's getting away. Pat us down if you must but be quick.'

The policeman gave in and nodded to his colleague. They gave Will and Alice a cursory pat down and opened the door.

'Thanks Tom,' said Alice, and then they were in the crowd, heading towards their bogus suspect.

'They'll call it in. Bound to. So, we're going to have Dexter and security on our tail as well,' said Alice as they jogged towards the square.

'There's only twelve minutes,' said Will. 'We've just got to go for it.'

They weaved their way through the crowds until they were facing the stands that had been set up on three sides of the square, looking towards the House of Commons and Big Ben.

Will looked around in frustration and something close to panic. Although the crowds were thinning as more and more people took their seats, there were still several hundred people between him and the main presentation area. There was the West stand, the VIP one, with a line of armed police in front, and he could see the snipers on the rooftops around the square. But none of that was any use to him. The chances were they wouldn't see anything until it was too late. It took only a second to trigger a suicide vest, and if the bomber kept his nerve and didn't stand out in the crowd, no-one would know till it happened.

He glanced at his watch. Six minutes to go. No margin for error at all.

'Let's head for the VIP stand,' he said to Alice. 'It's got to be close to there.'

They hurried through the crowds, pushing their way through people patiently queuing for their seats, attracting more angry stares. But each time that Will locked onto their eyes, all he was saw was the bright sunny day, another smiling face enjoying the prospect of such an important celebration and then the blackness and the fire. No clues about who it was.

'They've timed it cleverly, as people are taking their seats. Maximum bustle, maximum casualties,' he said to Alice despairingly.

His only hope was the triangulation. He scanned the VIP stand, searching for the familiar features of the Home Secretary. There were ranks of dignitaries already in place, and Will recognised most of the Cabinet. The Foreign Secretary looked like he'd just finished a long and boozy lunch, although it was barely nine o'clock. And then he saw her, the Home Secretary already in position, her usual impatient half-smile on her face.

So, if she was looking right, and the man from earlier in the South stand was looking left, then it had to be in the angle between those stands near the podium.

The crowds were definitely thinning out now as people took their seats. They passed a group of schoolchildren seated in the front of the North stand and like a magnet, Will's eyes were drawn to the one child he didn't want to see among all others, Melanie.

Could it only be three weeks since he'd saved her from the bus, only to have her die here? He saw her pale blue cornflower eyes looking at him and the spark of recognition as she realised who he was. He saw her turn and whisper something to the woman sitting next to her, a teacher probably, and the woman's head jerk up and fix on him.

Not good. He moved on towards the join of the South and West stands. When he glanced back, he could see the teacher talking to a police officer and pointing at him. The officer reached for his walkie-talkie. Time was running out fast.

Alice pulled on his sleeve. 'Look,' she said, and pointed. There was a flurry of security guards and there was the Prime Minister and the President of the United States walking down the steps of the main stand to the front row. The only guest of honour left was the King. Will looked at his watch again. Three minutes. And then he worked it out. They would not wait for the King. He would only come when everyone was

329

settled. To go before he arrived would ensure there was still a bit of confusion. Will measured the distance from the line of armed police to where the PM and President were taking their seats. Barely ten yards. A bomb there just in front of the armed police would generate the carnage necessary, but where was the bomber?

At that very moment, Will saw the President turn to survey the scene and stare straight at him. Will ducked away. He couldn't afford to look into the President's eyes and see him die in a few seconds like all the others. He needed to find the bomber. Right now.

Suddenly Dexter appeared in front of him.

'Stop right there,' Dexter said, grabbing Will by the arm where he'd been shot. Will gasped and nearly fell, but then Alice shoved herself between Will and Dexter, separating them.

'Are you really going to get in the way of the one chance we have of preventing this?' she said in Dexter's face. 'I know you set me up to take the rap for Pavel's death when you ordered his murder.'

Dexter blanched. 'This isn't the time or the place. You both need to come with me.'

Alice didn't hesitate. She punched him very hard in the eye, and Dexter fell to the ground. 'Run, Will, run,' she shouted.

Will headed for the corner of the South and West stands, trying to ignore the throbbing pain in his arm. There was only one thing left he could do. Make himself the target. He stepped onto the restricted area of grass in front of the podium. A security guard appeared in front of him. 'You can't go there, sir,' he said.

Then another figure bumped into his back and Will turned to see an unexpected face next to him.

'Javanshir. Thank God you're here,' said Will. 'We have to find the bomber. It's almost due. He must be right here.'

Javanshir gave him a wide-eyed stare, and Will noticed beads of sweat on his forehead. And for the first time he looked straight into Javanshir's intense brown eyes.

And there he was, right in front of the podium, staring upwards, his hand moving inside his jacket, then there was the flash of white, the blackness and fire and Will felt the physical blow. This was the epicentre of the blast, and it was just twenty seconds away.

Will doubled over from the pain and the shock. It was Javanshir. He was the bomber. He had to be. That was why he had never wanted Will to look into his eyes. Will tried to clear his throat.

'You'll have to come with me,' said the guard, leaning over him.

'He's the bomber,' said Will, pointing at Javanshir who was walking towards the centre of the grass staring at the sky.

'He's part of the security team,' said the guard.

Will tugged at Alice, who had arrived at a run. 'Javanshir's the bomber,' he said, and her eyes flew open in shock and she whirled round towards Javanshir's retreating figure.

It was all too late. Nothing could stop it now. Will felt a sick fury, then he saw the guard's pistol holstered inside his

331

jacket. Instinctively he threw himself upwards, catching the guard on the chin with the top of his head, and as the guard's body was thrown back, Will reached into his holster and grabbed his gun.

He whirled round, flicking off the safety catch, and there was Javanshir standing in the same spot as in the vision, reaching into his jacket to trigger the bomb.

There was no time for anything else. Will blotted out his own pain. His army training flooded back. The only way to immobilise an enemy and guarantee no movement was a head shot. Will loosed off two shots in quick sequence, a double tap, and Javanshir's head exploded in a shower of brain and blood.

But even as the bullets punched home, Will could see the police in the armed row reacting as half-a-dozen machine guns were levelled and trained on him. He could hear the screams of the crowd around him panicking, and then there was an explosion of bullets slamming into his chest and a blinding pain in his guts.

He was thrown backwards to the ground. The crowd were running wildly to get out of the way. The last thing he thought was, there's going to be a stampede and how many will die in that? There's always a knock-on. And then he saw Alice's panic-stricken face and beyond that Melanie staring at him with her pale cornflower blue eyes.

He locked on to her hoping that after all this sacrifice she at least would have a long and happy life. But instead he saw an awful cataclysm, a horror beyond belief and he felt a pain worse than anything ever before that shook his body and blew it away.

Then there was darkness.

Chapter Thirty-Six

When Will finally came round, there was bright white light bouncing off white walls, and he thought he was back in hospital again, handcuffed to the bed. That was silly, surely. And yet this time he couldn't move either arm, and one of them felt numb.

He flexed his fingers. They were definitely functioning, yet when he tried to lift his arm, it was impossible. He opened his eyes further. White room, white sheets, and discovered there were drips cannulated in his arm and monitors wired to his head and chest. His arms were strapped down.

He was much too tired to struggle. His chest felt like he'd been run over by a truck, and his thinking was fuzzy, either sedation or a brain injury. He felt a terrible foreboding, something was very wrong, but he couldn't pin it down.

He made a small noise, trying to clear his throat, and Alice appeared at the foot of the bed, smiling.

'You're awake at last,' she said.

Will tried to raise a smile too, but it felt like a grimace. 'Why am I tied down?' he whispered.

'You were pulling the tubes out of your arm. They had to do it to keep you safe. Nothing sinister.'

She was still smiling, but there were the tracks of tears on her cheek. I wonder why, thought Will vaguely. She came and sat next to him, holding his hand. He wanted to gaze into her eyes and check that the nursing home was back with their son reinstated in their future. But she wouldn't look him in the eye and the looming sense of foreboding returned.

'What happened?' he asked finally.

'Most of the shots were caught by the bullet-proof vest. Lucky you were wearing it.'

'Thank you for forcing me,' he managed.

'But two got through. One winged your arm, the same one that was already wounded. No real problem. But the second hit you in the lower abdomen and tore through your intestines. That's taken a fair bit of patching up. The doctors were worried that you seemed in extreme distress. You were babbling a lot of nonsense, even though you were unconscious, and they were afraid your mind was damaged. They've given you a massive dose of sedatives so you may be feeling pretty woozy.'

'How long have I been out?'

'Two days,' she said.

Will thought back to the last moments, the screaming, the thump of the bullets hitting him. He remembered that he had been worried about the knock-on. 'Did anyone else die as a result? I thought there was going to be a stampede in the panic.'

'Twelve people in the crush and one hit by a stray bullet,' said Alice. 'Tough, but not a bad trade considering the hundreds you saved.'

Will wasn't so sure. Thirteen dead was still thirteen families in mourning. Still more pain that he had caused. And what might those people have done with their lives? The conundrum again – had he preserved the life of that future Hitler, or killed off a potential world saviour? He was swamped by the feeling he had made the wrong choice, but he couldn't work out why.

He took in the surroundings. Superficially, it looked like a hospital room but the pictures on the walls were a bit too good, the sheets a bit too soft.

'Where am I?'

'Back in the safe house in Surrey, away from the public gaze.' Alice looked away. Why wouldn't she meet his eye? 'Dexter is downstairs, eager to see you when you've woken.'

Will tried to laugh but it came out as a bubbly gurgle. 'Keen to thank me, I'm sure,' he said.

Alice glanced back. 'Not exactly. I'll leave him to tell you.' She grabbed his hand again and squeezed. 'I just want you to know that I love you, Will. Truly. And I'll stand by you.'

What on earth was she talking about? Will couldn't comprehend it. Surely Dexter was going to congratulate him on stopping the bomb, even if he had broken a few rules.

His eye drifted over to a TV in the corner that was playing silently. He saw his picture come up and thought, well at least I'm the hero for a change.

But then his eyes focussed on the strapline and a surge of adrenaline shot through his body like an electric shock. The headline read: 'KILLER DIES' followed by the sub-title, 'Bomber dies on the operating table.'

Will let out an agonised cry and Alice whirled round. 'Oh fuck,' she said.

Will couldn't believe it. They were blaming him. After all he'd been through, they were using him again. No vindication, no recognition, just more shit, a lifetime of opprobrium, except that he seemed to be dead, too.

'How could they do this? How could you let them?' said Will bitterly.

Alice shrugged. 'No choice. I'm sorry,' she said.

Then the door opened, and Dexter walked in. Will could see straightaway that he wasn't the same Dexter. He looked shrunken, bone-tired, a bluish tinge to his lips. He had a very large bruise round his right eye. His gaze swept the room apprehensively and took in Will glaring at him and Alice looking furious.

'He knows,' said Alice.

'Oh,' said Dexter. 'Well, let's cut to the chase, then.'

'You've put the blame on me,' said Will.

'It seemed.... the best way,' said Dexter with a little grimace. 'You were already the Angel of Death. You fitted the bill. No-one saw the explosive vest on Javanshir. We got his body away quickly. And then we let out that you were wearing it, and that you died on the operating table.'

'And the caesium-137 capsule he was carrying?'

'It was in the front of the jacket, and it hadn't broken. Your double tap was very efficient. He fell on his back, and it remained intact. I have to say you deserve our thanks for that.'

'Well, bully for me,' said Will bitterly. 'What about Zar?'

Dexter looked away.

'He killed himself yesterday,' said Alice. 'Just as you predicted.'

'And you let him do it?' he said to Dexter. 'Very convenient. Tidying up the mess for you. So Javanshir's gone, and Zar and the bomb maker. I'm the only loose end. Why on earth should I go along with this?' said Will incredulously.

'Here's the deal,' said Dexter. 'You agree and we get you away to the States. New face, new life. We have let a couple of senior figures in the CIA know your talents and they're keen to use you. It's easier if you are officially dead.'

'You've got to be joking,' said Will.

'I'll be going with you,' said Alice. 'This is my deal, too. Dexter and I have talked about what happened with Pavel, and this is my payoff. I want to be with you. There's nothing here for me now. I don't want to work for a murderer.'

Will was taken aback. 'You'd do that?' he asked. He was silent for a while. He should be happy about that at least but all he felt was a creeping fear.

'I could be a dead hero. Why do I have to be the villain?' he asked eventually, although he'd already worked out the answer.

'We wouldn't want it known that two MI5 officers were traitors, would we?' said Dexter.

'Leaving you in the clear?'

'I think you can rest assured that my career is going nowhere. Overseeing two jihadis and failing to uncover them has not endeared me to my boss. I expect I'll have to resign.' Dexter gave a ghost of a smile. 'That's my payback.'

'And if I don't agree?' Will said wearily.

Dexter looked at him with a strange sorrow. 'You're already dead. You could just...die,' he said finally.

The baldness of it seemed to stop them both in their tracks. Will and Dexter looked at each other like prize-fighters, exhausted after punching each other to a standstill.

'It really would be better,' Dexter said. 'I'll leave you to talk it through.'

After he was gone, Alice just held Will's hand for a long time, but she still wouldn't look directly at him.

'It's not exactly a choice,' he said finally.

'You can choose to be with me,' Alice said simply. 'And we can make a new life. With our son.'

'Ok,' said Will. 'I'd like that.' He hesitated 'Why won't you look me in the eye?'

Alice stifled a sob. 'I'm frightened to. I'm scared you won't see the future we had before. You were saying some terrible things when you were unconscious.'

Will felt a chill go through him, a deep atavistic dread. This must be the horror that he was trying so hard not to think about.

'What was I saying?'

Alice was crying now. 'Something you'd seen in Melanie's eyes. A terrible event in fifteen years' time.'

'And why was it so awful?'

'You said…' She stopped as if she couldn't face it, but finally she continued. 'You said it was the end of the world.'

And with that Will finally remembered. An extra-ordinary, world-shattering, obliterating wipe-out. So big, so vast, that he couldn't even work out if it was explosion, or disintegration or just nothingness. And the date – 4 April 2040.

He bit back the scream. Could it be for real or had it just been a reaction to the bullets and the terrible trauma of that moment in Parliament Square. He would have to find out, whatever the cost.

He grabbed Alice's arm and wrenched her round. 'Look at me,' he demanded.

She let out a little wail. 'But what if it's true?'

"I have to know. We have to know. There's no other way.'

Slowly she raised her head. Will thought then, even as his heart quailed at what he would see, that he had never loved her as much as she brought her tear-filled blue eyes into contact with his.

And then it hit him. Carnage like never before. The spectre of that first explosion in Afghanistan but a million deaths, a billion deaths worse. The pain ripped through him with the force of a nuclear bomb. He would surely disintegrate this time. Will could hear his screams coming back off the walls and see Alice's agonised face with her hands over her ears.

Then mercifully the darkness claimed him again.

When he came round it was night-time and the lights were low. He could see Alice asleep in the chair beside him. She was curled up, like a foetus, as if she was expecting a fatal blow any second. His heart ached for her.

He lay there playing in his mind the enormity of his last vision. He knew he must be drugged-up to the eyeballs

340

because he wasn't screaming. He could contemplate what felt like the end of the world with a tranquillised detachment, although the guilt still seared through him.

Was it his fault because he'd prevented the Parliament Square bomb? There had been no sign of such a terrible outcome before that. Had he saved someone – maybe the US President – who set in train some disastrous course of action that led to the coming apocalypse? Or was it someone he had accidentally killed, one of those who'd been caught in the stampede in Parliament Square, who might otherwise have survived and been able to prevent doomsday?

Either way he was going to have to find out, and then he must stop it from happening.

He looked over at Alice and knew he had to try. If the end of everything was in 2040 his child with Alice would be a teenager by then. He would have to find a way to save the world. For his son, for Alice, and for the rest of humanity.

Acknowledgements

Getting any book out into the world requires a lot of help. I would particularly like to thank Julian Alexander of the Soho Agency who recognised the potential in The Day You Die and helped me bring out the best in the story.

Laura Wilkinson of the Creative Writing Programme in Brighton was endlessly supportive and encouraging, and Phil Viner of the Goldsboro Academy was an energetic and inspirational teacher, a hard taskmaster in all the right ways.

I would also like to thank everyone at the Hove Writers Group for their warm and welcoming community, a haven of generous support and constructive criticism every Monday night that makes the writing life feel less lonely.

Thanks also to my fellow survivors of the City University MA course in Creative Writing, John Hobson, Mike Stevenson and David Cox for their advice and practical help as well as many long alcoholic evenings discussing our fledgling novels and how to put the world to rights.

Finally, my thanks to my wife Elizabeth and my son Robbie for their constant love and support. This wouldn't have been possible without you.

Coming soon, the next thriller with a supernatural twist from Clive Edwards. *See over.*

Lost In A Yellow Wood

Seeing your doppelganger is supposed to be a harbinger of death. But what if it's the doppelganger that's trying to kill you?

David Lorrimer is accused by the police of viciously attacking his wife Kate and leaving her in a coma. Then he's terrified to see out of her hospital window a figure looking up at him with his own face.

David fears he's having a breakdown, but the doppelganger appears again, this time with a woman who looks like his first girlfriend. Then he sees another doppelganger that may be connected to a former lover. Can he solve the mystery before his wife dies and the police arrest him for her murder?

To read an opening extract and find out more about the author go to cliveedwardsauthor.com.

Printed in Dunstable, United Kingdom